PRAISE FOR

Beverly Long and *Stay with Me*

"I loved this story and the characters from the moment Sarah drops into John's life until the surprising ending. Down-to-earth dialogue, a great deal of humor, and a heart-warming romance kept me up until the wee hours of the morning. For a book that will make you smile, do not miss *Stay with Me*. It's a perfect ten." —*Romance Reviews Today*

"I found *Stay with Me* to be one of the best time-travel books I've ever read. This story caught my attention from the beginning and held me spellbound until the surprising conclusion. I admire the way Ms. Long introduced her characters, then slowly expanded them throughout the story until you felt you knew them all personally." —*Romance Junkies*

"I am screaming this out loud folks, 'What a find!' New author Beverly Long comes soaring on to the time-travel romance scene with a sure-to-be bestseller . . . This book will keep you turning the pages, as it did with me."
—*A Romance Review*

"This debut romance is a wonderful romp into the past and an elegant analysis of layers of love and community. The pages fly by as one devours each plotline more quickly than the last. Ms. Long does an excellent job conveying the confusion and compassion a modern woman can have for life in the 1800s. The conflicts are not contrived, and the characters are convincing." —*The Best Reviews*

"You can't help but love Sarah Jane Tremont as she muddles through fitting into 1888, where fate has seen fit to fling her backward to. And, on top of that, deal with the sexy and rustic John Beckett she finds herself staying with . . . It's fun to watch as they both fight their attraction and lose the battle." —*Romance Reader at Heart*

"Beverly Long weaves a clever love story filled with the right amount of adventure. The love scenes are sweet and sexy. *Stay with Me* will encourage readers to seek out their own cowboy fantasy." —*The Romance Reader's Connection*

HERE WITH ME

BEVERLY LONG

BERKLEY SENSATION, NEW YORK

THE BERKLEY PUBLISHING GROUP
Published by the Penguin Group
Penguin Group (USA) Inc.
375 Hudson Street, New York, New York 10014, USA
Penguin Group (Canada), 90 Eglinton Avenue East, Suite 700, Toronto, Ontario M4P 2Y3, Canada
(a division of Pearson Penguin Canada Inc.)
Penguin Books Ltd., 80 Strand, London WC2R 0RL, England
Penguin Group Ireland, 25 St. Stephen's Green, Dublin 2, Ireland (a division of Penguin Books Ltd.)
Penguin Group (Australia), 250 Camberwell Road, Camberwell, Victoria 3124, Australia
(a division of Pearson Australia Group Pty. Ltd.)
Penguin Books India Pvt. Ltd., 11 Community Centre, Panchsheel Park, New Delhi—110 017, India
Penguin Group (NZ), Cnr. Airborne and Rosedale Roads, Albany, Auckland 1310, New Zealand
(a division of Pearson New Zealand Ltd.)
Penguin Books (South Africa) (Pty.) Ltd., 24 Sturdee Avenue, Rosebank, Johannesburg 2196,
South Africa

Penguin Books Ltd., Registered Offices: 80 Strand, London WC2R 0RL, England

This is a work of fiction. Names, characters, places, and incidents either are the product of the author's imagination or are used fictitiously, and any resemblance to actual persons, living or dead, business establishments, events, or locales is entirely coincidental. The publisher does not have any control over and does not assume any responsibility for author or third-party websites or their content.

HERE WITH ME

A Berkley Sensation Book / published by arrangement with the author

PRINTING HISTORY
Berkley Sensation mass-market edition / November 2006

Copyright © 2006 by Beverly Long.
Cover design by George Long.
Cover illustration by Jim Griffin.
Interior text design by Kristin del Rosario.

ISBN: 0-425-21287-4

BERKLEY SENSATION®
Berkley Sensation Books are published by The Berkley Publishing Group,
a division of Penguin Group (USA) Inc.,
375 Hudson Street, New York, New York 10014.
BERKLEY SENSATION is a registered trademark of Penguin Group (USA) Inc.
The "B" design is a trademark belonging to Penguin Group (USA) Inc.

PRINTED IN THE UNITED STATES OF AMERICA

10 9 8 7 6 5 4 3 2 1

For Gerry—
you make it easy to believe in love

ACKNOWLEDGMENTS

Touring the vineyards in Napa Valley is one of my very favorite things to do and each time I visit, I am filled with envy for those who get to live there year-round. It was a pleasure to write this book because for a short time, I could pretend.

I am grateful to the staff at both Shafer Vineyards and Robert Keenan Winery. I had a lovely time at the wine tastings and you were all so gracious about answering questions. Any errors or omissions rest solely with me.

I am also very appreciative of the editors at Berkley. First of all, thank you to Louisa Edwards, who bought this book, and thank you to Jessica Wade, who made it better. Also, I would be remiss if I did not thank my agent, Sha-Shana Crichton, who is as excited about my career as I am.

A big thank-you to all of you who read *Stay with Me* and especially to those of you who took the time to visit my website and then e-mail me a short note, asking about the next book. *Here with Me* is for you. I'd love to hear from all of you again (www.beverlylong.com).

ONE

GEORGE woke up flat on his back, feeling like he'd eaten a bad egg. He opened one eye, then the other, and with the last bit of strength he had, he rolled to his stomach, pushed himself up to his hands and knees, lifted his head, and, in the fading light of day, saw what had to be the ocean.

It was just as he'd heard it described and yet, altogether different. More gray than blue. Bigger, for sure. It went forever, until it reached a point where it bumped up against the setting sun and was sucked up into the violet- and pink-streaked sky.

He hadn't expected it to be so noisy, or so angry. Tall waves rushed the beach, slapping against the rocks, churning and foaming over the sandy shore. Birds, big silver-white ones with wings spread wide, swooped low, letting loose with high-pitched, plaintive screeches. One erratically changed direction and George turned his head to follow its path.

He winced when the strap of his camera, which had somehow become wrapped around his neck, tightened. He untangled himself and rested his hand on the sturdy case, feeling doubly grateful—one, that the damn thing hadn't strangled him along the way, and two, that it had come through time in one piece. It was tangible proof that he hadn't left everything a hundred-plus years behind.

The beach, a patch of sand fifty yards wide and stretching as far as the eye could see, was empty save a solitary figure at the edge of the water. Three hundred yards separated them, and the dwindling light of day combined with the white straw hat on the person's head made it difficult to tell if it was a man or woman. All George knew is that given how close the person sat to the rolling waves, his or her trousers had to be long past wet.

His own trousers were dry although there was a fresh hole in the knee, and they were stained with dirt. His heavy shirt had rips that hadn't been there when he'd slipped it on just as the wicked bitch of a storm had started.

His journey had not been an easy one. He had jagged memories of being sucked into utter blackness, of whirling and banging into objects he couldn't see or identify, of feeling like his insides were being ripped from his body.

Just when he'd been sure he couldn't take another minute, he'd seen the hand, somehow visible in the darkness. He'd recognized it immediately, because at one time he'd held it in friendship, claimed it in love, and clasped it in passion. His Hannah had not deserted him and he'd been desperate to feel his wife's touch one more time, to hold her in his arms, close to his heart.

But when he'd attempted to reach for her, his stupid arms and legs had refused to obey. His limbs had hung from his body, useless. Hannah had tried. She'd wrapped her long, slender fingers around his arm and tugged hard.

However, the dank and greedy darkness, a worthy enemy, had fought back and as seconds had turned to minutes, her touch had grown cold and weak. Hope had faded and a terrible emptiness had loomed.

Then, from out of the darkness, another hand had appeared. Not Hannah's. This one was that of an old woman's, with fingers bony and bent with age, and skin lined and spotted from the sun. It had brushed up against Hannah's hand, passing through it in a flash of silvery light, and the sudden heat that flowed from his wife's fingers, into his upper arm, had warmed him to the bone.

Then the old hand, its grip stronger than he'd imagined possible, had grabbed his other arm, and working together, Hannah and the Other had pulled him to the light.

Then they'd disappeared.

And it had been like losing Hannah all over again. Only this time worse than that terrible day he'd buried her in the cold North Dakota ground. Because this time, he'd known, had felt it all the way through his battered soul, that she was leaving him forever.

Her work was done. She'd brought him safely into his new world, into this strange place, this strange time. He was on his own to make of it what he would.

He guessed he best get to it.

He sucked in a breath, gathered his strength, and stood up. And promptly fell flat on his ass again. He felt dizzy and stomach sick and he thought he might have cracked a rib or two on his journey through time. It hurt like a son of a gun to breathe.

Damn it to hell and back. He'd promised Sarah Tremont that he'd come forward to her time and help eight-year-old Miguel Lopez but he wasn't going to be able to help himself, let alone a sick child, if he couldn't keep standing.

Keeping his breaths shallow, he stood up, a little slower

this time, and while the dizziness didn't leave him, it did fade and he remained standing. He situated his camera, letting the leather strap loop over one shoulder and the heavy box rest at his hip.

He gave the person at the water's edge one more lingering look. He or she was huddled over bent legs, head down. It dawned on him that the person had no doubt come to the beach, expecting solitude, and he had no right to intrude. Plus it wasn't like he didn't have any of his own business to attend to. He'd come to this time so that Sarah Tremont could stay with John Beckett. The love between those two had been so real that only a fool could have missed it. But Sarah had been torn, believing that she had to leave, had to come back to her own time, to fulfill her promise to the Lopez family. She'd had information that the family needed, information that would help the young boy.

George had come in her place. Somehow. Someway. And he'd managed to survive it. Now, he needed to find Miguel and his mother. He shifted his eyes, looking upward at the sky. It would be dark soon. He needed to get the lay of the land before the light was completely gone. Before he'd left Sarah, she'd told him about her house, saying it wasn't far from the beach.

He turned away from the person and walked toward the rocky cliff at the back edge of the beach. He found the steep steps leading skyward. Halfway up, his boots heavier with each passing second, he had to stop to catch his breath.

And coming from behind him, he heard a scream. He whirled around, so fast he almost slipped. The beach was empty and he caught a glimpse of white tossing around in the dark waves.

George scrambled down the stairs, his arm clenched to his side, holding his aching ribs. He ran and tried to keep the person in his sight. His camera banged against his hip and he dropped it in the sand along the way. He charged forward like a mad bull, not stopping until the water was waist-high and pushing at him, like it hoped to drag him under, too. Just when he thought he was too late, the wild beast of an ocean tossed up its bounty and he saw a flash of pale skin.

George dove into the water and grabbed. The person's arms were kicking and flailing and Christ, if he wasn't careful, he was going to get knocked silly. He grabbed the person tight into his body and kicked his feet hard. Three more kicks and he'd made enough progress that there was sand beneath the water. He staggered toward the beach, crawling the last three feet on his knees.

His eyes burned, his chest hurt, and his ribs ached worse than the time he'd been kicked by a cow. He ignored it all and sank back onto his haunches to look at what he'd dragged out of the sea.

Mother of God. It was a woman. With long dark hair plastered flat against her head. Her eyes were closed, her face pale, and she wasn't breathing.

He deposited her on the beach, rolled her over to her side, and rapped her sharply between the shoulder blades. It seemed to take an eternity but water gurgled out of her mouth and she started coughing and sputtering. He thought he'd never heard a more beautiful sound.

"You're safe," he assured her and felt bad when her body jerked and she fell flat on her back. Her wide-set eyes were open now and dark with fear.

"I mean you no harm, ma'am," he said. He braced his hands on his knees and tried to catch his breath. She wore dark trousers and a white blouse and both were molded to her body. She put her hand over her stomach, her eyes flashing wildly, and he saw the slight swell of her stomach. "Oh, Jesus," he whispered. "You're with child."

She licked her lips and swallowed. "I'm five months pregnant."

He started to shake. Felt like a damn fool but couldn't stop. He wrapped his arms around his body and prayed that he'd stay upright and not embarrass himself further by falling facedown in the sand. He had salt water rolling around in his stomach and fear chilling his blood. It made for some severe unpleasantness.

"You saved my life," she said. "My baby's life." Her soft voice trailed off at the end.

The thought of what might have happened if he'd been even a minute later made him shake all the more.

"I was so stupid. I got too close to the water and this huge wave came and it just wouldn't let go." She looked at him like she had just noticed his shivering. "You must be freezing," she said.

"I'm not cold," he said. "You scared me," he admitted.

She laughed, a light musical sound that drifted above the heavy dampness of the evening air. It calmed him. If she could laugh, surely she and her babe were not hurt.

She sat up and pushed her wet hair behind her ears. He saw how fine-boned her hand was and it made him worry that he'd rapped her back too hard, that he'd hurt her.

"I'm sorry if I was rough with you," he said.

"Oh, please," she waved her hand, dismissing his concern. She extended her arm, almost hesitantly. "I'm Melody, by the way."

He gave her small hand a gentle squeeze. "I'm George."

He thought she looked at him rather oddly. Without releasing his hand, she said, "Melody Song." She'd emphasized the last name.

It was an odd name and needed no emphasis. And he had the strangest sensation that he'd heard it somewhere before. It was the kind of name that stuck with a person.

"George Tyler, ma'am."

He could feel the tension in her small hand relax and when she smiled at him, the genuineness of it reached her eyes. "It's a pleasure to meet you," she said. "You know, you could have drowned right along with me."

He supposed if he'd taken time to think about it, he could have reasoned that out. When he'd heard the scream and realized what had happened, he'd known time wasn't a luxury the person had. "I suspect that's true enough," he said.

"Well, I'm sorry that my carelessness almost got you killed."

He didn't respond. He'd stopped caring six months ago whether he lived or died, so it didn't seem right now to pretend to be worried about what might have happened.

"I really should have known better," she said. Her voice dropped and he could hear something in her tone that hadn't been there before. "Especially here," she added.

Here was the place Sarah Tremont had traveled from and he had traveled to. Did she know something about that? The hair on the back of his neck stiffened. "Why's that, ma'am?" he asked.

She shifted her gaze and stared past his shoulder, out toward the ocean. He turned his body and settled down in the sand next to her. Just the tip of the setting sun remained visible and the violet and pink had turned into a smooth dark blue with just a hint of purple.

He'd been close enough to her to know it was just the color of Melody Song's eyes.

"A little over a year ago my best friend drowned at this beach," she said. "You might have read about it in the paper. Her name was Sarah Jane Tremont."

George was grateful that he was sitting, otherwise he'd have disgraced himself by falling down again. He knew where he'd heard the odd name. This was the Melody that

Sarah had told him about, the woman who had been her coworker, her best friend. But a year ago? Sarah had told him that she'd left California on April 17, 2005, and traveled back to that same date in 1888. He'd placed his feet in the footprints a little more than two weeks later, on the third of May, believing he was meant to come to her time.

Christ, he thought his head might just split in two it ached so badly. How could this have happened? Hannah had been there. She had guided him and she would not have led him wrong.

Melody put her hand on his arm. "Are you all right?" she asked. "You don't look so good."

No. His heart was racing, he couldn't think straight, and his stomach churned, making him think that his lunch would be on his boots soon.

Hell. He hadn't eaten for over a year.

Impossible.

"What happened?" he managed to ask. He needed to find out what he could. Needed to figure out what had gone wrong.

She didn't respond right away. When she did, he could hear the emotion of loss in her voice. "There was a big storm and the ocean was rougher than usual. As best we can figure out, she got caught up in the waves and washed out to sea. Her body was never found."

There'd been no body to find. It was safe and sound in 1888 Wyoming Territory.

"She was my best friend," she went on. "We were both social workers at the same grade school."

The school where Sarah had met Miguel Lopez. Perhaps Melody knew Miguel, knew where he could find the child and his mother. He couldn't just ask outright. "Were there many students at this school?" he asked, hoping that he could steer the conversation in the direction he needed it to go.

"Hundreds. But Sarah and I didn't work with all of them. There were a few special ones," she said, and he could hear a change in her voice.

"Like who?" he asked.

She gave him a half smile. "Tonight, the one I'm thinking about is Miguel. Probably because I'm here." She pointed to a large boulder that sat about thirty feet back from the water's edge. "Sarah's cell phone was found on the beach, wedged behind that big rock. When the police investigated her disappearance, they traced all the phone calls that she'd made. The last one was to a customer service representative at an insurance company. When the police told me that, I called him. He gave me some information that would have been important to Sarah, important to Miguel and the Lopez family."

Sarah had explained much the same before he'd left her and John Beckett in Wyoming Territory. She'd said that Miguel's mother wanted to care for her sick child at home, but that would have required special machines and nurses. A company, the one that had sold her something called insurance, had refused to pay for these things. They had said that Miguel must go to a hospital but the only hospital they would pay for was many miles from Miguel's home. Miguel's mother had no way to travel there and even if she did, she could not leave Miguel's younger sisters alone.

Sarah had accepted that Miguel was going to die. She could not accept that he would die alone. She had fought for Miguel and his mother and finally the company had agreed to pay for Miguel to be cared for at home, surrounded by his family. But Sarah had been swept off the beach before she'd gotten to tell Miguel's mother. "What did you do?" George asked.

"I did what Sarah would have done. I helped Miguel and his mother." She shrugged her delicate shoulders. "We became friends," she added, her voice very soft. "I stayed with them often. It was a difficult time. Especially toward the end."

Toward the end. He leaned forward, urgency ripping through him. "What happened to the child?" he demanded.

"He died. Five months after Sarah did." She said it simply but he knew from the way her shoulders tensed and the set of her pretty mouth that it hadn't been simple at all.

The water in his stomach surged upward and he had to work to keep from vomiting. Miguel was already dead. He'd come for nothing. Had left everything for nothing.

Melody stared at the ocean, oblivious to him. "You know, it's been more than six months now and I can still hear Miguel teasing his sisters," she said. "Or reading the newspaper to his mother. He desperately wanted to teach her to read and write English."

Sarah had told him that, too. George focused on breathing in through his nose and out his mouth and when he felt able, he asked, "And did his mother learn?"

"She did. Rosa Lopez knew that learning to read was her final gift to her child." She turned to look at him and he could see the sheen of tears in her pretty eyes. He understood why she was unaware of the affect of her words. She was dealing with her own pain and had no reason to think that what she was saying would be important to him.

"It was a horrible time but there were days that were wonderful," she said. "Days that were so full of love. In the end, he died in his mother's arms, and I think he was content."

George closed his eyes and prayed for the child who had fought the final battle and the mother who had watched him go. It made him remember the desperation he'd felt when Hannah and their unborn child had been killed. It made him remember the rage, the absolute sense of loss.

"I'm glad that you were there," he said. "I'm sure Sarah . . . your friend . . . would have been grateful."

"I'd like to think so. I miss her."

He had to tell her the truth. She'd already spent a year missing her friend. "There's something you should know," he said. "I—"

"You know what really helped me when Miguel died," she interrupted, "is that I knew that Sarah was already there waiting for him. I knew he wasn't going to be alone. It's the one thing that really gives me peace."

Was it his place to rip that peace away from her? Could he tell her that her friend hadn't drowned? That she'd been swept off the beach and traveled back to 1888 Wyoming Territory? That she'd met John Beckett there?

What would Melody think if she knew that George had met Sarah in a saloon? That he'd left his home in North Dakota months earlier and had been tracking a man who had killed his wife and unborn child, intending to avenge their deaths? Would she cower in fear again? Even though, in the end, when the man had been killed, it had not been by George's hand?

He'd never seen two more miserable people than Sarah Tremont and John Beckett when it looked like Sarah was going to have to return to her own time to help Miguel Lopez and his family. Then the footprints had appeared— but not for Sarah or John. No, it had been George who had taken first one step, then another, and had been whisked up into darkness.

"I'm sorry," she said. "I didn't mean to interrupt you. What were you saying?"

This woman had suffered two great losses but she'd obviously come to terms with both of them. If he told her the truth, would she miss her friend any less? Would it only cause her grief because the peace that she'd clung to for the past few months would disappear?

He knew better than most that peace was mighty hard to come by.

"Um . . . nothing." He rubbed a hand over his face.

"I came here tonight to tell Sarah I was leaving. I thought she'd want to know."

"What about your job at the school?"

"After Sarah's disappearance, the school expected me to cover her caseload. I already had all I could handle. There was no way I could spend the time I needed to spend with Miguel and his family. I took a leave of absence but ultimately the school ended up replacing both Sarah and me. So there was no job to go back to." She smiled at him. "It's for the best. I really need to go home."

"Where's home?"

"My grandmother has a place about two hours north of San Francisco. In the hills of Napa Valley. Have you ever been there?"

He'd heard of San Francisco, had even had a neighbor once who'd traveled there and back again to North Dakota. But he had no idea what this valley might be. He shook his head.

"It's a beautiful place. Even when the roads are jammed with traffic and there are tourists everywhere, it's a special place." She chewed on her lower lip. "I'm leaving early in the morning. I haven't come back here since Sarah's death but for some reason, I couldn't go until I came tonight. And when the water kept edging farther up onto the beach, I wasn't scared. It was like I was suddenly closer to her." She stopped and shook her head. "You must think I'm crazy."

"I don't think that." Crazy was stepping into footprints and traveling a hundred and eighteen years forward. Crazy was arriving a year too late. What the hell had happened?

Hannah had been there, directing, guiding. He was sure of it. She wouldn't have led him astray. Never.

He stared up at the now-dark sky dotted with sparkling stars and a quarter-moon. He'd never been a devout man, had counted on Hannah to take care of the praying for both of them. It didn't seem right now to suddenly start, no matter how much he wanted answers. He gave the sky one last, lingering look before turning to face Melody.

She stared at him for a long moment and he couldn't stop himself from staring back. She had strikingly strong features, everything from her expressive eyes to her high cheekbones to her full mouth.

"I guess I better be going," she said.

He stood up and held out a hand to help her up. Her skin was warm and soft and when she swayed, as if she wasn't quite steady on her feet, his heart thumped in his chest. He held on to her hand and her wedding ring felt warm against his palm. "Are you ill?"

She shook her head. "If I don't eat every three hours, I get a little light-headed. I think I'm about a half hour behind schedule. Once I get home, I'll have some crackers and hot tea and I'll be fine."

Hannah had loved tea. Every night before bed, she'd brewed a cup. She drank it strong and very hot. He wondered how Melody Song liked her tea.

But that wasn't his business. She had a husband who would know those things—would know whether she liked to sweeten it with sugar or cream, would know what cup she liked to drink from. "I imagine your husband will be worried about you," he said, wanting to distance himself from her female charm.

"I don't have a husband," she said. She pulled her hand away.

His hand felt suddenly cold. Oh, hell. "I'm sorry." He

looked deliberately at the ring. "I didn't realize you were a widow."

"I've never been married."

She said it without malice, without much emotion at all. He wasn't at all sure what to make of it.

"I bought this ring just today. Got a good deal on it. Nobody wants plain wedding bands anymore. At least that's what the guy at the jewelry store told me. I told him that I'd lost the ring that my husband had given me and needed to replace it quickly while he was out of town. I don't think he believed me. Probably because I was stumbling over my words. But it didn't stop him from selling me a ring, though."

It was a rambling explanation but he thought he understood now why she was going home to family. "It's not my place to judge," he said quickly. "Will your parents meet you at your grandmother's?"

She looked at her hands. "Sarah's death was the second time that the Pacific has stolen from me. Fifteen years ago, during a rainstorm, just an hour north of here, my parents' car slid off the road, right through a guardrail. They fell a couple hundred feet before they hit the ocean."

Life had dealt Melody Song her share of hardship. Sarah had told him about the square metal boxes on wheels that they called cars. The things must be hard to control. It made him realize that while he'd left a world that was sometimes hard and unforgiving, he'd perhaps come to a time of even greater dangers.

"After they died, I went to live with my grandmother," Melody said, looking at him once again.

"Does she know that you're with child?"

"She does. She's delighted. Of course," she added, shaking her head slightly, "she also thinks I'm married."

He was grateful for all his years of being a sheriff and

the many times he'd had to piece together bits of a story. It helped him now. "Because you told her that."

She rubbed a hand across her mouth. "I'm twenty-eight years old and I swear, it's the craziest thing I've ever done. But it just seemed like the right thing to do at the time."

"Why?" He'd met this woman less than thirty minutes ago but he felt like he had a right to know. He'd dragged her from the ocean, after all.

"My grandmother means everything to me. And while it might be 2006, Grandmother holds tight to the old traditions, the old beliefs. And of all the things she feels very strongly about, legitimacy of a child is right there at the top."

"And that's wrong?"

"Oh no. Trust me, she has very good reasons to feel that way. But I'm sure you're not interested in all that. Anyway, now she's . . . ill. Very ill. My aunt Tilly called a few days ago and said that Grandmother wanted me home. She wants to meet my husband."

It did seem like a hell of a mess. "What are you going to do?"

She shrugged. "Well, I guess unless I find a husband within the next twelve hours, I'll have to tell her the truth."

He heard the forced lightness in her voice and knew that Melody Song's burden was heavy. "Your grandmother will understand," he said, hoping he was right.

"She will." Her voice cracked at the end. "It's just that it's going to hurt her so much when she finds out that I've been lying to her. And then there's the whole thing about the baby not having a father. She's really going to hate that."

He was no expert on these things but he was fairly certain that not everything had changed that much in a hundred and eighteen years. "There *has* to be a father. Where is he?"

"Long gone. Probably still running. He took off about ten minutes after I told him I was pregnant."

That kind of thing had happened in his time, too, but George had never been able to abide a man who didn't handle his own responsibilities. "So, he left you and the child to fend for yourselves?"

"We'll be fine," she said. "Look, this probably sounds strange but I know that I'm better off without him. He's got . . . issues. What I know for sure is that he has no interest in being a father to this baby."

"Damn fool." Man didn't deserve what was his.

"Do you have children?" she asked.

He shook his head.

"A wife?"

"I did," he said. He realized it was the first time that he'd automatically thought about Hannah in the past tense. He suddenly wanted to tell Melody about his wife; not how she'd died, but rather how she'd lived. But he couldn't. She would have too many questions, then too many doubts, maybe even fear.

That wasn't how he wanted his time with her to end.

He had perhaps just minutes. Sarah had told him that the footprints in the sand, the ones she'd stepped into to travel back to 1888 Wyoming Territory, had appeared around the time the sun had set. She'd been at this very beach, perhaps in this very spot. It could happen at any moment. He needed to make sure Melody was safely off the beach first.

"It's getting late," he said. "I don't want to keep you."

"Yes. I . . ." She stopped and then smiled. Placing a hand over her stomach, she said, "*We* appreciate everything you did tonight." She paused. "Well, good night."

She turned and walked toward the steep steps at the rear of the beach. He watched her until she got to the top and disappeared over the edge. Then he looked around. The moon had slipped behind a cloud and the beach was even darker than before. He could hear the rush of the water and knew that behind all that noise was his world.

He felt very alone. He didn't belong in this strange place. Miguel was already gone. There was no reason to stay. He had no work, no money, no place to live.

George started walking, looking for his path home.

TWO

HOURS later, when the sky was black with only a quarter-moon to guide his path, when even the birds were quiet, George was still pacing up and down the beach. For hours, he'd walked a mile or so in one direction before turning back and doing the same thing in the other direction. He hadn't wanted to stray too far from the spot he'd arrived at and that Sarah had departed from. His stomach was empty, his ribs still hurt, and his soul ached with worry.

Finally, exhausted, he lay down on the cold sand, feeling more weary than he'd ever felt, even counting those terrible days following Hannah's death. He closed his eyes and later, when he woke, the soft gray of early morning washed across the still-empty stretch of beach. The sun was well over the horizon, although not yet warm with heat. He closed his eyes and continued to lay on his back, unwilling to let go of his dreams, of the peace the memories had brought him.

He'd dreamed of John and Sarah, of all the people he'd left behind. He'd dreamed of his job as sheriff of

Bluemont, North Dakota. And of Hannah and the baby she'd carried.

He realized with a start that the last person he'd dreamed about had been Melody. She'd gotten herself into trouble and now had a babe on the way. In his time, there were few choices for a woman on her own with a child. There'd be little money and even less acceptance.

He hated the thought of any woman having to struggle along with no man to help her. It wasn't right.

"George. Excuse me, George. Mr. Tyler."

His eyes flew open and he lifted his head. Melody Song, her arm in the air, waving to him, was climbing down the steep steps at the edge of the beach.

He sat up. For a minute, he thought maybe he was still dreaming. She was practically upon him before he grabbed hold of his senses. He scrambled to his feet, feeling like a clumsy fool.

She'd changed her clothes. She had on a bright yellow blouse, which was snug at the top but loose enough lower down to provide space for her growing baby. She had white trousers that ended at least six inches above her ankles and she wore some crazy kind of shoes that showed her toes.

The woman had nice feet. Small and smooth, with toenails painted pink.

The early morning breeze blew her hair across her face and she pushed it out of her face. "Good morning," she said.

Christ. She was real. He'd imagined that her hair was dark. But it was much lighter. It was the color of winter wheat, a rich honey, and it fell in thick waves past her shoulders. "What are you doing here?" he asked, and got embarrassed when his voice squeaked like that of a young boy's. It didn't surprise him though. Melody Song, with her smooth skin, her shiny hair, and her full breasts, made him feel as inept as a twelve-year-old.

"I don't know," she said, her voice subdued. "I got up early this morning knowing I needed to be on the road if I was going to make my grandmother's house by lunch. I was driving by, had almost passed the Fayetteville exit, and all of a sudden, I just knew I had to check. I had to know if you were still here."

"I am," he said, trying hard not to let her hear the desperation he felt.

"Do you know that I almost caused a freakin' wreck? I crossed two lanes of traffic without even looking." She waved an impatient hand toward him, like it was somehow his fault. "I never drive crazy. I'm a very careful driver," she added, like she might be trying to convince herself.

He couldn't stop looking at her hair. "You look different," he said. "Your hair."

"Took me a half hour in the shower last night to get it clean. Between the salt water and the french-fry grease from work, it had taken a beating."

French-fry grease? From work? None of what she said made any sense. She'd said she lost her job at the school. "Where do you work?"

"I have a friend who owns a little restaurant, sort of upscale sandwiches and fancy desserts. I'm a waitress there."

"Seems like that might be hard work for a woman who's carrying a child."

"I was grateful for the job. But you're right," she said, smiling at him. "It's getting harder and harder to lift those trays. Plus, I really need to find a position that offers insurance for me and the baby."

It sounded like Melody intended to work soon after the child's arrival. He wondered how she would manage. She'd be trying to juggle her new position, a new baby, and a sick grandmother. "Is there anyone to help you at your grandmother's?"

"Well, there's Tilly and Louis. They're my aunt and uncle and they have lived with Grandmother for the past seventeen years, ever since my grandfather died. They came for the funeral, stayed for lunch, and then never left."

"They must have been good company for your grandmother?"

"Yes, well, let's just say that generally I'm glad they were there. There's my great-aunt Genevieve, too. She's a couple years younger than Grandmother. Very independent, sort of a free spirit."

She talked fast but he thought he understood. It was, however, damn hard to concentrate on what she was saying. She was pure pleasure to watch. Her eyes seemed more blue than violet this morning and her face glowed with the healthy sheen of motherhood. Her bare arms were tanned from the sun and were sleek with feminine muscle.

When she gracefully sank to the ground next to him, his heart skipped a beat until he realized that she wasn't fainting, that she was just getting comfortable. She lifted her head and looked up at him. He felt awkward standing over her and there was no good reason for her to strain her neck. He sank down next to her.

"You slept on the beach," she accused.

It didn't seem to make much sense to deny it. "I've slept in worse places," he said.

She looked concerned. "You're lucky you didn't get mugged. The beach isn't safe at night." She stared at her pink toes. "Do you . . . uh . . . live around here?"

Not hardly. "No. Just passing through."

She stopped looking at her feet and instead looked at him. Her scrutiny made him uncomfortable. He figured he must be a sight. He had sand in his hair, stubble on his face, and his clothes were ripped and torn.

"If you need a ride somewhere," she said suddenly,

surprising him, "I'd be glad to drop you off. Just tell me where you want to go."

He had nowhere to go. He had to stay. Had to wait for the footprints.

Go. Go with her.

"Did you hear that?" he asked.

She blinked her pretty eyes. "What?"

Christ. "Nothing," he said. The damn wind was talking to him, making his heart jump and his skin heat up.

She needs you.

He rubbed his temple. She was going home to family. Her grandmother might not approve but she'd welcome her. That's what families did. "You get along with your grandmother?" he asked.

"Uh . . . yes," she said, obviously confused at his question. "She's wonderful, the best really. She has"—she paused and furiously blinked her eyes—"cancer. My aunt says it's very serious. Her doctors say that chemo wouldn't make a difference. She's had some radiation treatments but they didn't really help."

What she said made no sense to him but he knew that whatever this cancer was, it must be a ravaging beast. He hurt for her. Barely knew her, but still, hurt on her behalf. He watched her grasp a handful of sand and hold the weight in the palm of her hand. Then carefully, deliberately, she spread her fingers, letting the grains fall through. "She's going to slip away from me," she said, her voice heavy with emotion. "Like sand through my fingers."

He'd slid through time, like sand through a crack. Now he waited to be swept up by the wind, like wayward sand, and carried home, left to settle back into a world he knew.

His problem was that he'd never been especially good at waiting. He was a man of action and he didn't need any damn wind telling him what was the right thing to do. "You said yesterday that you were looking for a husband."

She cocked her head to the left. "What?"

"You said that you told your grandmother that you had a husband and she's expecting you to bring him home. That's what you said, right?"

She chewed on the corner of her bottom lip. "That's what I said."

"I've been a husband. It wouldn't be like starting from scratch."

Keeping her head tilted, she patted the side of her head with the palm of her hand. Then she made a production of leaning her head to the other side and repeating the motion before sitting up very straight. "I must have water in my ears still."

Now that he'd decided, he wouldn't be put off. "You need a husband. I've got a little time on my hands. We'd be helping each other out."

Her cheeks showed bright spots of color. "Oh, good grief. You don't know what you'd be getting yourself into. You've got to have better things to do."

What was there to do when a person was a round peg in a square hole? "My offer stands," he said.

"I'd be asking too much. Look, this isn't a weekend trip home. I don't know how long I'm staying."

That made two of them. He just needed to stay prepared, to be ready when the footprints back appeared. "If I need to leave, if something comes up suddenly," he said, "you can always give them an excuse. By then, they'll believe I'm the real thing."

She stood up, her movements less graceful than before. She started walking, making small circles around him. "This is nutty," she muttered, waving her delicate hands. "It'll never work." Another circle. "It's too much for me to expect." Another circle.

Christ, he was getting dizzy. But he couldn't stop watching her. The wind blew across the ocean, making her hair fly and pushing her loose shirt tight up against her frame, and he saw the slight evidence of her child.

She stopped walking. "What's in it for you?" she asked.

A sense of purpose, perhaps. He'd had that when he was sheriff and had the responsibility of taking care of a whole town. Had certainly had it when he'd been chasing after Hannah's killers. He'd been spurred on by the need for vengeance. But now, in this strange time, he had no town that needed him. And in 2006, the one remaining man of the three who had hurt his Hannah, was certainly long dead. He had no reason for continuing on other than to help Melody Song.

But she had every reason for questioning his offer. After all, by what she'd shared, there had already been one man who'd charmed her into his bed, only later to desert her. This was a woman who would be on guard, who would question a man's motives.

"My pockets are empty and I've got no job and no place to live," he said.

She nodded. "I would definitely pay you," she said.

He'd never cared all that much about money. "We'll work something out," he said. He looked down at his clothes. "I guess I'm not really dressed to go calling on family."

"That's easy to fix," she assured him. She played with the hem of her blouse. Then she did some more circles in the sand. Finally, she lifted her eyes to the blue sky and he saw her lips move in what he figured was silent prayer. As long as she wasn't asking God for another big wave to wash him away, it probably couldn't hurt.

It took her another minute before she looked at him. "Well, what do you say?" he asked.

She gave him a wobbly sort of smile, stuck out her hand, and said, "I think we just got married."

ON the way to her car, Melody examined her new husband. His shirt and pants, which had been wet and clinging to his body last night, had dried stiff. His dark brown hair, which was well over the edge of his shirt collar, was matted down in a combination of salt and sand. He wore cowboy boots with a one-inch heel and it looked like the worn leather hadn't yet dried all the way.

Last night when he'd said his name was George, it had startled her because he looked very much like George Clooney from his days on the television show *ER*. While it was unlikely to stumble upon a famous actor on a deserted beach outside Los Angeles, it wasn't impossible, and hearing his last name had been a relief. She wondered if that was why she'd missed the fact that he had lovely moss-green eyes with dark lashes so thick that if he'd been a girl, she'd have discreetly leaned over and asked for a recommendation on mascara.

It had been too dark to see that his skin was tanned with a few lines around his eyes or that when he smiled, his teeth were nice and straight with the exception of the slightest overlap of his lower two front teeth. Had he been the kind of boy who didn't have time for a retainer?

What she had noticed was that he had a nice voice and a wonderful sort of gentlemanly manner about him. That was hard to miss.

She wondered if he was homeless. It seemed rather obvious that he only had the clothes on his back. She'd realized she was taking a chance when she'd offered him a ride. But she couldn't leave him stranded when he'd risked his life to save hers.

They were just a few feet from the steps that would take them up the steep cliff when he stopped to pick up what looked to be a ten-by-ten square wood box. It had a latch and a long leather strap that he looped over his shoulder. "What is that?" she asked.

"My camera."

She'd seen old cameras in similar boxes at flea markets. "Oh, an antique one?"

He looked rather startled, like perhaps he hadn't expected her to ask that. "Yes, it is." He motioned for her to go first on the steps. She took them slowly, but even so, when she got to the top she was breathing hard, keenly aware of every one of the eight pounds she'd already gained.

"Maybe we should rest a minute," he said.

She smiled at him. "I know this will surprise you, but I used to live on the tenth floor of this huge apartment building. I did the stairs every day."

"Tenth floor," he repeated, like he could hardly believe her. She didn't blame him. Not when she was practically panting like a dog on a hot summer day.

"Fortunately for me," she said, pointing to her five-year-old green Grand Prix, which was the only car in the small lot due to the time of the day, "we're driving the rest of the way."

He stared at her car and his eyes showed a myriad of emotions she couldn't identify. She felt bad for him. Maybe he'd had to give up his own car when he'd fallen on hard times. Or God forbid, maybe he'd had to sleep in a car after he'd lost his home. She kept walking, wanting to give him a moment. When she reached the car, she looked over her shoulder. He was still standing in the same spot.

Not sure what else to do or say, she opened the door and got in on the driver's side. That seemed to spur him into action. He walked quickly to the other side, opened the door, and when he sort of sank, half-dropped into the seat, he almost hit his head on the roof.

"Careful," she warned.

When he leaned forward and placed the camera between his feet, she thought she saw his hand tremble. "I'm a very good driver," she assured him. "Just forget what I said earlier about cutting across multiple lanes of traffic." She fastened her seat belt and he did the same, although he fumbled around with the catch.

When she pulled out of the lot, he sat up in his seat and gripped the handle on the upholstered door. "There's a Target just up the street," she said, trying hard not to be offended. She *was* a good driver. "We can get some clothes there."

He kept staring out the front window. Ten minutes later she pulled into a crowded strip mall lot and found a space. When she turned to look at him, she was surprised to see how pale he looked. "Oh no," she said. "You're not the carsick type, are you?"

He shook his head. "I don't think so." He sat bone-straight in his seat.

Oh this was going to be such a fun drive. As weird as her stomach had become, if he threw up, it would be a matter of seconds before she joined him in sympathy.

How the heck had one little lie turned into this? Okay, it wasn't *one* lie and none of them were that *little*.

She'd always gone home for Christmas. But she hadn't this past year. On the twentieth of December, when her period, which always, always, came every twenty-eight days, was six days late, she'd taken a home pregnancy test. She'd promptly gone to the store and bought two more and repeated the test on the twenty-first and twenty-second of December. All three of them had said the same thing. She was pregnant. On the twenty-third of December, still reeling from the shock, she'd called her grandmother and told her that she had to work at the restaurant over the holidays and wouldn't be able to come home this year. That had been the first lie.

On the fifth of January, her grandmother had called for her weekly chat. A day earlier, Melody had seen her doctor and he'd confirmed that in late August or early September, her child would be born. She'd left the doctor's office and called Alexander, the man she'd met a month after Miguel had died.

When she'd told him about the pregnancy, he'd gotten very quiet, not at all like the fun and carefree man who had swept her off her feet when she was still reeling from grief. After a minute, he'd blurted out that he already had a sixteen-year-old and a nine-year-old. Oh yeah, and a wife, too. That had come up some time later in the conversation. That's when she'd felt really stupid. Of course, he'd been fun and carefree with her. His worries were back home in Ohio.

So when her grandmother called less than twelve hours later, hurt and fear and pure craziness had spilled out of her mouth. She'd told her grandmother that an old boyfriend had surfaced a few months earlier and that one thing had led to another and they'd eloped on New Year's Eve. Lie number two.

Her grandmother had been surprised but gracious, offering her congratulations first and then second, demanding to know when she could meet the new husband. Melody had promised soon, hung up the phone, and cried for an hour.

In mid March, she'd played the *we're pregnant* card. In a rare moment of truth, she'd told her grandmother that she was already almost fifteen weeks along. Her grandmother had quickly done the math and realized that Melody had already been a month pregnant on New Year's Eve, when she'd eloped. Her grandmother had taken the news in stride and Melody had understood. It wasn't important when she'd gotten pregnant. What was important was that she was married now. The baby would have legitimacy—something that her grandmother had never had.

Her grandmother had begged her to come home but she'd come up with one excuse after another. More lies. Her plan had been to have the baby, and then, quietly, without much fuss, claim irreconcilable differences and get a quick divorce. It wasn't perfect but it could have worked.

But she hadn't ever dreamed that her grandmother was sick. There'd been no mention of it. When Tilly had told her, the word *cancer* had seemed to vibrate in her ear, to go on forever. When Tilly had said that her grandmother wanted Melody and her husband to come home now, Melody had agreed without question. It was only hours later, when she'd finally stopped crying and started thinking, that she'd realized what a truly horrible predicament she was in.

Then she'd met George, and now she was taking her new husband home to meet the family. They were going to be late, however, if he wouldn't get out of the car. He had relaxed his death grip but he continued to just sit and stare out the front window at all the cars going past.

"I told my aunt I'd be there for lunch," she reminded him. She started to reach for the door and stopped suddenly when she felt the movement of new life. She'd first felt the delicate flutter around twenty weeks and every day in the two weeks since, the movements had become stronger, making it more real.

She pressed her hand to her stomach and like always, joy blossomed, pushing despair aside. However it had happened, whatever had been the consequences, what mattered was now. She was having a baby.

But first she needed to take her new husband home. "Let's go, George." He didn't answer but he did get out. Once inside the store, he wandered up and down the aisles, like a little kid, touching things, looking at price tags. When they got to the men's section, she turned to him. "What size of pants do you wear?"

He shrugged and she had no choice, really none, but to take a really good look at his body. His belly was flat, his hips trim, and his legs long. "I'm sort of out of my element here," she said, "but I'm guessing about a thirty-four-inch waist and a thirty-six-inch length. How's that sound?"

"Fine," he said, but made no move to pick anything out. She looked at his ugly flannel shirt. "Large in shirts, right?"

"I imagine," he answered.

She waited another minute before she simply picked out a pair of tan pants, some jeans, a couple shirts, and shoved them all into his arms. "Okay?" she asked.

He nodded. As they walked up to the checkout, she'd added a package of briefs and some tee shirts, never making eye contact. At the last minute, she detoured to the sundry items and picked up a handful of the basic things he'd need.

It cost her a hundred and forty-two dollars and when she handed over her credit card, George's mouth literally dropped open. When the clerk handed her the sack, she pulled him to the side and pointed to the restrooms at the front of the store. "Why don't you change here," she suggested.

Fifteen minutes later, she realized he cleaned up real well. When he walked out of the men's room, she barely recognized him. He'd put on the jeans and tucked the long-sleeved white shirt into them. He'd shaved and maybe even washed his hair. It was wet and pushed away from his face.

She'd been right about the sizes although the jeans looked just a little loose at the waist.

Easy for a lover to slip her hand inside.

Damn. Where had that thought come from? She sat down so hard on the red plastic bench lining the wall that she felt the vibration all the way up her spine. He crouched in front of her and reached for her hand. "Is it the child?" he asked, his voice thick with concern.

How could she tell him that she'd just had a thought that no woman who was pregnant with another man's baby should be having about a man that she'd met just a day before? "I'm fine," she said. "I get tired when I stand too long," she lied.

He helped her up and kept his hand under her elbow as they walked out of the store. When they got to the car, he opened her door, waited until she got in, then carefully shut it.

She thought it was so sweet that she didn't even get mad when he got in, fastened his seat belt, and grabbed the door handle again, like he was hanging on for dear life.

He didn't let go for three hundred miles. He held on and stared out the front window and every so often sucked in a breath of air like he was gasping for oxygen.

He'd spoken once. They'd been on the road for several hours when he turned to her and asked, "Should you eat something? It's been more than three hours."

She looked at her watch and realized he was, give or take fifteen minutes, right on the mark. That freaked her out since she'd noticed he didn't even wear a watch. It freaked her out even more that he'd remembered what she'd said the day before. Like he really cared.

She reached her hand behind her seat and fished a box of crackers out of a bag. "Want some?" she asked, holding up the box.

He shook his head. "You go ahead."

She dumped ten or so onto her lap and then tossed the box over her shoulder. "I guess we should get our stories straight," she said.

"Probably be a good idea."

"We got married on New Year's Eve. A small ceremony at City Hall. You'd recently returned to the Los Angeles area and we'd rekindled an old college relationship."

"I see." He paused. "We'd courted for some time in the past?"

Courted? "Yes, I guess we did."

He was quiet for the next few miles. "Were you and your child's father together for a long time?"

"I met Alexander shortly after Miguel had died. With Sarah gone, too, I was lonely and sad and when I was with him, I could forget that." She glanced over and he was studying her with interest, and perhaps a little sympathy. It was the latter that she couldn't stand. It was the kind of look she'd gotten too often after her parents had died. She hadn't deserved the sympathy then, she didn't deserve it now. Alexander had fooled her and she'd been careless. "It wasn't love. We both knew that," she lied.

The tip of his nose got pink and she wondered if she'd shocked him. Good. Shock was way better than sympathy. But if that shocked him, her family and its very strange dynamics would push him over the edge. She gripped the wheel with a growing sense of dread. This was never going to work.

It was just that he'd been so darn convincing on the beach. He'd looked at her with those intense green eyes and she'd started to think that maybe he was the answer to her prayers. What had possessed her to do something so crazy?

She drove north for another ten minutes before flipping on her turn signal. She slowed the car down, made a right-hand turn, leaving the main road. "We're almost there," she said, "another fifteen minutes at the most. Grandmother's house is up in those hills."

He nodded, his attention on the grapevines, supported by their trellis system, that flanked both sides of the paved road. The man just did not talk much. "You know," she rambled on, "over the river and through the woods to Grandmother's house we go."

He didn't even blink.

"Except there's no river and no woods. Just grapes," she added, like an idiot. She put her foot on the brake and stopped the car. "George, let's just admit it. This is never going to work."

THREE

"WE'RE not even there yet and you're giving up?" he asked. Before she could answer, he let go of the door handle and turned his head to glance out the window. "Pretty country," he said.

It was beautiful country, so lush in the springtime. Summer would bring the heat, which would be almost unbearable, but so necessary if the grapes were to ripen and sweeten. Fall would bring the rains. There'd be a push to bring the grapes to harvest before that happened.

"The closest bus station is less than a half hour from here," she said, trying to get him back on topic. "I'll drop you off and you can . . . uh . . . pick up your life where it was before I so rudely interrupted it."

"So grapes are the only crop?" he asked, his head still turned toward the window.

There was no time for a horticulture lesson. "Mostly. There are a few olive trees, for the heck of it. I mean, after all, this *is* wine country."

"I don't see any grapes on those vines," he said, sounding concerned.

"It's too early yet. What will be grapes are now just buds."

"What's that?" he asked, his eyes focused a hundred yards out.

"A wind machine. Sort of a really big fan. Frost is a vineyard manager's worst nightmare. These machines can mix the warmer air, which lingers somewhere about twenty feet above ground, with the colder air at the surface. Many times that's all that's needed to ward off significant damage to a grape crop."

He finally turned to look at her. "I don't know much about growing grapes."

He should stop worrying. He wasn't staying that long. "There are plenty of people here who do," she said, dismissing his concern.

"Like your aunt and uncle?" he asked.

"Uh . . . no. Tilly and Louis mostly work on the business end and leave the grape-growing to others."

"You don't sound all that fond of them."

Damn. Either he was more perceptive than most or she hadn't been as careful as usual. "We've never been close. It'll be even worse now."

"Why is that?"

"Because of the baby. They weren't able to have children. Tilly resented that her sister, my mother, was able to. It probably didn't help that once my parents were gone, Grandmother doted on me. Now that I'm pregnant, it'll be just one more reminder."

He glanced at her foot, which still rested on the brake. "So the father doesn't want the child and your family will resent it. Seems like quite a burden for the unborn."

She pressed her hand to her abdomen. "I'll protect my child," she said. She frankly didn't care what Tilly and

Louis thought. She'd stopped doing cartwheels for them a long time ago once she'd figured out it was them and not her that were the problem.

"Does your grandmother know that there's friction between you and your aunt and uncle?"

"She knows we're not great friends but we're all very civil to one another. As long as they're nice to Grandmother, it's not important how they feel about me." It was her grandmother's opinion that mattered. The woman had given her a home and loved her unconditionally. "Look, I'll admit that it's not the best circumstance," she said, "but I can't worry about the things I can't change. I won't waste my time."

"Speaking of time, shouldn't we be going?"

The enormity of what she was about to do made her chest hurt. She was about to take a stranger into her family's home and pass him off as her husband. More important, from his perspective, she was about to subject this poor man to an inquisition better reserved for insurgent rebels. "George, I don't think this—"

Her cell phone rang and she grabbed it out of her purse. George jerked back and bumped his shoulder against the car door.

"Hello," she said.

"You're late. Your grandmother is worried and Louis and I have plans this afternoon."

As usual, Tilly's voice was loud and just shy of shrill. Maybe that was why George was staring at the phone like it was about to sprout wings. "Tilly, please let her know that I'm close," Melody said.

"You know we eat at one o'clock."

"I know. I'll be there in . . ." She looked at her watch. It would take her another hour by the time she turned around, dropped George off at the nearest bus station, and returned.

"Go ahead and eat without me," she said. She'd lost her appetite anyway.

"You're alone?" Her aunt's voice rose, in interest and raw speculation.

"I'm . . ."

George put his hand on her arm. His skin was shockingly warm. She looked at him and he was shaking his head.

She felt sick and dizzy and knew it was because she was teetering on the edge of reason. Was it really possible that she could pull this off, that she could convince her grandmother and the rest of the family that she was a happily married woman?

She knew she had to try.

"I'm showing my husband the grapes," she said. "We'll be along shortly."

She heard Tilly's hiss, then a click, then nothing. "Oh boy," she said, feeling like her head wasn't connected to her body any longer, "now I've done it."

George sat forward on the seat and grabbed the door. "We should probably be getting on. You need to have your noon meal. You're eating for two now," he said, his voice even kinder.

Melody pounded her fist on the steering wheel. "Yeah, but, don't you see? Now you're stuck. I'm stuck." She stopped pounding and pressed her fingers to the bridge of her nose, willing herself not to cry. "I've never lied to my grandmother. Ever. Until now. I . . ." She sucked in a breath. "I don't want her to die being disappointed in me."

She closed her eyes and focused on breathing and swallowing. It would be the icing on the cake if she lost her cookies, or more appropriately, her crackers, in the poor man's lap. She heard him unlatch his seat belt and then the sound of his door opening.

And she knew that he'd decided that walking back to the bus station was preferable to sitting in the car with a crazy pregnant woman. It was what she wanted, right? How could it hurt so much?

There was a soft knock on her window. He stood there, waiting. She reached for her purse. Of course, she'd owed him for his time this morning. He probably needed it for bus fare. She pulled out forty dollars, opened her door, and handed it to him. "Good luck," she said and meant it. None of this was his fault.

He ignored her hand and the money in it. "Take my seat," he said.

"What?"

"You're in no shape to operate this car. I'll take us the rest of the way."

"You're staying?"

"I gave you my word." He motioned with his hand for her to get out. "Please."

Feeling numb, she got out and walked around the car. By the time she got in, he was already behind the wheel, with his seat belt buckled. He waited until she buckled her own belt before he pressed his foot to the gas.

The engine of the car raced.

A dull red crept up the man's neck.

"It helps if you put it in Drive," she said.

He stared at her blankly. She pointed to the console between them. He grabbed the lever and moved it to Drive. They took off with a jerk and she was glad she was strapped in.

"You don't drive much, huh?" she asked.

"Not much," he said. His hands were wrapped tight around the wheel and he sat too far forward on his seat to be comfortable. He had, however, managed to even out the pace and now they drove a sedate twenty-five miles an hour down a road that most people took at sixty. She looked behind them and was relieved to see that they were the only car on the road.

The man probably rode mass transit every day. Many of her friends in the city didn't even have cars. "George, I guess I should know what you do for a living," she said. "Since we're married," she added lamely.

He drove for another minute. "I used to be a sheriff," he said. He said it simply. Proudly.

"But not anymore?" she asked.

He shook his head. "No."

She wanted all the details but knew she didn't have the right to ask. He'd probably had a desk job and ultimately became a victim of the bottom line. Every community in the country was cutting back on their public services. No wonder the man looked down and out.

"When this little charade is over," she said, "I'd be happy to help you find something. I've helped people with job searches before."

He nodded. "I'll keep that in mind."

"Turn at the next right," she said, directing him to the road that would take them out of the valley and up into the hillside. He took the turn, which was sharp, without braking. She grabbed the handle of the door, just as he had done for the entire morning, and hung on.

She didn't want to be bossy but she'd been driving this road since she was sixteen. "This gets pretty curvy and narrow in spots," she warned. When he gave her a quick glance, she made a point to look toward his feet and added, "Gives the brakes a good workout."

They almost jerked to a complete stop at the next turn. She felt like she was back in driver's ed. She'd been partnered with Judy Barnitski, who'd never really ever gotten the hang of the brakes either.

"They can be a little touchy," she said, not wanting him to feel bad. He didn't answer and she braced herself for the next curve.

It went remarkably well. She didn't let go of the door handle but she did start to breathe again. He was clearly a faster learner than skinny Judy had been.

"What name did you call your husband by?" he asked, after they'd negotiated two more turns successfully.

It was considerate of him to pretend that there had been a husband. "Michael Johnson. I wanted something very common so that if someone tried to Google him, there would be a thousand hits."

He looked absolutely perplexed.

"Not a lot of computers at the sheriff's office, huh?"

He didn't respond. "Michael Johnson," he repeated. "I guess I could get used to it."

"Don't worry about it. I'll tell them that your full name is Michael George Johnson but that you prefer to go by George. Then you only have to remember Johnson."

"I'll remember. So you're Melody Johnson?"

She could feel the heat all the way up to her ears. "I guess I am."

He took his eyes off the road long enough to turn and smile at her. "It's a pleasure to meet you, Mrs. Johnson."

THE house was a pale gray wood with white shutters and white trim on the immense wraparound porch. It sprawled across the land, two or three stories high in some places, bigger than any house he'd ever seen before. It was surrounded by green grass. Off to the far right side, there was a fountain like he'd seen in picture books. It was built of stone and had to be at least fifteen feet wide at the base and twenty feet in the air. It was an angel in flight, and water flowed from her wings. The light breeze caught the spray and carried it across the empty bench that sat in front of it.

He slowed the car down and turned to Melody. "This is your grandmother's place?"

She gave him the same wobbly smile that he'd seen on the beach. It made her look very young and he was more thankful than ever that he was there to help her.

"I guess I didn't mention that Grandmother owns one of the most successful midsized wineries in the Valley. Sweet Song of Summer wines are sold across the country. Song is my grandmother's last name. This ranch is called Songbook Serenade."

"Ranch?" It didn't look like any ranch he'd seen.

"That's what the people who live here call their land. It's sort of a shorthand way to refer to a neighbor's property."

"And your grandmother named it?"

"Her father did. Grandmother kept her maiden name when she married my grandfather and my mother did the same. Pretty unusual for my grandmother's generation but pretty much old stuff by the time my parents got married in the mid 1970s."

He'd married Hannah in the mid 1880s. She'd taken his name with pride. "And they named you Melody. Melody Song."

She rolled her eyes. "First grade was not a good year for me."

He understood. He'd stuttered until he was eight. "Children aren't always kind."

She patted her stomach. "Mine will be," she said. She waved a hand toward the house. "The house has been added onto over the years, but the original structure is almost a hundred and thirty years old," she said. "Can you believe that?"

He wasn't all that far behind. "I guess I can," he said. "What's over there?" he asked, pointing to the largest of the outbuildings. It was painted red and had a steeply sloping, shiny tin roof.

"That's the wine shed." She smiled at him. "Not a very fancy name, I know. There's office space inside, storage space for extra barrels, and the bottling operation in the rear. You can't see it from here, but there's a large cement paddock behind the shed where the grapes are processed as well as a couple fermentation tanks, too."

It was a far cry from the corn and bean fields of North Dakota. He struggled to know which question to ask next. "How many people live here?"

"Bernard and Gino each have suites in the east wing. Bernard is our winemaker and Gino manages vineyard operations."

"And your family lives in the rest of the house?"

"Grandmother and Great-Aunt Genevieve share the central quarters, although Grandmother has always chosen to spend her time outside. You won't find her in the kitchen. In years past, she worked the vineyard alongside my grandfather. More recently, she spends her time in the gardens."

There were beds of color—all kinds of pinks and purples—and large, practically overflowing pots on the porch. A sudden wave of homesickness came over him and he fought to control it. "Your great-aunt?" he asked.

"I just call her Aunt—she said the Great makes her feel old. Anyway, Aunt Genevieve never married and she lives on the top floor."

"She doesn't help your grandmother with the gardening?"

"I don't think I've ever seen her in the garden. I mentioned before that she's sort of a free spirit. I know it sounds crazy but sometimes she disappears for days. She locks the door of her bedroom and nobody goes in and she doesn't come out. Then, unexpectedly, she'll join the family for dinner and act like nothing happened. She's sort of odd in that way."

"And your aunt Tilly and uncle Louis?" he reminded her.

"They have the run of the west wing and," she paused and pointed, "see that smaller building to the left of the shed?"

It was gray like the house with a blue awning stretched across the front. There were chairs and tables out in front with more flowers. "Yes."

"That's a small gift shop. We offer tours and wine tasting by appointment and Tilly handles that out of there. Louis has an office in the back. He works in sales and does most of the advertising and promotion work. When he's not doing that, he mostly whittles away the day by bothering Bernard and Gino. That is, whenever he and Tilly haven't skipped off to Reno for a quick weekend."

"Reno, Nevada?"

"Yeah. Don't play cards with them unless you've got some money you want to lose. They've had a lot of experience."

Ah, gamblers. Not everything was different in this time. "What's that?" he asked, pointing to a good-sized white building that stood another two hundred yards back from the gift shop.

"That's the bunkhouse. Years ago, the field workers lived on the property in that building."

"But not anymore?"

"No. Grandmother feels strongly that the workers will be more satisfied and stay longer if they have roots in the community. She helps them buy small houses in town. The building isn't empty, though. We store equipment in there and there's a big table for the workers to eat their lunch inside, out of the hot sun."

She pointed to the bricked circle drive. "You'll want to park there."

He got her car stopped and tried to pull the keys out, wanting to make sure the machine wouldn't lurch forward on its own. Out of the corner of his eye, he saw her reach toward the lever between them and moved it forward, all the way to P. "That should make it easier," she said.

He yanked the keys out and dropped them into her pretty little hand. He hoped like hell that was the last time he ever had to travel like this. Because of what Sarah had told him about cars, he'd been prepared for the shape but not the speed at which they'd hurtled down the road. He'd watched Melody all morning and had thought he had it figured out, but obviously he'd missed a few things along the way.

Give him a horse any day. He liked feeling the wind in his hair, the sun on his face. Liked knowing that with a sharp tug on the reins, he had control.

Two brown-and-black dogs, their markings identical, ran toward them. They were big, full of muscle, and barking like crazy. "Do they bite?" he asked, thinking it was a damn shame if they did. He'd just have to take his chances because he wasn't sitting in this car for one more minute than he had to.

"Don't worry. They make a lot of noise but they're not mean. Unless you're in Aunt Genevieve's face. They're pure-blood German shepherd, and very loyal to her. She got them when they were pups. When she's in her room, they plant themselves outside the door. Once I saw Louis try to get into her room and I swear, he almost lost a leg." She smiled at him and he was once again struck by how pretty she was. "I think that's why I've always had a soft spot for them."

The front door opened and out stepped a woman. Even from the distance, George could see Melody's resemblance to her. There was the same strong bone structure, the same tilt of her chin. The woman's hair, thick and a brilliant white, blew around her face. "Your grandmother?"

"Yes. Oh my gosh," she whispered, her mouth barely moving. "She's lost so much weight."

It didn't stop the woman from practically running to the car. "Dionysos, Hermes, that's enough," she said, shushing the dogs. They stopped barking immediately. She jerked open the door. "Thank goodness you're here," she said. "I've been wearing a rut in my living room rug."

Once Melody was out of the car, the two women hugged and kissed. George opened his door and was halfway around the car when he saw the older woman pat Melody's stomach gently. She turned toward him and reached out her arm. "Michael, I presume?"

He moved quickly around the front of the car and returned the shake. Her fingers were small like Melody's and he made sure he didn't squeeze too hard. "It's my pleasure, ma'am. It's Michael George," he added, sticking to the story, "but I prefer George if you don't mind."

She looked him over. "Michael was the name of the first young man who dumped me, left me in the middle of a dance twiddling my thumbs. I think I prefer George myself. And please," she said, waving her hand, "there's no need for formality. Call me Grandmother or Pearl, either one is fine." She smiled at him.

He wasn't staying long enough to call her Grandmother. "Pearl it is, then."

The house door slammed and the dogs started barking again. George looked up to see a woman walking toward them. She had hair as black as night and it fell past her shoulders, even longer than Melody's. She wore a red shirt, red trousers, and a big gold belt pulled tight around her middle.

It made him think of a fifteen-pound pig stuffed inside a five-pound sack.

"So, you made it," she said.

It had to be Aunt Tilly. He recognized her voice as the one that had come out of the little machine Melody carried in her purse. The woman's red-painted mouth had a pinched look and he could see the puffiness under her eyes and the skinny blue lines, just under the surface of the skin, zigzagging across her cheeks.

She had the same look he'd seen on cowboys who had their noses too often in whiskey bottles. He supposed she'd been a pretty woman at one time, although her face probably had never had any of the softness that her niece carried so naturally.

Melody stepped out from behind her grandmother. "Tilly," she said, her voice cautious. "How are you?"

Tilly studied her niece, her gaze coming to rest on Melody's slightly rounded stomach. "Are you pregnant?" she asked, her voice stiff.

George realized that Melody had been right. The woman was not happy.

"I . . . yes. Um . . . this is my husband, George Johnson."

The woman folded her arms, pushing her abundant breasts up so high that George feared they might just pop out of her shirt. "Well, George," she said. "You didn't waste any time."

George had learned to read people, everybody from troublemaking cowboys to lonesome saloon girls. This woman was mean-spirited, no doubt about it. "No, ma'am. Didn't see the need."

A nasty shade of purple-red crept up her neck. She turned back to Melody. "I thought Mother said you got married on New Year's Eve."

"We did," Melody answered.

"When is your baby due?"

Melody didn't flinch. "Early September."

Tilly looked at her mother and smiled but there was no joy there. "Well, I guess it's true what they say about babies—for most of them it takes nine months but the first one can come anytime."

He heard the breath leave Melody's body.

"Tilly," Pearl said, her voice steady. "I'm going to have a great-grandchild and you're going to have a great-niece. That's what we need to be focused on."

The purple-red crept another two inches higher. "Of course. Congratulations, Melody, George." She turned, giving them her back. "Bessie said lunch is ready."

He didn't think she'd probably come late to too many meals. He looked toward Melody, but her attention was focused on a man coming from the wine shed. He favored his right leg when he walked and his hair was gray. George pegged him at around Pearl Song's age, give or take a couple years.

Melody met him halfway and she threw her arms around the man. George looked at Pearl. "Uncle Louis?"

She snorted. Took him a bit by surprise, her being such a lady. "That's Bernard. He's our winemaker. He's been here for almost thirty years. We owe much of our success to his efforts. Melody adores him and it's mutual."

She hooked her arm through his. "They'll want to catch up and it's been a good long time since a handsome young man walked me to my door. Come along. They'll follow soon enough."

He did as instructed, being careful to keep his stride short and his pace slow. The woman felt frail on his arm, as if a good, strong wind could blow her away.

When they got to the house, she opened the door of her home with a flourish. If he'd been surprised at the outside, the inside damn near stunned him. It was huge, with fancy wood flooring and floor-to-ceiling windows. There were hanging chandeliers and all kinds of pictures on the walls. She led him through the foyer into another room. The furniture was big and soft-looking, and it seemed as if ten people could be in the room and not be crowded. A big black piano sat in front of the bay window and to the left of it were double doors, which led outside onto another porch.

"Have a seat," she said. "I'll check on lunch."

He was glad he'd put on the new, clean clothes. He'd have been afraid to sit if he'd had his old trousers on. He lowered himself down onto the edge of the sofa.

He'd been there less than a minute when an old woman, stick-thin with dark brown hair cut so short she could have been a man, entered the room. She wore a blue dress that dragged on the floor and she carried a black cat in her arms. "So you're the husband?" she asked, her voice husky with age.

He stood up, feeling off-kilter. Her lips were painted bright orange, her eyes rimmed with black, and she had two yellow feathers stuck behind one ear. "I am."

"My great-niece is a special woman," she said. "I expect you know that."

He nodded.

"Don't disappoint her," she said, her voice suddenly hard. "If you do, you'll have me to answer to." She bent down and placed the cat on the floor. It walked toward him, its tail high in the air. Two feet away, it stopped and let out a sharp hiss.

"Oh for goodness sakes, Genevieve. Call off your cat." Pearl stood in the doorway. "The poor man needs a chance to catch his breath. He's had a journey." She turned toward him. "George, this is my sister, Genevieve. Melody's great-aunt."

Sort of odd. That's how Melody had described her. It was nice to know that his new wife wasn't prone to exaggeration. He extended his hand. "It's a pleasure, ma'am."

She stared at his hand long enough to make him uncomfortable. Then she extended her own thin arm. Her hand was bony and spotted from the sun. It reminded him of . . .

He jerked his hand back. Christ, he'd seen a similar hand not so long ago. It had wrapped around his arm and pulled. She smiled at him and he felt the chill run up his spine. He swiveled toward Pearl. She had her own hand in the air, waving it toward the hallway. Her hand was thin like the rest of her, and it looked very much like her sister's.

"This way," Pearl said. "Lunch is ready."

His stomach growled. Lunch would be the first food he'd had in a very long time.

Aunt Genevieve walked over to stand next to her sister. "Well, George?" she asked, her head tilted to the side, as if in challenge.

The absurdity of the situation didn't pass him by. He'd faced down bank robbers, cattle rustlers, and more liquored-up cowboys waving their guns than he cared to remember. And he'd never run from any of it. But now, two old women, one sick, the other half-crazy, had him about to tuck his tail under and run for the hills. Or in his case, the damn beach.

He'd never thought of himself as a coward. It wasn't an appealing picture. He looked them both in the eye. Neither woman flinched nor seemed overly aware of the panic that threatened to overtake him.

Of course not. They'd had nothing to do with getting him here. Any minute now he'd be seeing ghosts in the corners.

He squared his shoulders. "I'm looking forward to the meal," he said. "I appreciate your hospitality."

"It's our pleasure," Pearl said, as she walked out of the room. He followed her and as he walked past Aunt Genevieve, she said, "Welcome to the family, George."

FOUR

WHEN they got to the dining room, there was already a man sitting at the table, a half-eaten piece of buttered bread in front of him. "What a surprise," said Aunt Genevieve, her voice edgy with sarcasm. "George, this is Tilly's husband, Louis."

The man took his time chewing while he looked George up and down. Finally, he swallowed. "My wife tells me congratulations are in order."

The man had said it nice enough. "Thank you, sir," George replied. Uncle Louis looked like he could use the extra pounds that his wife was carrying. And with his bald head and fair skin, George bet the thin man took red in the sun. He turned to Pearl. "If you don't mind, I'd like to wash up before we eat."

She nodded toward the side door. "Through there and then down the hall. It's the second door on the right."

George found the way easily enough and slipped quietly into the small room. He'd seen the flush toilets at the store so that didn't surprise him but the gold handles on the sink took him back a peg. He pulled one forward, then the other, and when the water was warm, he squirted some fancy-smelling soap out of a bottle that sat on the edge of what had to be a marble sink.

Damn, these folks were rich.

He scrubbed his hands. Melody Song's baby would want for nothing. That is, nothing except a father. He rinsed the soap off and then shut off the water.

He eyed the green towel hanging on the hook and almost hated to get such a fine thing wet. However, since the alternative was his trousers, he reached for the fancy cloth. Once his hands were dry, he reached out and flipped the switch on the wall, the way he'd seen Melody's grandmother do when they'd entered the dining room.

The small room went completely dark.

He flipped it again. Light.

Back off, then on, and back off again. It was magic and it made him feel like a little child. For the hell of it, he flipped it twice more before he opened the door.

Melody, her arms crossed, her head cocked to the side, stood three feet away, her back against the wall. "Having trouble with the light?" she asked. She pointed to the sliver of space between the floor and the heavy door. "From this angle, it looked like it was flickering."

"It's fine," he said, feeling like a fool. "I wanted to wash up before the meal," he added, praying that she'd let it go.

"Grandmother and Aunt Genevieve spirited you away before I could introduce you to Bernard." She stepped a foot closer and lowered her voice. "He's anxious to meet the man who stole my heart." She didn't look happy. "This is harder than I thought," she whispered. "Are you sure we can pull this off?"

He wanted to tell her that he'd spent the last six

months acting, that this was just one more performance, one more lie.

After all, he'd successfully posed as the town drunk while he'd searched for the three men who had raped and killed Hannah. He'd found the first one, already on his deathbed from consumption. That man had led him to Mitchell Dority and ultimately to Sarah and John Beckett. Within weeks of arriving in Cedarbrook, he'd watched Dority get shot by an angry father, half-crazy with rage after Dority had raped his seventeen-year-old daughter. The bastard had bled to death before George could question him about the third man.

At least pretending to be Melody Song's husband gave him something new to lie about.

"Your grandmother seems like a fine woman," he said.

Tears filled her pretty dark blue eyes and it made his stomach lurch. He hadn't meant to make her cry.

"I hate it that she's sick," Melody whispered.

"I suspect she hates it, too," he said. "But she's dealing with it. I think the rest of the family can only do the same."

"Bernard said that she's been like her old self these last couple days, ever since she heard that we were coming." She reached out and touched his arm and he felt the jolt clear to his toes. "We can't let her know that this is a lie. We just can't."

She had nice hands. Her nails were painted with a lighter pink than had been on her toes. Even in her trousers, she was so feminine, so delicately built. "It'll be all right," he said. "Go and dry your tears," he said. "It won't do for her to think that you've been talking to your husband and that he made you cry."

She took a step toward the privy but then stopped, her face serious. "I don't know what I would have done if you hadn't volunteered to come with me."

"You'd have figured something out," he said.

She shook her head. "I don't think so. If I haven't said it yet, thank you. I really appreciate everything that you're doing."

"It's my pleasure," he said and meant it. It *was* nice to think that she'd been the reason that he'd been pulled forward to this time. That maybe helping her was a chance to make up for the despair and hatred that had consumed him after Hannah's death. "I'm glad I could—"

"What are you two doing back here?"

Melody jerked back so fast it was a wonder she didn't knock her head against the wall. George turned and saw Tilly at the end of the hallway, her hands on her ample hips.

"I . . . uh . . . we . . ." Melody stammered.

He turned back toward Melody. Well, she was no good at pretending. No wonder she'd been worried.

She ran a hand through her hair. "I . . . mean, we were just—"

George did the only thing he could think of to shut her up. He kissed her.

It was a brief brush of his lips across hers. It should have meant nothing but when he heard the catch of her breath and felt the warmth of her skin, it made him think about things that he hadn't thought about in many months. And when she put her hands on his shoulders and pulled him even closer yet, he felt his own skin heat up.

"How sweet."

Melody jerked away from him.

He looked over his shoulder at Tilly. She didn't look like she thought there was anything sweet about the situation. In fact, she looked like she'd eaten a sour pickle, and he realized that she didn't take the trouble to guard her feelings so carefully when Pearl wasn't around.

"I'm sorry to delay the meal," he said, embarrassed that

his own voice was a little shaky, "but I couldn't miss the opportunity to spend a couple minutes with my wife."

"Oh, please. Can we just get this meal over with?"

"We'll be along shortly," he said. He stared at the woman until she turned and walked away. Then he turned back toward Melody. She looked pale and she had her hands clasped so tight in front of her that her fingers were white.

"I apologize," he said. He'd had no right to take such liberties.

"Oh, no," she said, shaking her head. "You saved me from myself. I never have been able to handle Tilly. She always seems to know how to push my buttons."

Push her buttons? He didn't understand the words but the meaning was clear enough. It made him want to shake the woman for giving Melody even one moment of grief. "Worry can't be good for your child," he said. "Just forget about your aunt. I'll take care of handling her."

She studied him. "Others have tried."

"Trust me," he said.

"I do," she said. "Maybe more than I should. There's something different about you, George. Something I can't quite get my arms around."

Her arms had felt just about right when they'd been wrapped around his neck. "Nothing much here, Melody. I'm just a man about to enjoy a meal with his wife and her family."

She didn't look convinced but nor did she press the issue. She put her hand on his arm and pulled him toward the dining room. "Well, then, we better hurry. It'd be a good idea to get to the chicken before Tilly does."

SHE had been kissed before. Melody tried to remember that as she passed first the chicken, then the potatoes and the green beans, and finally the fresh-baked bread. With her plate full to the edges, she focused on her food and tried to ignore that her heart was beating too fast and that the tips of her fingers tingled.

Thankfully Grandmother had put George directly to her left. If he'd have been across the table, if she'd had to for even one minute look up and see those eyes and that mouth, she might make a fool out of herself.

It had to be hormones. In the last few months, she'd read just about every book ever published on the topic of pregnancy. All of them said it. Pregnancy caused normally well-behaved hormones to pitch a fit. Well, when she finished eating, she was going to bring her stuff in, unpack her books, and find the one that explained exactly how to get the little renegades back in line.

She maybe could have understood her reaction if it had been a push-you-up-against-the-wall-and-stick-my-hand-under-your-shirt kind of kiss. But it had been sweet. Nice. Gentle.

"Melody!"

She dropped her fork. It clattered when it hit the thick edge of her plate. She looked across the table at Bernard. The man was frowning at her.

Oh, boy. Had he seen that she was practically squirming on her chair? "Yes," she said.

"Honey, I said your name three times. Where were you?"

Halfway there. And with just a kiss. Amazing. "Just enjoying Bessie's cooking," she lied. "What did you say?"

"I was asking whether or not you might be able to help with some data entry—we're way behind on our computer work. Gino had a girl from town helping but she broke her hand. He's maybe too proud to ask for help but I know I could use it."

"Where is Gino?" she asked. Generally, at mealtime, both Bernard and Gino joined the family.

Louis leaned forward in his chair, gave Bernard a deliberate look, and then focused his attention on Melody. "Hopefully making sure those field hands of his don't wreck anything else."

She looked at her grandmother but the woman's face was carefully neutral, as if what she cared most about in the world was spreading butter on her roll. Melody felt, more than saw, George shift in his chair, and knew that he'd picked up on the hostile undertone.

"What do you mean, Louis?"

"A couple of them ruined one of our trucks last week. Evidently there's no word for oil in Spanish," he added sarcastically.

"They're migrant workers, Louis," Tilly said as she dumped another big scoop of potatoes onto her plate. "What do you expect?"

Aunt Genevieve made a choking sound. Grandmother gave her sister a warning look and then carefully laid down her fork. "Tilly," she said, "they are not migrant workers. Most of them have been with this family for more than ten years."

"Well, you'd think they'd have learned a little of the English language by now. Live in America, speak American."

Melody looked at both her grandmother and Bernard, who was shaking his head in disgust. "I'd be happy to help."

"I knew I could count on you," Bernard said. He pointed across the table. "Pass me that chicken, George."

He dutifully picked up the plate and passed it. Melody couldn't help but notice the nice shape of his hands, his broad fingers with nails trimmed short. When he'd shaken

her hand the night before at the beach, she'd felt the rough
texture of calluses on his palm.

This morning, she'd woken up with the feel of his hand
against her cheek. Her bed had been empty but it was as if
his warmth, his gentle strength, had lingered about her.
That's what had driven her to almost jump out of bed, rush
through her shower, and literally throw her things in the
trunk of her car. The only thing she'd been really careful
with had been the photograph, the one that had hung in the
office that she and Sarah had shared. It had been found in
the trunk of Sarah's car when the vehicle had been discovered parked at the beach more than a year ago.

It was a simple-enough scene. A cowboy in a long
leather coat, his foot perched on a stump stood watching a
woman who warmed herself in front of an open fire. The
woman's back was to the camera but the cool evening sun,
half-set behind the mountains, had offered the photographer just enough light to capture the man's profile.

The picture had a haunting sense of longing about it.
Sarah had loved it, though, and Melody had not wanted to
leave it behind in her empty apartment.

"If there's work for me to do," George said unexpectedly, "I'd be glad to help, too."

Melody started to assure him that it wasn't necessary
but stopped herself. The man would be bored silly sitting in the house with Grandmother and Aunt Genevieve.
She watched as Grandmother looked to Bernard for in-
struction.

The older man, the man who'd been as kind to her as
any father or grandfather could have been, cupped his
weathered chin with the palm of his hand and considered
George. "I'll speak to Gino," he said after a minute.

Louis took a sip of water. "Maybe he could help you,

Bernard. You're always complaining that you've got enough work for two people."

Bernard didn't even answer and an uncomfortable silence fell over the table. Out of the corner of her eye, Melody looked at George. No doubt he was regretting his offer to play husband. She had tried to warn him.

Grandmother smiled at George. "It's kind of you to offer, George. I'm sure we've plenty to keep you busy. I know I could use some help with one of my chores. You don't happen to have any experience with animals?"

George nodded. "Some."

"I've always kept a few riding horses but . . . well, lately it's been a struggle to give them the kind of attention that they're used to. Do you ride?"

George sat up straighter in his chair. "I have," he said.

Tilly, who'd been wiping her plate clean with a piece of bread, paused. "I thought horses were finicky. That it takes them a long time to warm up to anybody new. Exactly how long are the two of you planning on staying?"

With a loud scrape, Aunt Genevieve scooted her chair back from the table. She stood up and whistled, and the cat, which must have been under the table, jumped from the floor to the woman's skinny shoulder.

"It doesn't matter how long, Tilly," Aunt Genevieve said, her voice hard. "What matters is that they're here." She looked at her sister and Melody caught the gleam of tears in her great-aunt's watery blue eyes.

For the first time, Melody thought about how difficult it must be for Genevieve to watch her sister have to give up the things she loved, to have to slow down. It had to be a startling realization that they were both of an age where frailty and ultimately, death, beckoned.

When Tilly and Louis turned to stare at Aunt Genevieve,

Melody pushed her chair back suddenly, unwilling to let them examine the woman too closely. It was her right to grieve without these two intruding. "I'm going to get our things from the car," she said.

Before she could barely move, George was standing next to her. They were popping up like jack-in-the-boxes. "I'll carry them," he said.

"Your old room is ready," Grandmother said. "If you don't mind, while you're unpacking, I think I'll lie down for a while."

The grandmother she'd known would have suggested a walk through the fields or a trip into town. It made her realize how life had changed, and she was grateful that she'd made the decision to come home, that she hadn't had to disappoint the woman. "I'll see you later," Melody promised. "After I show George around."

"That would be fine, honey." Her grandmother stood, more sedately than everyone else had. "I'm so happy to have you here. We all are."

Melody doubted that Louis or Tilly shared her grandmother's sentiments but she refused to let it bother her. She'd keep out of their way as long as they kept out of hers.

On her way through the foyer, Melody grabbed her keys from the entranceway table. She reached for the door but George, hot on her heels, reached around her and opened the door for her.

He was way too nice for this family.

"I tried to tell you," she said as they walked outside.

He shrugged and didn't look overly concerned. "Bernard and your uncle Louis don't seem particularly fond of one another."

"It's been that way for years," she said. She pressed the trunk-release button on her key ring. The trunk sprang open and George stopped abruptly and grabbed for her hand. Heat streaked up her arm.

"What?" She turned and looked at him. He was staring at the trunk, like he half expected a monster to emerge.

"How . . ." his voice trailed off.

"How much stuff?" she finished his question, wanting to be helpful. "Not that much. Two suitcases, a box of books, and another box of miscellaneous. Come on," she said, and attempted to pull him forward.

It was like a hungry ant trying to carry home a slice of bread. Too little against way too much.

"George? What's wrong?"

He shook his head.

"Are we going to get my stuff?"

"Sure." He started walking but he didn't let go of her hand. When they were three feet from the car, he moved fast, stepping in front of her, placing himself between her and the trunk.

Oh good grief. What was his problem?

"Let me," he said, reaching into the trunk.

"If you can get both suitcases, I can carry the books and the other box," she said.

"No," he said. "You shouldn't be lifting," he added, his tone a little gentler.

She wondered who he thought had loaded all the stuff into the trunk. "Oh, fine. Can I at least carry that?" She pointed at Sarah's photograph, which she'd wrapped in a brown sack from the grocery store. "It's very light, I promise."

Before she could move, he'd reached into the trunk and pulled out the sack. He held it in his hands a minute longer than necessary and suddenly, as odd as it seemed, a whiff of pine floated past her.

"Do you smell that?" she asked.

He frowned at her. "What?"

She grabbed for the photograph. "Never mind." She was losing her marbles. She walked around the car to open the passenger-side door.

"I'll get my camera," he said, coming up fast behind her. He reached around her, grabbed the box, and slung the strap over his shoulder. Then he walked back to the trunk, hauled both suitcases out, and picked up one with each hand.

They were halfway to the house when the door opened and Tilly walked outside. Melody prepared herself for another smart remark but Tilly just brushed past them. When they got to the door, Melody turned around and saw that Tilly was checking the mailbox.

She led George directly to her room on the second floor. Grandmother hadn't changed it much in the last couple of years. The walls were painted a light yellow and the white comforter with small yellow and green flowers looked as thick and warm as ever. Next to the bed was a sturdy night-stand with a phone and her old clock radio. Across the room, her cherrywood dresser, obviously freshly polished, gleamed as the bright afternoon sun bounced off of it. The thin, white ruffled curtains had been pulled back and the window was open a few inches, letting in the fresh spring air.

It was a girl's room and George Tyler looked big and uncertain standing in the middle of it. Still holding the two suitcases, he turned around, taking it in. His eyes rested on the Raggedy Ann doll that sat in the corner of the window-sill. It was missing one leg and someone had taken a scissors to her hair.

"It was my mother's," she explained, sure he must think her silly for hanging on to such things. After her parents' deaths, her grandmother had given it to her. She had clung to it night after night and cried. Until it seemed like she just couldn't cry anymore.

He bent his knees and set the suitcases on the floor.

When he straightened, she noticed that his right hand rested on his camera and his thumb stroked the worn case almost absently. "I imagine she'd be glad to know that you have it," he said, his tone somber.

His eyes held the look of a man who'd known loss. "George?" she asked, not wanting to intrude.

"Where do you want your cases?" he asked abruptly, letting her know that he didn't intend to let her get too close.

She waved a hand. "On the bed is fine. I'll unpack later. But definitely before I . . . we . . . go to bed." Like a fool, she felt her face heat up.

It was one thing to sit at a table and pass him off as her husband. It was a whole other thing to sleep in the same bed. She'd been so worried about him meeting her family that she hadn't thought the whole thing through. Her grandmother would expect them to share a room, to share a bed.

Her legs suddenly feeling weak, she sat down on the edge of the bed. The mattress squeaked under her weight. This was perhaps even more awkward than the morning she'd walked into her friend's restaurant, smelled bacon cooking, and promptly thrown up on the straw dispenser.

"I guess the fair thing to do," she said, determined to not make it harder than it needed to be, "is to take turns sleeping on the floor. It's no big deal," she said hurriedly. "The carpet is clean and thick and I know where my grandmother keeps the extra blankets. It'll be like camping."

He looked at her as if she'd lost her mind.

Her baby, almost like he or she had heard the comment and liked the idea, did a little flutter kick. She spread her hand over the roundness. "Jingle here thinks it will be fun."

"Jingle?"

"I wanted to call him or her something other than *the baby*. But I didn't want to set him or her up for gender issues later on."

"Beg pardon?"

She'd read that phrase in a book before but she wasn't sure she'd actually ever heard anyone use it. It should have seemed odd, sort of feminine or something, but from George, it seemed right. Polite. Very gentlemanly.

"I didn't want to call him by a girl's name if he's a boy or a boy's name if she's a girl. So I came up with Jingle. You know, 'Jingle Bells' and all that. I found out I was pregnant right before Christmas."

She gave her belly a little pat, letting her child know that she appreciated the acrobatics.

He rubbed his chin in contemplation. After a minute, he said, "I imagine Jingle expects his or her mother to sleep in a bed." His eyes shifted downward. She realized that it was the first time that she'd seen him really look at her belly. Now that he'd started, he couldn't seem to look away. However, when he realized that she was watching him, he turned a pretty shade of rose, starting from his neck to the tips of his ears.

"I was almost sixteen weeks along before I started to show," she said, trying to make conversation to put him at ease. "Even then, I was able to wear my regular pants as long as I kept the top buttons undone."

He nodded and she saw that his green eyes had taken on the same intensity she'd seen that first night at the beach. It was like she was telling him something important, something he needed to know. And she realized it was the first time she'd shared any of the details of her pregnancy. Before, there'd been no one who cared. "Now, six weeks later, I've given in to elastic waists and loose shirts. Most people probably just think I'm plump."

He shook his head. "Your arms and your face are still slim."

It was silly but it seemed nice that he'd noticed that. She

resisted the urge to tell him that her normal 34B-cup breasts had somehow turned into a full-fledged C-cup. If he started staring at them, she'd be the one whose face would be turning pink. "Here's the deal," she said, redirecting the conversation back to where it had been. "Whether I'm sleeping on the floor or in a bed, it's all about the same to Jingle so it's crazy not to take turns."

He looked her in the eye. "If there's sleeping on the floor to be done, *I'll* be the one doing it."

He'd said it in a way that made her realize that it would be useless to argue. "Fine. I'm going to wash my face while you get the rest of our things. Don't forget the Target sacks are in the backseat," she added.

Once he'd left, she immediately walked into the attached bath. She didn't really need to wash her face but she figured if she'd told him that she needed to pee, he'd have sunk right into the floor.

The man seemed to embarrass awfully easy. Once her bladder was empty, she washed her hands. In the mirror that hung over the long vanity, she saw that her grandmother had painted the bathroom at some point. It had been a dull taupe when she'd left and now it was a beautiful sage green. The goldenrod-colored fixtures that had been there as long as she could remember had been replaced with classic white.

She turned off the water, dried her hands on the thick burgundy-and-sage towel, and walked back into the bedroom. She'd laid Sarah's photograph on the dresser when they'd come in. She walked over, picked it up, unfolded the brown sack, and pulled it out.

It really was lovely. She held it flat against the wall, like it would look hanging. No. That wouldn't work. It looked weird next to the dresser. She walked over to the eighteen inches of bare wall that stood between the two large windows. She positioned the photograph in the middle.

She heard the downstairs door slam and then the sound of George coming up the stairs. When he entered the room, she looked over her shoulder and asked, "How's this look?"

He dropped her box of books. They hit the floor with a jarring thud.

He didn't look like he even noticed. He was staring, first at the photograph, then switching to her, then back to the photograph again. His eyes moved so fast, it made her dizzy. "What's wrong?" she asked. She pulled down the photograph and turned to get a better look at him.

"Where did you get *that*?" he asked, his voice husky.

If he'd been pink before, now he was so pale she wondered if somehow his blood had all seeped out. If she looked out on the stairs, would there be a trail leading from the car to her bedroom?

"It was Sarah's. It hung in our office. When they found her car at the beach, this was in the trunk."

He walked over, took it from her, and ran his fingers lightly across the photograph. It surprised her when she saw that his hand was shaking.

She sniffed. There was that smell of evergreens again. Someone had to be trimming trees somewhere. It was just odd since there weren't all that many evergreens in this part of the state. She walked over to the window and closed it.

"It's nice, don't you think?" she asked, motioning to the photograph. "Even though it's in black and white," she rambled on, wondering exactly what she would do if all six feet of him decided to topple over. "I can just imagine what the sky must have looked like. Probably a mass of reds and oranges."

He nodded and swallowed so deliberately that she could see his throat muscles working. "I expect you're right," he said after a deafening moment of silence.

"I'm not sure what this is," she said, pointing to a series

of squiggly lines about an inch from the bottom, on the right-hand side. "At first I thought it was the photographer's signature but I can't make it out."

He looked at the picture more carefully. "I don't know," he said, sounding concerned. He carefully laid it on the bed and backed away a step, then another. Hell, if he weren't careful, he'd back himself all the way out the door and roll down the stairs.

"Grandmother is going to expect me to show you around," she cautioned. "I don't want her to think there's anything odd going on."

He jerked his head, his eyes shifting quickly from the photograph and settling on her. For a minute, he looked almost wary.

"George, is everything okay? Please don't tell me you're going to back out of this now."

He pulled himself up straight and his broad shoulders seemed even wider, to take up more space, to spread maleness in the midst of what had always been purely female. When he shook his head, she could feel the warm relief flow through her.

He inclined his head toward the bed. "You going to hang that photograph?" he asked.

"Yes. If you don't mind," she added. "I mean, it's your room, too." Brother. Could she be any more awkward at this?

He didn't say anything for a minute. Finally, he looked at her and gave her one of his gentle smiles. "I think I'd enjoy seeing it," he said. "Reminds me of home."

FIVE

BY the time they got halfway to the large red shed, George could feel his lungs start to work again. For a minute, when he'd seen Melody holding that photograph up against the wall, he'd thought all the air had been sucked right out of him.

He'd taken the photograph of John Beckett and Sarah Tremont the night before he had gotten into a stage with them headed for Cheyenne. The plan had been for Sarah to get on a train there and return to California, to her own place, hopefully to her own time. John Beckett was to have returned home to his ranch in Cedarbrook, Wyoming, and George was to have gone back to his position as sheriff of Bluemont, North Dakota.

But instead, they'd gotten halfway to Cheyenne before the storm had started. Before he'd seen the next dawn, he'd placed his feet in the footprints and traveled more than a hundred years forward, to Sarah's place, to Sarah's time. And the photograph, made from the glass plate he'd put in his bag with the intention of giving it to John once Sarah had left, had been waiting for him.

How did things like that happen?

"Let's find Bernard," Melody said, breaking into his memories. "You can learn more about winemaking from him in ten minutes than you could from most people in ten days."

"He and Pearl seem fond of each other."

"I think it's a lot of mutual respect. Grandmother knows that Bernard works like crazy and that Sweet Song of Summer wines wouldn't be half as successful without him. Bernard knows that Grandmother trusts him implicitly— she never second-guesses his decisions."

Maybe it was the photograph or maybe it was hearing her describe the relationship between Bernard and her grandmother so simply that suddenly made him homesick. He'd had that kind of relationship once. With a whole town. He'd liked the people of Bluemont, North Dakota, and he'd worked hard to earn their respect as sheriff. In return, they'd trusted him. At least until he'd left, a mere day after he'd buried his wife.

He'd taken their trust, their respect, and set it aside because the fire, the pure need for revenge, had burned hot in his belly. Probably some of the good townspeople had disapproved, him being a lawman. But most knew, most understood, that a man couldn't go on when his soul was gone.

He'd left them and spent six months chasing the three men responsible for murdering his wife. Two were now dead. The third was still out there somewhere.

And that had the power to haunt him.

Melody stopped walking and grabbed his arm. Her skin was warm and her touch gentle. "You're awfully quiet all of a sudden," she said. "Do you want to do this later?"

"No. Now is fine." They'd reached the building and entered through the open, ten-foot-wide door. Barrels, each three feet in diameter, stacked twelve feet high, flanked them on either side. A young man, no more than sixteen, he guessed, sat eight feet off the ground, on top of a big yellow machine that made more noise than the car. Wide silver forks extended from the front of it and a barrel rested on them. George watched the young man pull a lever on the machine and the fork raised higher still. In less than a minute, he'd moved the barrel up to the top of the stack.

Melody waved at the young man. "How goes it, Montai?"

He gave her a big grin. "I get to run the forklift this year," he yelled.

She smiled at him. "Excellent. I'll see you later."

They walked another ten feet. "Montai's father has been working here for over twenty years. Montai and his sister were both born here. His mother helps Bessie in the kitchen."

When they were three-quarters through the shed, they saw Bernard. He was talking with a man who looked to be about his age, maybe a few years younger.

"Gino," Melody said.

The man looked up and a smile crossed his weathered face. "Well, if it ain't Sweet Pea," he said. He held a clipboard in one hand, and with the other, he patted her head and ruffled her hair, like one might a small child. "Good to have you home."

"It's good to be home, Gino. How are the grapes?"

He smiled. "It could be one of our best years yet. But the season is young."

"I know, I know. Don't count your wine until it's bottled and corked."

The older man laughed and turned toward George. "Welcome," he said, holding out his hand. "Know much about grapes?"

"No, sir," George said. No sense trying to kid this man. He had a look in his eye that told George he didn't suffer fools lightly.

"Good. Then I can train you right." He put down the clipboard. When he looked at Melody, his eyes were serious. "So, you've seen your grandmother?"

"Yes."

Bernard and Gino exchanged a glance before Gino again turned to Melody and said, "Your grandmother is sick. Really sick. She won't complain and she sure as hell won't tell you the truth about being scared or being so weak that she can't walk out to get her own mail."

Melody's pretty eyes, which had been so bright just minutes before, filled with tears. "How much time?" she asked, her voice husky.

Bernard shook his head. "We don't know," he said. "But she told me that she doesn't expect to see the fall harvest."

Melody's body swayed and George moved fast. He wrapped an arm around her shoulders and pulled her tight up against his body. "Steady," he said, his voice low. This couldn't possibly be good for her child.

"I'm all right," she protested and moved out of his reach. He let her go but stayed close enough that he could easily catch her if she fell again. Her face was pale and she was blinking her eyes furiously.

She looked first at Bernard, then at Gino. "Thank you both for being here for her, for taking care of things the way you always have. I know that must be a comfort to her."

Gino shrugged. "Having you here is what's a comfort. Especially you being married and pregnant. When she told Bernard and me about it, her face just lit up."

Pearl hadn't told Tilly, her daughter, yet she'd told her hired help. Very interesting.

"Maybe the thought of having a great-grandchild will

give her something to live for," Gino said. "Sort of romantic how the two of you got together again after having been apart for a couple years."

George stood close enough to Melody to sense her body stiffening. *A couple years.* Try a hundred and eighteen.

But it was the story she'd told. Given that, he'd have thought she might be a little more adept at keeping false about it. She wasn't too skilled at this kind of thing.

Like a calf facing a branding iron, she looked like she might bolt if given the chance. He put an arm around her shoulder. "I'm grateful she waited for me," he said, smiling at her.

Melody's upper lip twitched nervously in response.

"Maybe we should check on your grandmother," he suggested.

She gave him a grateful nod. "I'll see you later," she said to Gino and Bernard. "You'll both be at dinner, right?"

"Wouldn't miss your first dinner home, Sweet Pea," Gino said. "I imagine Bessie's going all out, probably fixing every one of your favorites."

Melody's eyes filled with tears again and George tightened his grip. "Come on," he urged. With his arm still around her, he turned her body toward the door. Sensing that she might want a minute to compose herself, George kept the pace slow.

They were close to the door when Bernard called after them. "Hey Melody, when can I show you the data entry that needs to be done?"

They both turned. Bernard stood in the same spot where he'd been. There was no sign of Gino.

"I can come tomorrow," Melody said. "How about at—"

Bernard held a hand up to his ear, telling her that he couldn't hear. Melody slipped away from George and took several steps back toward her old friend.

And what happened next, happened so fast, that George didn't have time to think, barely had time to react. He heard the sharp *whoosh* of air moving and looked up to see a heavy barrel rolling from the top of the stack. It was gathering speed, headed straight for Melody.

George sprang forward, wrapped his arms around Melody, and hauled her back. He hit his shoulder on the oak barrels directly to his left and the pain shot down his arm. He saw the now-airborne barrel fly across the center aisle.

It hit less than a foot in front of them. There was a sharp crack of oak against oak, then a dull thud as it dropped to the cement floor. George stared at it and knew that if it had hit Melody, it would have killed her.

If he'd have been a fraction of a second slower, he would have been too late. The realization made him swallow hard, twice.

Then, the realization that she had her back to his front and he had one arm wrapped just under her breasts and one around her middle, made him afraid to breathe. It was wrong to hold her so, to be so forward. To hold her in the way that a man holds a woman when that woman is his. To hold her in such a way that all he had to do was arch his hips and he'd be pressed in behind her, her curves suddenly a part of him. To hold her in the way a man holds a woman when he wakes up in the middle of the night and his need is great and her body is warm and welcoming.

"George," she said, her voice a mere whisper.

He kept his hips right where they were supposed to be. "Yes," he said. He was afraid to breathe, afraid to jar their careful balance.

He could hear her take a deep breath and he felt her chest expand. She turned her head, and her lips were just inches away from his. And for the briefest moment he thought that she was going to kiss him, like he had kissed her before lunch, and his whole body started to shake.

He let his hands drop back to his own sides. What the hell was he thinking? He took a step back, giving them both space.

She smiled at him. "It seems a bit inadequate, but thank you."

He wanted to come up with something witty or smart to say but it had been too close a call. He managed a nod and was grateful when Bernard ran toward them and Melody's attention was diverted to the older man. His face was pale and his hand shook when he held it out to touch her face.

"Are you all right?" Bernard asked.

"I'm fine," she said.

Bernard whirled around. Montai was off his machine and standing thirty feet away, his face much paler than his bare arms.

"Damn it, Montai. What the hell happened?" Bernard demanded.

The boy shook his head. George could see he was plenty scared. "I don't know. I wasn't anywhere near that barrel. I put my load at the end, just like you showed me how to do."

Bernard walked to where the barrel had rolled from and looked up. Then he looked over his shoulder, back at George and Melody. "Somebody forgot to set the chock. Who the hell could have done something so damn stupid?"

Montai shook his head. "I never touched them," he said, his voice quivering.

George looked across the aisle. Sure enough, in front of every remaining barrel, there was a small angular piece of wood, propped just so, to keep the barrels in place. It was pretty easy to see what had happened. Montai had dropped his load on the opposite end and there'd been just enough vibration to start a chain reaction.

Bernard walked over and kicked the oak barrel. It didn't even roll an inch. The metal banding around the two ends and in the middle was bent but the lid had stayed on. "I've been doing this for forty years and I've never see anything like that," he said. "If it would have been full, it would have never budged, but these barrels are empty. We'll use them this fall."

Montai wiped a hand across his mouth. "I'm so sorry, Melody. I would never want to see you hurt."

"I know that, Montai," she said. "It was a crazy accident. It's not your fault." Her voice sounded surprisingly strong.

George was grateful for that because his knees felt pretty damn weak. When Melody turned to look at him, he wondered if she somehow knew.

Her eyes looked concerned. "Was that your head that made that thump?"

"My shoulder," he said, relieved that she was focused on something else entirely. "It's fine," he lied. He was going to have a hell of a bruise. It would match the bruises on his ribs that he'd seen in the mirror when he'd changed clothes at the store.

"Empty, those barrels weigh almost a hundred and fifty pounds," Bernard said.

"Well, it didn't hit me so there's no sense worrying about how much it weighs. Whatever you do, don't tell Grandmother," Melody said.

She'd no sooner finished speaking before the dogs, followed by Tilly and Louis, bounded into the shed. They ran up and sniffed the barrel, then ran circles around it, like nobody needed to tell them that something was wrong.

George noticed that Montai had slipped into the shadows of the wine barrels.

"What's going on?" Tilly asked.

"Barrel slipped off the stack," Melody said, her voice very matter-of-fact. George didn't miss the warning look she sent Bernard's way.

Louis propped a foot on the barrel. "Thank goodness it wasn't a full one. Could have been a waste of a promising Cabernet."

"You stupid idiot," Bernard said, evidently deciding to ignore Melody's warning look. "That barrel almost hit your niece. And would have, too, if George here hadn't pulled her out of the way."

Louis had the decency to look shocked. "I had no idea," he said. "I'm glad you weren't hurt, Melody."

Tilly took a step closer, her eyes bright with speculation. "What happened?"

"Nothing," Melody said. "Nothing happened. It was a stupid accident and we all need to forget about it."

No one said a word. Finally, Louis smiled, showing all his teeth. "Fine. I got an e-mail from Marty. Orders are pouring in for the 2004 Chardonnay. He wants another forty cases."

Bernard ran a hand over his face. "The next time that damn woman writes a cookbook, I hope she'll let us know in advance that she plans to put our bottle on the cover."

"What woman?" Melody asked.

"Rebecca Fields," Louis answered. "She has the hottest cooking show on cable right now and her book is flying off the shelves."

Show on cable? George tried to remember if Sarah had mentioned anything about cables.

"And she likes our wine?" Melody asked. Her eyes,

bright with excitement, looked more purple than before. "That's wonderful."

"I was already busier than a one-armed paper hanger," Bernard complained. "Now I got every Rebecca Fields wannabe calling me at all hours of the day."

George saw past the man's words, straight into his proud soul. This woman, this Rebecca Fields who had written a cookbook, had somehow given him recognition that he publicly disdained but there was little doubt that he privately enjoyed.

"All I know is the price of that wine just went up 20 percent," Louis said. "Oh, by the way, she's coming to dinner tonight."

"Who?" Melody asked.

"Rebecca Fields. Your grandmother has been wanting to meet her and she was free tonight."

Tilly rolled her eyes. "I don't know what the big deal is."

George saw the quick flare of anger in Louis's eyes. But when he spoke, the man's voice was calm enough. "The big deal is that she's helping to put Sweet Song of Summer wines on the map. We need that, Tilly."

She stared coldly at her husband. "I know what we need." She turned and walked out the door. Louis hesitated for just a second before he followed her out.

They were barely out of the door before Bernard took off his straw hat and swatted it across his pant leg. "I'm sorry, Melody. But I just can't stand that son of a bitch."

She stood on her toes and kissed his cheek. "Don't worry about it. Look, I'm going to go check on Grandmother."

George walked by her side, keeping a watchful eye on the barrels. When they reached the door, Melody was silent for another hundred yards as they crossed what looked to be a freshly mowed yard.

There was just enough wind that wisps of her hair blew gently around her face. In the wine shed, he'd held her close enough that he knew that her hair smelled like strawberries. It was the smell of his boyhood, a smell of pleasure. Strawberries had grown in the patch behind his mother's house. They'd been sweet and pure and damn tempting.

Just like she was.

"What are you thinking?" she asked, looking at him.

There were times when the truth just wasn't the right thing. "That you were lucky," he said.

She put a hand on his arm and it was crazy, but he could feel the heat all the way to his toes. "That's the second time you've saved my life," she said.

She made him feel big and powerful and because he was afraid that he might have a stupid look on his face, he looked toward the house. "I imagine your grandmother is up from her nap."

"I imagine," she said, her voice soft. "You know, I'm not sure I can hide it from her."

"I wouldn't worry about it," he said. "I don't know your aunt and uncle very well but I suspect expecting either one of them to keep a confidence is a little like a man in a clean shirt spitting in the wind. Just foolhardy."

She laughed, like he'd hoped she would. It made his heart beat a little easier. "I think you're right," she said, "but that's not what I meant. I'm worried that I can't hide that I know she doesn't expect to see the fall harvest."

They were less than fifty feet from the front door. "Maybe she wants to talk about it," he said.

She stopped. "I know that people are supposed to be able to rise to the occasion but I'm not sure I've got it in me. I don't want to make it worse for her because I can't handle it well. I don't want her worrying about me and what's going to happen to me when she's gone."

He wanted to assure her that he'd be there to help her but knew that he couldn't. The footprints, the path back home, could come at any time. He'd make no promises that he couldn't keep.

"You'll handle the conversation just fine. I know you will."

"I hope you're right," she said as she pulled open the front door. They found Pearl and Aunt Genevieve in the room with the big piano. Pearl sat facing the window with a stack of newspapers on her lap. Her sister sat across from her, the cat slumped over her shoulder, back paws visible, front paws hidden by the woman's body. She was flipping the pages of what looked to be a catalog.

Melody knelt on the floor next to her grandmother and reached for the woman's hand. "Did you sleep?"

"For a little while," Pearl said. She tapped the newspapers on her lap. "I hadn't made it all the way though the Sunday paper yet so I've spent the better part of the last hour doing that."

Sunday paper. Good lord. It had to be two inches thick. Was there so much happening in 2006 that they needed all that space to tell about it? His fingers itched to get hold of the newspaper, to somehow get his bearings in this strange world.

Aunt Genevieve looked up from her catalog. "So, what do you think of our little winery?"

"I think you both should be very proud," he said.

She nodded, like she was satisfied with his answer. Pearl set her papers aside and slowly stood up. "It's been a labor of love," she said. "Now how about I show you the horses. Genevieve, are you coming?"

"No. I'm going to my room." She whistled and the cat, going completely boneless, slid off her shoulder. It landed in her cradled arms and she held it like one would a baby.

The animal never even opened its eyes. George tried not to stare as the woman, who had considerably more ease and agility than her sister, stood up.

"Mona knows I'll catch her every time," the woman said, in way of explanation as she looked at the cat. "Complete trust, George. That's what it takes."

GIVEN the questions George asked Grandmother about the horses, Melody assumed he'd grown up with the animals. When they got to the corral, he opened the wide gate and stepped inside, then did nothing but stand there, letting the horses get used to him being in their space. She and Grandmother stayed back. When her grandmother folded her arms, placed them on the top rail, and leaned her weight against the fence, Melody did the same.

He was patient and one by one, all six of them finally wandered over. He let them smell him and bump their heads up against his shoulder and his chest. Then he murmured a few words and gave them a brisk rub between the ears.

"That's Brontë," Grandmother said, pointing to the one who came up last. "I used to ride her every day."

"She's a beauty," George said, running a hand across the brown mare's sleek coat. He hadn't taken his eyes off the horse. "I had one very much like her," he said, his voice soft. "Ran like the wind."

Grandmother smiled at Melody. "As does she. There are several saddles to choose from in the barn," she added.

George looked over his shoulder at Grandmother. "Are you sure?" he asked. And Melody knew he wasn't asking about the saddle. He was asking permission to take what had up to now always been Grandmother's.

Grandmother unfolded her arms and pushed her body away from the fence. She stared first at the horses and then at George. She had a soft smile on her face. "I can't think of anything that would give me greater pleasure."

George hesitated for a brief moment before taking off for the barn, his long stride eating up the distance. Grandmother turned toward Melody. "I imagine your days of riding are temporarily over."

She patted her stomach. "I don't think Jingle is so inclined."

"Jingle?"

"Gender-neutral," Melody explained.

"Of course."

It had always been like that with her grandmother. There'd never been any need for long explanations. There had been simple understanding, unwavering acceptance, unconditional love.

Truth.

Until now. Recently neither one of them had been very forthcoming with that.

She dug her foot into the soft earth and stared at the almost-unidentifiable shape of the oak trees that lined the far edge at the property. "You should have told me right away that you were sick."

"I'm old, Melody. Old people get sick."

She could feel the hot rush of tears and knew that it would take a miracle to keep them back. "I'm so sorry," she said. "I wish I could do something."

Her grandmother reached over and patted her hand. "You're here. It's the biggest something I could have asked for."

She turned to face her grandmother and with an impatient hand brushed off the tears that would not be denied. "I love you," she said.

"And I love you, darling. As you will love your child and then years from now, his or her children. You know

what they say? Children never know how much they were
loved until they have children of their own."

Melody gently wrapped her arms around her grandmother's body and pulled her close. "I will be here as long
as you need me," Melody said, wiping a tear away. "I
promise."

"How does your husband feel about that?"

Melody swallowed. *Truth.* This was her chance.

SIX

"HE . . . he . . ." she stammered. *He's not my husband.* She couldn't do it. She would not give her grandmother something new to worry about. "He knows how important you are to me."

Grandmother smiled. "That's lovely." She reached for Melody's hand. "You've gotten yourself a good man."

Her good man had gotten a saddle from the barn and was making short work of getting Brontë saddled. With one final tug, he tightened the cinch. He put one foot in the stirrup and swung the other effortlessly over the horse's back.

"He sits a horse well," Grandmother said.

Oh boy. Did he ever. His back was straight and strong and his butt seemed made for the saddle. When he used his legs to guide the horse, Melody had no trouble imagining what it would be like to have those same legs wrapped around her.

She felt warm in places the sun couldn't possibly reach. George Tyler was handsome, smart, and polite. Perfect.

It was really too bad this was just a temporary assignment for him.

"Will you walk me back to the house?" Grandmother asked. Her voice sounded tired.

"Of course." Melody put her arm under her grandmother's elbow. With one last long look at George, she turned back toward the house.

When they got inside, her grandmother lay down on the big green leather sofa and Melody took the far end. She sat quietly long after her grandmother had fallen asleep. Bright sunshine, split into streaks by the almost-closed horizontal blinds, danced across the hardwood floor, skipped over the backs of chairs, and finally settled on her face.

She felt safe and warm and very thankful to be home. She knew she was wrong to lie to her grandmother. But knew too that she'd do far worse than lie in order to make the woman's last few months on this earth worry-free.

She didn't know how long she sat there but at some point she closed her eyes and didn't wake up until the front door closed with a slam. She straightened up, realizing immediately that her neck had been at a most unusual angle for sleeping. She gently turned her head side to side, easing the kinks out. She saw then that the afternoon sun had lost both its height and intensity as the day faded into early evening.

Tilly and Louis walked into the room. Tilly's hair was windblown and she wore dark sunglasses. Louis was carrying his keys in one hand and a half-drunk bottle of beer in the other. Melody figured they'd been out in their convertible—drinking and driving. It made her want to wrap her arms around her stomach and always protect her unborn child from all the fools like them.

Melody glanced at Grandmother just in time to see her open her eyes, realize who was coming, and close them again. Melody figured that perhaps she was debating whether or not she should pretend to still be asleep. Having been cooped up inside, away from her horses and the myriad of other chores that would normally have occupied her time, had no doubt given Grandmother plenty of opportunities to chat with Tilly and Louis.

Melody decided to help her out. She put a finger up to her lips. "Be quiet. Grandmother's sleeping."

However, either Grandmother's impeccable manners kicked in or she'd just plain lost her common sense because the woman sat up on the couch. She rubbed her eyes. "Where were you two this afternoon?" she asked.

Tilly's head jerked up. "Nowhere. Why do you ask?"

Grandmother shrugged. "Just making conversation, Tilly."

"Where's your husband?" Louis asked Melody, before he tipped his beer up and drained it.

"Getting acquainted with the horses," she said.

Tilly sat in the chair opposite the couch. "That's so convenient, isn't it, that he's had experience with them?"

Coming from someone else, it would have been casual conversation. From Tilly, Melody knew it was the prelude to a full-blown inquisition.

"Your grandmother mentioned that the two of you dated a few years ago. I don't believe I ever heard you mention him before."

Bingo.

She'd never been good at party games. She stood up. "I'm sure I must have mentioned him," she said. Before the next question came, she turned to her grandmother. "I've still got unpacking to do. I'll see you at dinner."

"Of course, darling. By the way, we're having a guest. It's Rebecca Fields of cookbook and cable television fame."

"Louis mentioned it earlier."

Her grandmother smiled. "I thought it was the least we could do. She's really lovely on television and Bessie's even tried some of her recipes. I think that speaks to her powers of persuasion."

Bessie didn't like admitting that anybody knew anything about cooking that she hadn't already forgotten. "It should be fun to meet her," Melody said. "Do you still eat at seven?"

"Absolutely."

On her way out of the room, Melody heard Tilly ask Grandmother if she wanted her to rub her back. Grandmother answered with a grateful-sounding yes. It made Melody less irritated with her aunt. Whatever else Tilly had ever been, she'd always been kind to her mother.

Melody stopped at the desk in the foyer and grabbed the telephone book out of the top drawer. She did need to unpack but she also needed to find an obstetrician. She'd seen her own doctor three times. He'd listened to the baby's heart, pronounced Melody sound, and sent her on her way with prenatal vitamins big enough that they looked remarkably like the horse pills her grandmother kept in the stable cupboards. But every day she forced one down, followed by at least six crackers and a glass of milk.

Once she got to her room, she sat on the edge of her bed, opened the phone book to the yellow pages, and ran her finger down the list of physicians. Fortunately, she had a name. Her friend, who had owned the restaurant where she'd been working, had a sister in Napa who'd had a baby the previous year. She'd raved about her obstetrician.

Melody found the name she was looking for and dialed the office on her cell phone. When the receptionist answered, she explained her situation and waited while the woman checked availability. She had expected to have to wait a couple weeks but was delighted when the woman said that she could take a cancellation the day after tomorrow. She ended the call and had just flipped her cell phone shut when there was a light knock on the door.

Thinking it could be Tilly, she debated feigning sleep but decided it was an okay short-term but a darn poor long-term solution. She couldn't stay in her room forever. Jingle had gotten used to eating every three hours. There'd be some serious consequences if she missed dinner. "Come in," she said.

The door opened slowly and George stood there. His hair was messed and his cheeks had a hint of pink from the sun. He carried an old straw cowboy hat in his hand. Grandmother had always kept extra in the barn. "Your grandmother said you were likely unpacking," he said. He made no move to come in.

"Just started," she said. She was glad she was sitting. George Tyler did the windblown cowboy look very well. She could smell the sweet mix of horse and fresh grass tangled up with the scents of budding wisteria and wild mustard. He'd been in the meadow. "Enjoy the horses?" she asked.

"I did," he said and for a minute, his eyes didn't look so serious. "I'm grateful to your grandmother for letting me ride."

"I think she thinks *you're* the one doing her a favor. I don't have to tell you how lucky you are to have landed that particular job. I'll be getting carpal tunnel while you're galloping across the valley." She said it so that he'd know she was teasing.

"Carpal tunnel?" he repeated. If anything, he looked even more serious.

Had no one in the sheriff's office ever had a worker's compensation injury? "Never mind," she said.

He continued to stand in the doorway.

"George, come in. It is your room, too," she whispered.

If anything, his cheeks took on a slightly pinker hue. But he came in—far enough that he could shut the door behind him. He leaned his very fine rear end against the edge of the dresser.

When he didn't say anything, she got nervous. Like a fool, she held up her cell phone. "I got a referral from a friend. You know, for an OB-GYN. I . . . uh . . . just called him and set up an appointment."

He chewed on the corner of his bottom lip. "An O. B. G. Y. N?"

He said each letter like it was a separate word. Good grief. The man had said he was married. Surely his wife had had an occasional doctor's visit. "An obstetrician-gynecologist. You know, somebody who delivers babies."

His head jerked up. "Did I grab you too hard earlier?"

"No. I'm fine," she said and tried to squelch the rush of heat that started to spread outward from her belly button. He acted like he really cared, that it wasn't just a job for him.

"I'm sorry about that," he said.

"Not your fault. Just some kind of crazy accident."

He crumpled up the brim of his cowboy hat. "Maybe. Maybe not."

What? "George, you were there. You saw what happened."

He shook his head. "I don't want to upset you or to worry you needlessly. But just a few minutes ago, when I came into the house, I heard your aunt and your uncle talking. They weren't in the room with the piano or the dining room. It was the room off to the left."

"That's a little sitting area," she said.

"Yeah, well, they were sitting in there and talking about

you. I heard your aunt tell her husband that it might have been nice if the wine barrel had hit you—that their problems would all be taken care of."

"Oh." After a minute, she said it again. "Oh." Then she felt stupid that that was the only word she could think of. It was just such a hateful thing for Tilly to have said. "What did Louis have to say?" she asked, rather inanely. What did it matter?

"He told his wife not to worry. That he had it under control."

"I see. You know, if you hurry, you've got time to shower before dinner," she said.

"What?" He looked at her like she was crazy. "Did you hear what I said?"

She shrugged her shoulders. "First of all, what happened in the wine shed was an accident. There's no way that Louis and Tilly could have known that I was going to be in the shed at the exact moment that Montai was moving barrels. And second of all, it's not news that Tilly and Louis can't stand me. But they aren't going to hurt me. That's too crazy, even for them."

"People do crazy things. Bad things," he added. His voice was hard and he said it like he'd had some experience with bad people or bad things, or maybe both.

"They can't hurt me with words. I'm not thirteen anymore," she added, before she thought better of it.

He moved a step closer to the bed. "What happened when you were thirteen?" he asked. His green eyes were narrowed and his jaw set.

She played with the zipper on her suitcase. She did not want to get into this—it was ancient history. But she thought it quite possible that if she didn't, George would go find Louis and keep at him until the man told him what

George wanted to know. "Oh, fine. Shortly after my parents died, Louis told me that it was my fault that my parents were killed."

"That's ridiculous," George said. "You were just a child."

"Well, true. I mean part of what he said was right. He said that they'd have never been on that particular stretch of road, that particular night, if it wasn't for me."

"I don't understand."

"We lived about a hundred miles north of Los Angeles. The summer I turned thirteen, my best friend moved to Los Angeles and we'd made plans for me to go spend a couple weeks with her in the summer. They'd dropped me off at her house and were on their way back, when they crashed over the side of the road."

"But you weren't even there. You had nothing to do with it."

She so didn't want to talk about this. "Look, it was a stormy night and my parents didn't really want to make the drive there and back. But I begged and begged. I missed my friend and I'd waited months to see her. I didn't want to wait another night."

"It wasn't your fault," he said again, like he was determined to convince her.

"What I've come to realize over the years is that it doesn't really matter whose fault it was. What matters is that my grandmother lost a daughter, Tilly lost a sister, and the world lost two really wonderful people."

He looked mad. "That's a heavy burden for a young girl. Your family should have been the ones telling you that it wasn't your fault. Not the other way around. Did you ever tell your grandmother what Louis had said?"

She shook her head quickly. "No. I knew it would cause trouble between Louis and Grandmother, which would have ultimately caused trouble between Tilly and Grandmother.

Tilly and Louis had been living here for about two years when this happened. Within twenty-four months, my grandmother had lost her husband and a daughter and son-in-law. I didn't want to do something that would cause her to have a rift with her only living child."

"That was pretty grown-up of you."

It felt good to hear him say that. "Losing both your parents at one time forces you to be mature, whether you're ready or not. When you love someone and they die, it changes you."

He sucked in a breath, almost like he'd taken a blow to the stomach. Had he lost someone special? "Did I say something wrong?" she asked, feeling bad.

"It's fine," he said.

She knew it wasn't. Could tell by the stiff way he held his shoulders. She waited for him to say something else but he didn't seem inclined to tell her any more.

The need to touch him, to comfort him, was strong. She got up off the bed and walked over to him. Reaching up, she tucked a piece of his wayward hair behind his ear. She let her hand trail down the length of his strong jaw. His skin was warm against the tips of her fingers.

"I'm sorry, George, if what I said makes you think about things you'd rather forget. I'd like to think I'm not normally so careless or hurtful with my words."

He stood as still as a statue. "You're neither careless or hurtful, Melody," he said. "But you're right. Losing someone you love does change you."

His voice was soft but she could sense the underlying tension in his big body. She didn't know what to say to him, what would make it better. All she knew is that she didn't want this man whom she'd known for less than a day, to hurt.

The overwhelming urge to help him surprised her. Was

it as simple as the innate need of one human to comfort another human in his time of need? Was it something more? How was that possible? They barely knew each other.

He stared at her. They stood close. So close that she could see that he had a small white scar at his hairline and another one, an inch long but barely a hair wide, running horizontal under his full lower lip. She moved her hand from his chin and ran her index finger across both. "What happened here?"

He closed his eyes and took two deep breaths. Then, very deliberately, he reached up, gently circled her wrist with his fingers, and lowered her hand back to her side. In the process, the back of his hand brushed against her slightly-rounded belly.

He looked startled. "I didn't mean to . . . uh . . ." His voice trailed off.

It was the first time she'd heard him grasp for words, and it made him seem unsure and vulnerable. It was an appealing combination and before she did something absolutely stupid, like touch him again, when he so clearly didn't want that, she took a step back. She felt warm and off balance and she knew she needed to get out of the room. "I'm going to leave so you can get showered," she said.

He nodded. "That's probably a good idea," he said, his own voice sounding a little strained. He reached for the hat he'd put on the dresser and held it in front of him, waist-high, his hands gripping the brim so tightly that the tips of his fingers were white.

"We need to finish our conversation, Melody. I'm not going to let your uncle cause you any trouble. It's not right."

In one short day, she'd realized that George Tyler had a very strong sense of what was right and what was wrong. "Just ignore him. It's what I do."

"I'm going to watch him," he said.

"Well, that shouldn't be too difficult. If I know Louis, he's going to be doing the same to you."

"Why is that?" His words were quick, like he didn't like the idea of Louis studying him.

"Louis likes to think he's in charge. That's why he and Bernard don't get along. Louis thinks that since he's family, he should have more to say about how things get done. I heard him say once that he hates it that Bernard acts like the place is his."

"I'm not going to be acting like this place is mine," he said. "I wouldn't do that."

He almost sounded hurt. She wanted to tell him that while Louis was a lot of things, he wasn't a fool, and that the man had no doubt already figured out that George wasn't going to be easily dismissed. There was a rock-solid quality about the man.

But she couldn't tell him that. It was too personal.

Not that it wasn't sort of personal that she could somehow still feel the gentle grasp of his fingers around her wrist. Not that it wasn't *really* personal that she could somehow imagine what it would feel like to have him hold her wrists the same way, her hands above her head, his grasp pinning her to the bed, while they lay naked together.

Thank god the man couldn't read minds. He'd be running for the door.

She'd been so lucky that it had been George Tyler on the beach last night, that he'd been there at a time when she needed him and he was willing to be here now, playing the lead in this rather absurd drama she'd created. She didn't want to make him any more uncomfortable than she'd already made him.

"Why is he going to be watching me?" he asked again, bringing her back.

"Louis doesn't like stray dogs in his pen," she said, for lack of a better way to put it.

He cocked his head to the side. "As long as he behaves, I'll just run the fence. If he treats you badly, I'm going for his throat." Then, very calmly, like he hadn't just threatened her uncle, he added, "And if you don't mind, I think I will get cleaned up."

"Good plan," she managed. George didn't have to say much to get his point across. Whew. She resisted the urge to fan herself. She was living proof that hot flashes weren't reserved for women in menopause.

"I like your hat," she said, rather inanely.

He stared at her, so tall, so broad-shouldered. So silent. "It serves a purpose," he said finally, his voice soft.

She might be crazy but he looked a little warm, too. There was altogether too much heat in one small room. "I'll see you later," she said, backing toward the door.

He nodded.

She turned, opened the door, and got the heck out of there. She made it four feet before she stopped, turned so that her back faced the wall, and leaned her whole body against the smooth, cool plaster. She closed her eyes.

Holy tomatoes. The man had her already wild hormones dancing. And no box step. They were doing the tango, with big dips and turns. They were wearing flashy red and three-inch-spike heels.

Her hormones understood that George was taking care of her. And furthermore, while it was such a girl thing to do, they knew, too, that she liked it. Which was crazy.

She didn't need anybody to take care of her. After her parents had died, and her grandmother had taken her in, she'd worked so hard to make sure that she wasn't a burden. She handled things. Well. Always.

But George made it seem like it was okay to let him take care of her. He made her feel—

"What are you doing?"

Melody opened her eyes and stood up straight. Tilly stood at the top of the stairs, one hand on the railing, the other wrapped around a glass of red wine. She raised one professionally-shaped black brow. "Trouble in paradise?" she asked.

"Pardon me?"

She took a sip. "Did that handsome husband of yours lock you out?"

"He's taking a shower."

Tilly swirled the wine in her glass. "A man like that shouldn't shower alone. You know, his name fits him. He looks a little like George Clooney did in that movie about the ship that sank in the storm. Sort of rough around the edges but damn sexy."

The Perfect Storm. Something in her aunt's tone made her snap. "I don't really see the resemblance," she said.

Her aunt lifted one corner of her mouth, in a half smirk. "That's a shame. You know I've got a good eye for faces," she said.

The problem was, her aunt didn't just look. She knew the woman slept with other men. When Melody had first heard the rumors, she'd worried for a long time that Louis would find out. She'd been a senior in high school, just weeks shy of graduation, when she'd overheard them fighting one night. She'd realized then that Louis knew—had known for a long time.

The pair had hurled angry words at one another and it didn't take her long to realize that Louis had had at least one affair as well. It had made her sick. It wasn't the kind of marriage her parents had. It certainly wasn't the kind of marriage she intended to have.

As distasteful as it had been, it had been almost a relief to find out the truth. It had made it so much easier to accept that they didn't care about her. They didn't even really care about each other.

"Did you want something, Tilly?"

"Our guest has arrived. Your grandmother sent me up to tell you."

"We'll be there in just—"

"Fine," her aunt said. She turned quickly and literally ran down the stairs. It took Melody a minute to realize that the telephone was ringing. Her aunt snatched it up and turned, so that her back faced Melody.

Good grief. It wasn't like she cared who Tilly was talking to. Melody looked at her watch. If they were going to make dinner, she needed to finish getting ready.

She'd give him another couple minutes. She hoped George Tyler was the type who got dressed fast.

SEVEN

IT took George at least three minutes to figure out how to turn on the shower. He felt silly standing there as naked as the day he was born, twisting and turning knobs, only to finally discover that there was a lever that also needed to be lifted.

It was like the damn car—too much to remember.

The water hit his shoulders and back, almost scalding him. He turned the right knob and got it to a warm temperature, which soothed his tired muscles.

He couldn't figure out what hurt more, his shoulder or his ribs. He rubbed the bar of soap between his hands and washed his hair first. Then, using the soap and the thick washcloth he'd found under the sink, he cleansed his body. Not knowing how long the water might last, he made quick work of it.

He soaped up his still-half-hard cock. It had stiffened the minute Melody had reached up and tucked his hair behind his ears. And then when she'd run her fingers across his face, all he'd been able to do was think about kissing her a second time and it had practically sprung out of his trousers.

When she moved away, he'd taken great care to hold his hat in front of him.

He should have been relieved. It had been more than six months since his body had hardened for a woman, six months since he'd felt a woman's softness. He'd wondered, after a spell of four months or so, when he'd been half-crazy with wanting to kill the men responsible for Hannah's death, if it would ever happen again.

Had told himself that he didn't care. That he'd never bed another woman again. And now, here he was, acting like a stallion with a mare.

Except some other man had already gotten her pregnant, had already planted his seed. Then he'd left her. No doubt she wouldn't be welcoming another man between her legs.

Even knowing that, however, did nothing to keep his cock from wanting. He just needed to make sure that he kept his need private.

He turned the warm water off and rinsed off with cold. Then he stepped out, rubbed his hair almost dry with a thick towel, and pulled his new clothes out of the bag. He ripped the tags off. Damn, but things were expensive in this time. Melody hadn't batted an eye at his clothes costing what would have been three months of wages. It hadn't been just her. The store had been crowded with shoppers— mostly women—and almost all of them had been wearing trousers along with shirts that left their arms bare.

He wondered if people used paper money anymore. Melody had slid some kind of card into a machine and when he'd looked around, it had seemed like most everyone was paying in the same manner.

He put on fresh underclothes and then pulled his new shirt over his head and stepped into the lightweight pants. He put on socks and slipped his familiar boots on. They felt solid and comfortable. He walked over to the big window and pulled back the lacy white curtain.

Grapevines stretched as far as the eye could see. From this height, they looked like a mass of green, crawling up and over the hillside. Up close, from the back of his horse, he'd been able to see the delicateness of each plant, their thin trunks braced up by steel posts and wood rods, and their vines, supported by rows of thin wire, spreading wide.

He'd read books about how people turned grapes into wine. He just didn't have any damned idea how it happened. He turned away from the window just as there was a soft knock. He opened the door. Melody stood outside, her hands together, the thumb and index finger of her right hand twisting the slim silver band she wore on the fourth finger of her left hand.

"Oh, good," she said. "You're dressed."

"I don't generally answer the door otherwise," he said.

She blushed, looking younger than her twenty-eight years. "I . . . uh . . . wanted to change before dinner and I didn't really want to wait out in the hallway too long. It might look odd . . . you know . . . since we're married."

He could still remember the first time he'd seen Hannah undress. They'd been married for all of three hours and had finally pushed the last wedding guest out the back door. He'd helped her that night, had slipped the tiny buttons through their holes.

His hands had shaken. With fear. With delight. And until the day she'd died, he'd loved watching the feminine fussing that went along with starting the day and the nightly rituals that ended it.

It seemed wrong, somehow, that he should share that

with another woman. But it was her home, her room. "You shouldn't have to wait out in the hallway like some naughty child. I can turn my back."

She looked at the timepiece on her wrist and stepped into the room. "Yeah, well, we'll work on that. Right now, I'm just going to change in the bathroom and then we're going downstairs. That woman who wrote the cookbook is already here."

"I wonder if Bernard is still pretending to be mad at her?"

"So you picked up on that? He's so funny when he tries to act as if it's not important to him to have his wine, his baby, appreciated." She walked over to the closet, opened it, and pulled out a blue dress the color of a North Dakota sky on a clear summer day. "This will just take me a minute," she said as she walked into the bathroom and closed the door behind her.

It took three. When she came out, he saw that she'd not only slipped the dress on but that she'd gathered her long hair up and pinned it with some kind of fancy silver clip. She looked lovely. The dress was tight enough that it hugged her small belly and he had to tell himself not to stare. In his day, women hid their condition beneath skirts and petticoats. He'd always thought that was proper but he had to admit, there was something very attractive, almost seductive, about a woman who was with child.

The dress stopped just above her knee and she wore no stockings. Her bare skin was tanned and he could not tear his eyes away from the gentle curve of her calf muscle and then lower still, to her slim ankle.

He had a sudden vision of her naked in his bed, those legs draped over his shoulders.

"Ready?" she asked.

Oh Christ, yes.

"Jingle's hungry," she said.

It was a good thing Jingle didn't know what kind of thoughts he was having about the mother. George walked out of the room, grateful that she'd interrupted his thoughts. Another minute and he'd have had to eat dinner with his hat in his lap.

DINNER at her grandmother's had always been more formal than lunch and tonight was no exception. In fact, Melody didn't know if it was her homecoming or Rebecca Field's visit, but it seemed even more ornate than usual.

The lights in the dining room had been dimmed and several sets of candles lit the long table. Light bounced off the crystal wineglasses and water goblets that anchored each place setting. A vase of fresh flowers, flanked by two bottles of Sweet Song of Summer Reserve Cabernet, already opened, marked the middle.

The chairs around the table were empty. Melody could hear voices from the family room so she led George in that direction. Louis and Tilly had claimed the couch. Her aunt's glass was full and she balanced a plate of Brie cheese and crackers on her knee. Louis had switched from beer to wine but his glass sat in front of him, appearing yet untouched.

Melody quickly figured out why. He was too busy staring at the woman across the room who was having an animated conversation with Gino. At least she looked animated. Gino just looked uncomfortable, like he wasn't at all used to having a gorgeous woman talk to him.

And she was gorgeous. Rebecca Fields was tall, slim, and sort of exotic-looking. She had straight dark hair that reached her shoulders, and dark eyes. Her skin was pale with barely a hint of color except her lips, which were a soft shade of coral. She wore white slacks with a gold belt and a white shirt that had enough buttons undone that it was easy to see why her cable television show had men running to find their mixing bowls.

She wondered if George liked to cook.

If implants were flammable, this woman was in serious trouble. Or, if she leaned too far over. *Oh, pardon me, sir. It appears I've dipped my breast in your crème brûlée.*

She turned to see if George had noticed the assets across the room but found him already in conversation with her grandmother. She heard the word *Brontë* and knew Grandmother couldn't help quizzing him about her beloved horse. She turned back toward Rebecca Fields just as Bernard walked into the room.

He was wearing a suit. She hadn't seen Bernard wear a suit since she'd graduated from high school. She wasn't sure, but she thought it might be the same suit he had on now. She walked over to him.

"Looking pretty spiffy, my friend," she said.

He shrugged. "It is your first night home."

It was, but then again, over the years she'd had other first nights home and there'd never been a suit. No. Given the way his eyes had quickly searched out Rebecca Fields, *that damn woman*, his sprucing-up had little to do with Melody's homecoming and much more to do with a certain television celebrity.

It made Melody nervous. Bernard had never married, had never even dated as far as she knew. To coin a phrase from George, Bernard *courted* grapes.

"It's none of my business," she said, "but—"

"You're right," he interrupted. "It isn't any of your business."

Her feelings were barely even bruised. How could they be when she was so worried? She loved Bernard and she didn't want to see him get hurt. And while she knew better than to pass judgment, something told her that Ms. Fields wasn't the type of woman likely to be interested in Bernard—if for no other reason than she had to be at least twenty years younger.

She plucked at his sleeve. "Bernard, just be careful. Okay?"

He looked her over. "Maybe I've been a little too careful my whole life. Maybe it's time for me to stop being cautious." He reached over, took a glass of wine off the tray that Bessie was carrying past, and calmly walked away from Melody, leaving her with her mouth hanging open.

Oh, for goodness's sake. Couldn't the man just take up surfboarding or skydiving? There was no need to be crazy here.

"Darling," her grandmother said, coming up behind her. "Come with us. I want to introduce you and George to our guest." She had George firmly anchored on her left, and she hooked her right arm through Melody's.

Up close, the woman was even prettier. "Rebecca," her grandmother said, "may I introduce my granddaughter, Melody, and her new husband, George Johnson."

Rebecca extended a soft hand with absolutely perfectly manicured fingers. It took everything Melody had not to hide her own bare, sort-of-short, sometimes-chewed fingernails.

"I'm delighted to meet you," Rebecca said, her voice so on-camera sweet that Melody thought she might have stumbled upon a sound stage. "I've heard so much about you."

Since Louis was the woman's contact, Melody could just imagine what she'd heard. "The pleasure is mine."

Rebecca released Melody's hand and immediately turned her attention to George. She extended her hand. "My, my," she said, "why is it that all the gorgeous men are already married."

"Ma'am," George said, nodding his head at her.

She winked at him. "It's 'miss.'" She had yet to release his hand.

The absurdity of the situation hit Melody like a seven-year-old running full speed toward home plate. An absolutely stunning woman was interested in George, who would be a crazy man not to be interested in return, but he could do nothing. Otherwise, she'd have to tell her grandmother that she was a liar. And an unwed mother-to-be.

It really wasn't fair to George.

Melody pulled gently on her grandmother's arm. "Let's go talk to Aunt Genevieve. She's standing over there all by herself."

Grandmother looked between George and Rebecca Fields, like she was afraid to leave the two of them alone.

"Don't worry about Rebecca," Melody chattered brightly. "George can entertain her."

She didn't look back until she'd reached Aunt Genevieve's side. Then she was sorry she did. Rebecca and George were sitting on the couch, their heads close together. She turned back to Genevieve. Mona was draped around her neck, her front paws folded nicely on one side, her tail flipping furiously on the other.

"There's a name for women like her," Aunt Genevieve said.

"She's just outgoing," Melody said. "Probably was a cheerleader in high school."

Aunt Genevieve rolled her eyes. "It's a shame your baby is using up all your oxygen. Must make it hard to reason things out."

She ignored the comment and pretended to be fascinated by the tray of crackers and cheese on the table next to where her grandmother stood.

"I think we better have dinner," her grandmother said.

"Good idea," muttered Aunt Genevieve. "Before that one thinks it's time for dessert."

Within minutes Grandmother had them moving toward their chairs. She sat at the head of the table with Aunt Genevieve at her left. Then it was Bernard, Gino, and Louis rounding out the side. Grandmother waved Rebecca to the seat directly to her right and then motioned for Melody, George, and Tilly to file in.

George had his hand already on his appointed chair when Melody slipped into it, leaving George to sit between Rebecca and herself. He gave her a look but obligingly sat next to Rebecca Fields, who wasted no time in leaning his direction and saying something in her soft, aren't-I-sexy voice.

There'd been no good option. No way in hell was she letting Tilly sit next to George. Not only had the woman practically drooled over him on the stairs, she'd also had time to prepare a full arsenal of questions. George wouldn't stand a chance and the whole charade would be uncovered. She couldn't let that happen. However, now she'd have to spend an hour watching Rebecca Fields charm George.

"Melody, would you like to lead us in prayer?"

Dear God. Please make Rebecca Fields pick her teeth at the table. "Absolutely, Grandmother." She looked around the room. Bernard was staring at Rebecca, Tilly at the potatoes, and Aunt Genevieve had her eyes narrowed at George. He was the only one with his hands together and his head bent.

What was he praying for?

"Melody?" her grandmother prompted.

"Okay." She ran her tongue across her teeth. "Heavenly Father. We . . . uh . . . we thank you for this opportunity for our family to be together." She made the mistake of looking up. Louis looked amused. "And we . . . uh . . . thank you for this food." Now what? "Please watch over us," she finished and quickly unfolded her hands.

"Amen?" her grandmother prompted.

"Yes. Amen," Melody added. George turned his head and smiled at her.

It was the last time he looked at her. His attention shifted to Rebecca Fields when the woman put her hand on his wrist. Melody tried very hard to pretend that it didn't bother her. Or that later, when she heard George laugh at something the woman said, that it wasn't hard to swallow her roast beef.

Bessie had just cleared the dirty plates when Gino's cell phone rang. It startled Melody because one, Gino rarely carried a cell phone and two, everybody knew Grandmother hated those kinds of interruptions at the table.

She looked at her grandmother but she didn't see irritation in the woman's eyes. Instead, it was pure concern. Gino pushed his chair back and was halfway out of the room when he answered on the third ring.

"What's going on?" Louis asked.

Grandmother didn't answer. Aunt Genevieve looked like she wanted to speak up but a quick shake of her sister's head had her silent as well.

Bessie had delivered dessert and coffee by the time Gino came back. Melody felt scared when she saw that his eyes were red.

"It's over," he said, looking at Grandmother.

She nodded. "I'm sorry, Gino. You know I want you to take as much time as you need."

"It could be four weeks," he said, looking uncomfortable.

"Go." It was Aunt Genevieve who issued the terse order. "Your mother needs you."

It was Gino's turn to nod. "I've been trying to stay ready, to be prepared. I've got a good list made of what needs to be done over the next couple of weeks. Arturo can handle it."

"What's going on?" Louis repeated his question. His voice was louder, more agitated than before.

"My father is dead," Gino answered. He stood straight, rather stiffly, like he didn't want to talk about it.

Melody understood. She knew the story. Gino hadn't spoken to his father in over thirty years. Grandmother had told her that they'd had a terrible falling-out when Gino had left the family vineyard in Italy and had come to work for Grandmother. Gino had always kept in contact with his mother, talking once a week on the telephone, and he'd paid for her to come visit him in the United States several times.

"Arturo can barely read English," Louis said. "He certainly can't manage fifteen other men or the complexities of the vineyard." The man looked at his wife.

"Louis will have to do it," Tilly said. "Somebody in the family needs to be in charge."

Nobody at the table said a word. Bernard looked like he'd eaten something sour and Grandmother and Aunt Genevieve exchanged another look that told Melody neither woman thought the suggestion was a good one.

Grandmother, ever the professional, turned to Rebecca Fields. "Rebecca, I'm sorry but as you can see, we have some business to attend to." She glanced across the table. "Bernard, would you be willing to share dessert and coffee with Rebecca in the living room?"

Under normal circumstances, Melody knew it would take an earthquake to remove Bernard from a discussion about the vineyard. Every winemaker knew that the secret to wonderful wine was wonderful grapes. And wonderful grapes didn't just happen. They needed tender loving care in the form of just the right amount of sun, the right amount of water, and vigilance against the insects and other pests that threatened a growing vine.

He looked from Gino, to Louis, then back again to Grandmother. Ultimately, Rebecca was a force that could not be denied. He picked up his cheesecake and his coffee. "I'd be happy to," he said.

Rebecca had the good grace not to make a scene. She stood up, picked up her own dessert and coffee, and smiled at the group. "It's been a pure delight," she said. "Thank you so much for inviting me."

Melody noticed that the woman's utterance of delight had happened at exactly the same moment her gaze had reached and settled on George. She looked around to see if anyone else had noticed, but all eyes were on Grandmother, wondering what the heck she was going to do.

Grandmother waited until the door was shut behind Bernard and Rebecca before turning toward Louis and Tilly. She licked her lips and when she spoke, her voice was surprisingly strong, reminding Melody of the Grandmother of old. "Arturo is a fine young man. And if Gino thinks he's ready, then he's ready."

Louis turned red. "But—"

"But since," she interrupted him, "it is my name on the bottle and my reputation, I don't see any harm in having a family member working with him, side by side."

"Louis doesn't prune vines, Mother," Tilly said in a disgusted tone.

Louis's face had toned down to a dull pink. "No, but I sure as hell can tell somebody else how to do it."

"Of course you can," Grandmother replied smoothly. "But last week when we needed help spraying sulfur after that rain, you told me you were much too busy with the mail-order business."

"But this is different," Uncle Louis said.

Melody knew what was different. Last week he'd have actually had to work. Now he was gleefully contemplating bossing their trusted employees around. Gino would be lucky to come home to a crew.

Grandmother turned slightly in her chair and looked first at Melody and then George. "I believe we all agree that one of the family should take over for Gino. George, can you do this for us?"

Melody could feel her ears grow hot. George had straightened in his chair and she sensed his discomfort with the request.

It was all her fault. She'd told everyone he was family. He certainly hadn't signed on for this. He was supposed to show up, pretend to be a husband, earn a few dollars, and be on his way.

"Ma'am, with all due respect, I don't know much about grapes."

There was a grunt of satisfaction from Louis's end of the table.

"Gino is right in that Arturo does know what needs to be done. I just want you there as a second set of eyes and ears. Please."

George turned to look at her and Melody resisted the impulse to apologize. Instead, she looked him in the eye. "It's your decision, George. No one will think less of you if you say no."

"That's true," Grandmother said.

"That's good to know," he said. "However, if you think I can be of assistance, I'd be happy to help."

EIGHT

TILLY left the table without finishing her dessert. Louis, always better at keeping his feelings under wraps, settled back into his chair and sipped his coffee. "Work starts early in the vineyard, George."

"I imagine it does," George said, his tone even.

Gino looked at his watch. "I'm catching a red-eye out of San Francisco tonight but I have enough time to take you out and introduce you to Arturo."

Louis straightened up in his chair but before he could speak, Aunt Genevieve pushed her chair back and stood up. "Gino, grass is growing under your feet. Just go. I'll take care of introducing him around tomorrow morning. You know I'm always up."

Gino nodded and he looked first at George, then at Grandmother and Aunt Genevieve. "I appreciate this," he said. Then he looked at Melody. "I'm sorry I didn't get to spend more time with you, Sweet Pea. Next time, okay?"

She got up and gave him the hug that she'd been wanting to deliver for the last fifteen minutes. "Take care," she said. "We'll be thinking about you."

Gino shook his head and awkwardly patted her belly. "I'm happy for you." He glanced at George one last time and his eyes were serious. "You've got Sweet Pea and her baby and now my grapes to take care of. I hope to hell you're a good man."

It was the kind of statement that didn't require a reply and George didn't give him one. Gino hugged Melody and was out the door.

Nobody said anything for at least a minute. Then George pushed back his chair.

She figured he was going to go look for Rebecca Fields.

"I didn't get much sleep last night," George said, "and since work does start early, I think I'll retire for the evening if no one has any objections."

Retire for the evening?

Grandmother smiled at both her and George. "I imagine you're both tired. You had a long drive this morning and it's certainly been an eventful day."

Well, that was clear enough. Her grandmother expected her to *retire with* her husband. Given that her other option was chatting it up with super-thin Rebecca in the other room, it was no doubt the thing to do.

Melody walked over and kissed both her grandmother and her aunt on the cheek. "I'll see you both in the morning," she said. She glanced in Louis's direction. "Good night."

As they walked upstairs, Melody repeated one thought. *I can do this. I can do this.*

She had done this.

In college, the summer between her junior and senior year, she'd shared an apartment with Gavin Blake. They'd met through a mutual friend. He'd cooked, she'd cleaned, he'd showered at night, she in the morning. It had been perfect. Each had slept in his or her own bedroom.

She knew how to do the roommate thing.

And this was sort of the same. Her room at her grandmother's house was about the same size as the two bedrooms at that tiny college apartment. So, really, all she was missing was a wall.

Some drywall and a coat of paint. Nothing much.

She stopped in front of the big linen closet. "I'm just going to grab that extra blanket," she said. It was on the top shelf. She reached for it and he put his fingers on her forearm and gently pressed her arm down.

Heat.

Big dip, big sway. Tango in progress.

"I'll get it," he said. He pulled out the blue-and-gray quilt and tucked it under his arm.

"Drywall and a little paint," she mumbled.

"What?"

"Never mind."

When they got inside her room, he closed the door with a quiet *thud*. When she turned to look at him, he was staring at the picture on the wall. He seemed so far away.

"I figure Colorado 'cause of the mountains," she said.

He continued to stare at it. "I saw some mountains like that once in Wyoming," he said.

"I've never been to Wyoming."

He didn't answer.

"Sounds like you have, though." She pushed, unwilling to let him close her off.

He nodded absently. "Spent a few weeks there."

"When?"

His head jerked toward her. "A few years ago." His tone suddenly seemed guarded.

Who knew how long he'd been out of work? Maybe he'd drifted around for a while and the memories weren't all that pleasant. She walked over to the dresser and grabbed the pajamas that she'd put in the top drawer earlier. There was no sense putting this off indefinitely. He was tired. So was she.

"I'm going to change into my pajamas in the bathroom." She said it so nonchalantly that she was sure a casual observer would have assumed that she had men in her bedroom every night.

It struck her that George might think that very thing. After all, she'd obviously had at least one, at least once. "Um, George."

"Yes." He put the quilt down on the seat of the chair that sat next to the dresser.

"I'm not . . ."

"Yes," he repeated.

"I don't sleep around," she said. Well, that was probably blunt enough. "I mean, I know I'm pregnant and all and there's no husband, no boyfriend, no nothing."

He sat there. Waiting. Finally, he spoke. "Yes."

Oh, good grief. "That's three times. If you say that word again, I'm going to smother you with a pillow tonight."

He opened his mouth, but then shut it quickly.

Great. It wasn't like the man had talked all that much to begin with. "Never mind," she said.

She had the bathroom door open before he stopped her. "Melody."

She didn't turn around.

"What I think," he said, "isn't all that important but if it matters to you, I guess I'd just want you to know that I think you're a fine woman."

She threw up every morning, her bra was getting too tight, and in a couple of months, she wouldn't be able to see her toes. But suddenly, she felt sort of like delicate porcelain china.

Or like a new rose in the garden in early June.

She was a champagne bubble.

She was *fine.*

WHEN she finally got out of the bathroom, after changing into her pajamas, and running cold water across her wrists for about three minutes, he was already on the floor, covered up by the quilt. He lay on his back, his dark hair brushed back from his face, a stark contrast to the yellow pillowcase.

She looked at her watch and then back at him. He had an eight o'clock shadow. She knew he'd shaved that morning at Target so he must be the kind of guy who could go about twelve hours before he started taking on the very sexy, I-need-a-woman-to-remind-me-to-shave look.

"I can't believe we're going to bed and it's only eight o'clock," she said.

"I'll try to be quiet when I get up in the morning."

"I'll set the alarm."

He looked confused.

"Don't tell me," she said. "You're one of those people who just knows what time it is. You don't even need an alarm clock to wake you up?"

He shook his head. "Not usually," he said, sounding wary again.

She walked over and lowered both shades. The room darkened, lit only by the bathroom light, which she'd left on. She climbed into bed. "Even before I got pregnant, I hated to get up in the morning. Now, it takes something just shy of dynamite to get me up."

He didn't answer. She lay on her back and stared upward, looking somewhere past the darkness.

She hadn't bought him any pajamas.

So, he was either sleeping in his clothes or something less. And it was the something else that was causing her to feel sort of hot and bothered, even though the air-conditioning appeared to be working just fine.

She matched her breathing to his. It was crazy, she knew, but she didn't want him to hear her breathing. It was too intimate. She'd never heard Gavin Blake breathe.

Because there'd been a wall.

"Melody."

His voice was quiet, like he wasn't sure she was awake.

"Yes."

"I like your grandmother."

She smiled in the darkness. "That's cool. I think she likes you, too."

GEORGE woke up when he heard Melody cry out. He threw back the quilt, stumbled over to the bed, just in time to see her grabbing at her bare lower leg. She'd thrown back her covers and her normally smooth face was twisted in pain.

"Jesus. What's wrong?" he asked.

"Leg. Cramp," she said, between clenched teeth. She massaged her leg with the heel of her hand.

"Let me," he said. He moved quickly, sitting cross-legged on the bed with her leg across his lap. With both hands, he rubbed the back of her leg, from the hollow behind her knee, all the way to her delicate ankle.

He could feel the tension in her whole body. He'd had a leg cramp or two in his lifetime. He knew she had to be in terrible pain and that knowledge pinched at his heart.

It took all of three minutes before her body relaxed and she lay back in the bed, clearly exhausted. He continued to rub her leg, although with less force, knowing that even though the cramp had passed, it would have left her muscles sore. He skimmed the bottom of her foot with his knuckles.

She laughed and he realized that he'd tickled her. He did it again, grateful to hear her joy rather than her pain.

She opened her eyes. "Stop that," she said. "I'm ticklish." She pulled her leg back, resting her foot on his thigh.

Oh Lord. Another three inches higher and her toes would be tickling his balls. He didn't need them to start laughing right now. He gently shifted her foot toward his knee.

There was enough light in the room that he could see that the wisps of hair around her face were dampened with her own sweat. She was smiling but the leg cramp had taken its toll. "This happen often, Melody?"

She shook her head. "It just started recently. I thought it was because I'd worked an extra-long shift at the restaurant. Also, I read that leg cramps sometimes happen to pregnant women when they haven't had enough water to drink during the day."

He hated to think that she'd been alone dealing with this kind of pain. "You need to be more careful. Make sure you're not on your feet too much."

"I know."

"And that you drink enough water."

"Yes, Mother." She smiled at him and using her hands, scooted herself up to a sitting position.

His lap felt suddenly empty. And when her eyes settled on his bare chest and then drifted lower still, to linger on his unsnapped jeans, he could feel his body react in a most expected way.

He got hard—for the second time that day, proof positive that the first time hadn't been a fluke. He felt warm and wondered if it was lust flowing through his body or simply relief that he could want again for a woman.

"I'll get you some water," he said, shifting and moving, making sure that his need wasn't staring her in the face. He stood next to the bed, his body half-turned away from her, while he pretended to be busy straightening up the quilt.

"You don't have to do that," she said.

What? Get water or act like a man who'd taken leave of his senses? He wasn't about to ask for clarification. He picked his shirt up from the chair where he'd hung it the night before and put it on. "I'll be back in a few minutes," he said, never looking at her.

He took the steps quickly but quietly. The house was dark but several of the blinds had been left partly open and bright moonlight slipped in. He passed the piano room and looked longingly at the newspaper that Melody's grandmother had left next to her chair. He badly wanted to read it, to try to figure out this world he'd been thrown into, but he didn't stop. Melody needed water first.

When he got to the kitchen, he got the biggest glass out of the cupboard and filled it completely. Then he set it aside and splashed cold water on his face and ran his hands and wrists under the steady stream.

He needed to cool off, to get control. He sure as hell couldn't be reacting like some randy bull in a pasture full of heifers every time he touched her or she happened to touch him.

He was thirty-four years old and his cock was acting like he was fourteen again—jumping up and down like a damn puppet on a string. At fourteen, he'd gone behind the barn and handled it the way he figured most fourteen-year-old boys did. At seventeen, he'd had his first woman and that had been the last time, so to speak, that he'd taken matters into his own hands.

Hannah had wanted to wait until they were married. He'd taken her to bed that first night and almost exploded in her hand.

But as much as he'd wanted her, he'd never, ever, hardened so fast as he had when Melody had touched him. There was probably only one thing he could do. He picked up the glass and started walking back upstairs.

He had to make sure that the two of them didn't touch again.

When he got back to the room, she'd had the light on and she was sitting up in bed, a notepad of sorts on her lap. She was scribbling furiously on it. He paid her activity scarce attention, he was more interested that she'd pulled the sheet up, covering her almost to her neck. Had she seen his cock about to burst out of his pants? He thought about apologizing but decided it might be better if they both just ignored it.

"What are you doing?" he asked.

She looked up, clearly startled at his sudden appearance, and flipped the pad over. "Nothing. Just . . . making a list of things the baby needs."

"Drink it all," he said, as he handed her the glass.

She looked at the glass, then at him. "I'd wet the bed if I did that."

He knew he was in trouble when even that made his cock twitch.

"Drink what you can," he said. He stood there and she obediently tipped the glass up. She drank about half of it and then handed him the glass.

"If you leave it on the nightstand, I promise I'll finish it by morning," she said.

Not wanting the glass to leave a mark on the fine wood, he reached for the notebook that Melody had tossed aside. He heard a squeak from the bed.

"What?" he asked.

She shook her head.

He flipped the notepad over, set the glass on it, and was about to walk away when the words caught his eye. NAILS. BOARDS. SCREWS. TRIM. DRYWALL. PAINT. WALLPAPER. Then she had written the word WALL about ten times. He glanced at her. Her face was pink but she didn't look like she was in pain. If he'd had to guess, she was embarrassed.

"These are things for your baby?"

"Yes. Yes, that's what I said, isn't it?"

She sounded a bit flustered. He looked at the list again.

"I'm really tired," she said. "Can we just turn off the light?"

It had been a long day. They could both use the sleep. He turned off the lamp and lay on the floor, his back to the bed. Even though it was too warm for the quilt, he got under it.

"Melody," he said, his voice soft. "If your baby needs a wall, I'll help you build it."

She didn't respond for a moment. Finally, she said, "That would be great, George. Good night."

He lay perfectly still. It was maybe ten minutes later that he was certain by the steadiness of her breathing that she was back asleep. He waited another five. Then he eased out from under the quilt and stood up, as silent as if he was stalking a deer.

He knew what he should do. But he couldn't walk out the door. Not without looking at her one more time. She was on her back, with the sheet still pulled up all the way to her neck.

It didn't make any difference. He didn't need to see her skin to remember the silkiness or the soft warmth. He didn't need to see her breasts to remember their fullness. He didn't need to see her body to imagine what she looked like naked, beginning to ripen with child.

Her long hair spread across the pillow and he couldn't stop himself. Ever since he'd woken up on the beach and seen her walking toward him, her light brown hair blowing in the wind, he'd been aching to touch her hair.

He knew what it smelled like. Her scent had surrounded him when he'd held her in the wine shed. Now, he lifted a long strand and gently rubbed his fingers together.

Silk. And for the third time that day, he felt his body react. Christ, but wasn't he making up for lost time, then.

He dropped her hair and took a big step back, then another, until he was safely out of the room. He took the stairs fast, staying close to the edges to avoid any creaking in the middle.

On his way to the newspaper, he passed the big window in the piano room. The drapes had been left open. With the house being like it was, perched on a hill, he knew on a clear day he would be able to see for miles into the valley.

Tonight, with just a quarter-moon to guide him, he could make out the grapevines that grew closest to the house. And he knew from when he and Melody had driven up the long and winding road, that rows and rows of grapes extended far beyond what his eye could see.

He'd arrived on the beach just a little more than twenty-four hours ago and had stared at the same moon that was now lingering over the valley. He'd waited for the footprints to take him home and had been disappointed when he'd woken up, still on the beach.

Then Melody had come and everything had changed. Suddenly, he had a place to stay and work to do.

Not that he wanted to stay. He belonged in his own time, in his own town, in his old job. When the footprints came back, he would put his feet in them and let them take him back.

In the meantime, he'd do the best he could to take care

of Melody and her unborn child. He'd feel better prepared to do so if he understood this time better. He gave the valley one last glance and was about to turn away when out of the corner of his eye, he saw the dogs.

There were three of them, running hard, their strides long, their motion fluid. They were not more than three hundred yards from the house, at the very edge of the lawn. He was sure that he recognized Dionysos and Hermes, but wondered just how that could be. There'd been no mention of a third dog. But the dog running alongside them looked enough like them to be a brother or sister.

He watched until he lost sight of them as they moved farther around the house. He sat down in the chair, turning on the small light next to the chair, just the way he'd seen Melody's grandmother do.

He read for at least an hour until his head was almost spinning on his shoulders. There were soldiers dying in countries he'd never heard of, there was concern about something called the ozone layer, and a hundred thousand people had had their identities stolen when hackers had breached some company's firewall. What the hell?

Yet not everything was different. There was news about robberies, and weddings, and deaths. Articles about people doing the things that people did.

His eyes felt heavy by the time he got to the glossy pages that were clearly advertisements. He thought at first that he must be seeing things. How could a pair of ladies' shoes cost more than a hundred dollars? And when he looked at the food advertisements, he wondered how a man could afford to feed his family.

He closed the newspaper, set it aside, and felt even more unsettled than before. He understood the present a little better now and he surely wasn't convinced that things were better than they'd been in 1888.

Feeling weary, he closed his eyes and leaned his head against the high back of the chair. When the front door opened it startled him so, that he dropped the newspaper.

It was Genevieve, with Dionysos and Hermes at her side. The dogs' fur gleamed with sweat that came from a hard run. He stood up and the woman stopped suddenly, looking very surprised.

"I didn't realize you were up," she said.

"Melody needed a glass of water," he said.

"Of course." She looked at her dogs. "Dionysos and Hermes needed some exercise."

He didn't tell her that he thought he'd seen the dogs earlier or that there'd been a third dog with them. He couldn't. He could barely speak at all, because his tired mind was playing tricks with him.

How had he not noticed before that her hair, stick-straight that it was, was the very same color as the dark coat of the dogs? And her eyes, the same gold brown.

Damn it. It wasn't possible. A woman couldn't turn herself into a dog and then back again. But then again, he'd never believed a person could travel a hundred-plus years forward either.

"Doing some late-night reading?" she asked, looking at the newspaper.

"Yeah," he managed.

"You might want to get a few hours of sleep. You're going to have a big day tomorrow."

Couldn't be much bigger than today. He'd woken up on a beach outside of Los Angeles, decided to play at being a husband, and suddenly found himself in charge of fifteen men.

The only thing that seemed right about it was meeting Melody. She was sunshine and sugar and a hot drink on a cold day. She was perfect.

And hopefully still asleep. "I should turn in for the night," he said.

"Be on the front steps at half-past four. I'll take you down to meet Arturo."

"Gino seems to think he's a good man," George said.

"Gino's generally right. But I suspect, George, what somebody else thinks doesn't sway you much. You're the type who needs to make those kinds of judgments for himself."

There was something in her voice, a challenge of sorts.

"With all due respect, ma'am, I suspect you're the same."

She threw her head back and laughed. The dogs lifted their heads in surprise and Dionysos growled softly. "Shush," she said to him, putting out her hand and rubbing his head. "It's all right. George and I are just coming to a mutual understanding of our strengths and weaknesses."

He wasn't sure anymore what his strength was but he was damn certain his weakness was lying up in her bed. He nodded his head at Genevieve. "Good night, ma'am."

She smiled and looked very satisfied. "You're going to do just fine George, just fine."

"Beg pardon?" he asked.

She threw her head back and laughed for the second time that night. "Go to bed, George," she said, as she left the room with the dogs close on her heels.

NINE

❧

GEORGE had been getting up at the crack of dawn since he was knee-high to a grasshopper. Even in the days following Hannah's death, when well after midnight he'd drunk himself to sleep, he hadn't had any trouble waking up. So why he didn't crack an eye open until he heard a knock on his door was beyond him.

It took him just seconds to realize that night was passing and full-blown day beckoned. It meant that he was living up to Louis's low expectations.

He threw off the quilt, grabbed his shirt off the chair, and was halfway to the door before he realized that the quilt and his pillow were still on the floor. Moving fast, but quietly, so as not to wake Melody, he placed the pillow next to her. He made the mistake of looking at her and that stopped him.

She was so damn pretty. She'd kicked off her sheet sometime during the night and her pale yellow nightgown was wrapped around her body. She lay on her side, her knees pulled up, her shoulders rounded slightly. Her long hair was bunched underneath her head and for one crazy minute he thought about lifting her head and spreading her hair out across the pillow.

Then he remembered. *No touching.*

He moved away, throwing the quilt at the bottom of the bed. When he opened the door, Aunt Genevieve, wearing black trousers, a loose black shirt, and a black hat, stood outside. She wore yellow gloves with the fingertips cut off. She had purple feathers behind her ear and a green and yellow bandanna draped over one arm.

"It's time," she said. She handed him the bandanna.

He tied it around his neck. "I'm sorry," he said, keeping his voice low. "I must have overslept."

She stretched, not even pretending that she wasn't looking past him. He was grateful that he'd remembered the pillow and the quilt.

"Melody looks more like her mother every day," Aunt Genevieve said, her voice soft to match his. "It's good to have her home."

"I think she's glad to be here with you and Pearl," he said.

She looked him in the eye, then motioned for them to take the conversation out into the hallway. Once she closed the door, she turned to him. Her mouth was a tight line, her shoulders stiff. Over her shoulder, less than ten feet away, he saw Dionysos and Hermes waiting at the top of the staircase. They looked alert and watchful.

"She needs to understand that she's not going to have her grandmother much longer," Aunt Genevieve said. Her voice was strained with the emotion of loss. "God help me," she continued, "but I can't tell her."

He understood. Because to tell Melody, Aunt Genevieve would have to say the words. And she couldn't do that. "You don't have to tell her. She knows."

Relief showed in her gold-brown eyes. "It's still going to be hard on her," she said. "You need to be here for her, George. You need to stand by her."

He wouldn't make promises that he couldn't keep. "I'll do the best I can," he said.

"You're going to have to do better than that." She plucked a feather from behind her ear and handed it to him. "Purple provides strength of purpose."

He took it from her fingers, considered it, then put it in the pocket of his shirt.

"Good call," she said, giving him her back. She started down the steps at a pace that belied her age, both dogs on her heels. "Arturo's men will be quick to judge. You walk out there with a feather behind your ear and they're going to think you're nothing but a crazy old woman."

ARTURO, who looked to be about thirty, sat on a bench in front of the bunkhouse. Dark-haired with skin tanned a deep red-brown, he had a slim, wiry build. He didn't speak when Aunt Genevieve and George approached.

Once they stood in front of him, Aunt Genevieve said, "Good morning, Arturo. You've spoken to Gino." It was a question but phrased like a statement.

Arturo nodded. He still hadn't made eye contact with George.

"This is George—Melody's husband."

George put out his hand. "Morning, Arturo."

"Señor." His voice was guarded, not hostile but certainly not friendly. His shake was brief.

Aunt Genevieve looked first at George, then at Arturo, her gaze holding several seconds on each man. "There's grapes to grow," she said finally. Then she turned and walked away.

Now what? George looked past Arturo, into the long rows

of grapevines. The sun, just sliding over the horizon, gave the vines a soft golden glow. A vineyard in the early morning was a peaceful place.

"May I?" George asked, motioning to the empty spot on the bench.

Arturo slid over.

For several minutes both men sat quietly. In the distance, George heard the familiar sound of horses waking up. He leaned forward, rested his elbows on his knees, and said quietly, "I don't know shit about grapes."

It took Arturo a minute to respond. "Gino told me that before he left."

There was just a slight trace of an accent in the man's words and George realized the man's earlier deferential Señor had been flavored with pretense. It explained the look that Genevieve had given Arturo. "So, about now, you're thinking I'm going to be one giant pain in the ass to have around?"

No response at all from Arturo, and George appreciated that the man didn't pretend to be happy. "I'm going to need your help," George added.

"I will not tell the men," Arturo said.

George turned his head. "I don't much care about that. What I care about is keeping these grapevines healthy and not making a mistake that's going to cause trouble for Pearl Song or her family."

Arturo stood up. "Then you and I want the same thing." His voice sounded less guarded and George thought he perhaps had passed the first test.

"What did you plan to do today?" George asked.

"The holding pond needs to be checked first. The pump has been giving us trouble."

"Okay. Let's go."

Arturo led him around the wine shed. He caught a

glimpse of the cement paddock area Melody had told him about. There were four very tall—at least fifty feet high—steel tanks. He could only assume those were the fermentation tanks that she'd mentioned. A smaller machine, probably ten feet high by ten feet wide stood next to them. "Is that a grape crusher?" he asked Arturo.

"Yes. A crusher/stemmer. It was new a year ago. In the fall, when the grapes come in, Benito and his son, Montai, are the only ones who get to operate it."

George didn't know if Arturo offered that last piece up as casual conversation or if it was meant to warn him to stay away from the expensive machinery. Sort of a gentle reminder that his incompetence might be tolerated in the field but not anywhere close to the wine-making process.

They walked another hundred yards and got close enough that George could see the pond. The sun was now fully over the horizon and the water shimmered in response. It was much larger than he'd expected. "How big is this?" he asked.

"It's a forty-thirty-acre-feet pond."

"How much water is that?"

"An acre-foot of water is about 325,000 gallons. So, maybe ten million gallons." Arturo made a sweeping motion with his hand. "We have drains in these hills and we capture every damn drop of water that falls. When the grapes are processed in the fall, we recycle all that water, too. Water never goes to waste. I make sure of it," he said proudly.

In the car, coming up to Melody's grandmother's, he'd seen the big rigs out in the fields, irrigating the crops. "Then you spray it on the grapevines?"

"No. Some vineyards may still spray. But it can make your vines mildew. We have irrigation hoses that take the water to the fields and then drip lines buried into the ground that spread the water to the root of the plants."

Arturo walked to a small building at the edge of the pond and when he opened the door, George could hear the pump running. Arturo checked the gauges and appeared satisfied. "It looks okay. We'll check it again later."

They closed the door and retraced their steps. "Now what?" George asked.

Arturo walked over to the truck and opened a big tool-box that took up most of the back. He handed George what looked to be short-handled snips. "We need to join the men. They knew to go directly to Lot D. The vines are loaded with buds. Too many, in some cases. They need to be thinned out so that the buds that remain get the sun and air they need."

By ten, his shirt was drenched with sweat and his shoulders ached. But it felt good to work again, to have a purpose as simple as plucking off shoots and leaves. He'd just reached the end of one row and was rounding the corner to work his way down another path when he heard the sound of men's voices.

They were speaking loud and fast in what he assumed was Spanish. It was frustrating that he couldn't understand a word of it. Then he heard the unmistakable sound of a fist hitting flesh. Nobody needed to explain what that meant. He took off running, and found two men grappling in the dirt, blood dripping from both their noses.

He grabbed the closest one by the back of the shirt and yanked, hauling him back several feet. Then he stepped between the two men.

"Stop it," he yelled.

He didn't know if they understood English but both men stayed where they were. He could see that they were young, probably just in their early twenties. Both had dirt in their dark hair and blood on their shirts. He looked at their eyes, expecting to see anger, and saw only fear.

Arturo came running around the corner, almost skidding to a stop. His eyes took in the scene and he spoke quickly in Spanish to each man. Both answered Arturo without ever taking their eyes off George.

George waited until there was a pause in the conversation before interjecting. "What's going on here?"

Neither of the young men answered. George looked at Arturo.

"They fight over a woman," Arturo said, his tone disgusted.

George waited but Arturo didn't continue. "And . . . ?" he prompted.

"She works in town at a hotel. She and Pedro"—Arturo gestured at the man on George's right—"made use of one of the rooms last night."

There was a rapid burst of Spanish from the man.

"At her invitation," Arturo added.

To which the man on George's left spat on the ground.

That made it clear enough. No doubt the man on the left had spent a night or two as well in one of those rooms. "These two ever get into it before this?"

"No. Pedro and Rafael have worked side by side for three years."

George untied his bandanna, unfolded it, and wiped the sweat out of his eyes. "Tell them to get back to work and to settle this on their own time."

Arturo looked down at the ground. "You need to know that Mr. Louis has a rule that anybody caught fighting gets fired."

Now George understood the fear that he'd seen in the men's eyes. But he also understood that men had been fighting over women since the beginning of time and that it wasn't likely to change soon. "Then I suggest that nobody tell Mr. Louis about this. Let's get to work."

At straight-up noon, the men stopped working and piled into the back of the pickup truck. Arturo and George took the front, with Arturo driving. It took less than ten minutes to get back to the homestead. Arturo was quiet until they pulled into the driveway. He stopped the truck, pulled the keys, and turned toward George.

"That was a decent thing you did," he said.

"What would happen to them if they lost their jobs?"

"Their families would suffer. Señora Song pays her workers fairly. They would not find another job like this. There are not many vineyards like this one."

He was starting to realize that. "Arturo, if a man wanted to buy land here in this area, what would it cost?"

Arturo looked surprised. "Are you thinking of buying?" he asked.

"Just curious," George said.

"Land like this, known for producing a quality grape, has recently sold for a hundred thousand dollars an acre."

George had been doing arithmetic since he was six but he was coming up with one big number in his head. "That would mean that two hundred acres would run twenty million dollars?"

Arturo nodded. "Got that in your pocket?"

George shook his head. He couldn't fathom having that much money.

"Don't feel bad," Arturo said. "Not many have that kind of money, except for people who don't know anything about grapes but they've made their money in computers or maybe the stock market."

Computers. Stock market. He didn't have a clue what Arturo was talking about.

"They're the dangerous ones," Arturo continued on, "because they're used to having their own way. All they think they have to do is snap their fingers and order the grapes to grow."

George shook his head and reached for the door handle. "Not many want to trim vines?"

Arturo shook his head. "Señor, I think you are one of the few." He motioned to the porch. "Maybe your wife waits for you?" he asked.

George saw that Pearl and Melody were sitting side by side on the porch swing, gliding gently back and forth. Melody wore a light green shirt that hugged her body with a white skirt that showed her legs from the knee down. She wore the same shoes she'd had on yesterday, the ones that showed her toes.

She stood up and extended her arm to her grandmother, helping the woman out of the swing. Arm in arm, the two of them came down the steps toward him. When he looked at Pearl Song, he knew how strikingly beautiful Melody would be in her later years. Strong bones, clear skin, proud stature. It was an appealing combination.

He got out of the truck and stood next to it. When they got close, Pearl waved to him. "How was your morning?" she asked.

He made a valiant effort to stop staring at Melody's knees. "Good. We spent most of our morning in Lot D."

She smiled. "Oh, the Cabernets."

Yeah, that's what Arturo had said. Not that George knew one kind of grape from another.

"Those are my favorite," Pearl added.

He thought she sounded a bit wistful. Melody, apparently hearing it as well, turned her head to look at her grandmother. A gust of wind caught her hair, whipping it across her face, and his arm was half-raised before he remembered. *No touching.* He lowered his arm and put his hand in his pocket.

She tucked her hair behind her ear. "I didn't even hear you leave this morning," she said, looking at him.

Good. Then maybe she hadn't seen him standing over her, staring like some fool. Not wanting to dwell on the image of Melody in bed, he said, "What are you ladies up to?"

"Just enjoying the day," Melody said. "Do you . . . uh . . . happen to have a few minutes that I could talk to you?"

Had he done something terribly wrong in the vineyard? Had word already made its way back to the main house? He looked at Pearl but her posture was relaxed. It was just Melody who seemed tense. "Of course," he said.

She grabbed his free hand and as hot as his skin had been under the full morning sun, her touch was warmer still. She must have felt it, too, because as soon as she'd led him around the back of the sprawling house and through an arbor that was covered in fresh-blooming wisteria, she dropped his hand. The garden was an abundance of color and life. There were white daisies and orange black-eyed Susans and big yellow sunflowers. There were purple phlox and bright pink zinnias.

His mother had taught him to love flowers. He'd grown up twenty miles east of Bluemont, North Dakota, in a place where most everybody had grown their own vegetables. His mother had done the same, but what she'd really loved was the flowers in her garden. When neighbors had come round for a visit, they'd always found themselves in the garden, picking a bouquet or digging up a plant to take home to their own garden.

He'd worked those flowers from the time he was old enough to pull weeds and deliver water. And he'd told his friends he hated it.

Then later on, practically in the dead of night, he'd

planted flowers in the small garden behind his and Hannah's house. He'd claimed once they started to grow that they were Hannah's flowers, that he was just tending to them to be helpful. Hannah, who thought flowers were a waste of time, had gone along.

He loved them. Loved watching them poke out of the hard ground and reach up for the sun. Loved watching them bloom and then lose their luster, only to bloom again.

"This is a pleasant spot," he said, not wanting to sound too interested.

Melody drew in a deep breath. "I know. Don't you just love flowers?"

"I do." It came out before he could stop it. He looked at her to see if she was embarrassed for him but she didn't even seem surprised.

"When I left home for the first time," Melody said, "the first thing I bought for my apartment was three big flowerpots. I had a little deck off my living room and every night I would sit out there, close my eyes, and smell the flowers. It was like I'd brought a piece of home with me."

"It sounds nice."

"What's your favorite flower?"

In all the time he'd been married to Hannah, she'd never once asked him that. "I guess there's nothing that smells much prettier than a lilac bush in spring." He had several outside his back door at home.

"Very true." They walked another thirty feet before she spoke again. "Come over here; there's something I want to show you."

She led him past bold pink flowers on strong stems that were almost her height and then past a wide patch of what looked like wild orange lilies. She stopped suddenly and said, "This is my favorite part."

He could see why. It was a pool of water, maybe thirty feet long by twenty feet wide with a waterfall at one end. Blooming lily pads floated on the water and purple hyacinth bloomed along the edge. Small fish, every color of the rainbow, swam near the surface. All in all, it was one of the prettiest things he'd ever seen.

"My mother had been working on the design of it before she was killed. Grandmother finished it in her memory. When I was living here, there was hardly a week that went by that I didn't come back here. It's the one place that I always felt safe. Loved."

His heart ached for the young girl who'd suffered so. "Perhaps that's why your grandmother finished it. Maybe she knew you needed this place."

She blinked quickly and he knew that she was holding back tears. "You're probably right," she said. "She's always known me better than anyone else."

It was the second time she'd said something like that. It might be true but it begged the obvious question. "If your grandmother knows you that well, how is it that she didn't know you weren't truthful about having a husband?"

She didn't look surprised. Instead, she pointed at the bench that sat at the far edge of the pond. "May we sit? My back hurts."

That scared him. "Should we get back? I could carry you."

She rolled her eyes. "Hoping for a hernia?"

"What?"

"Never mind. I'm fine, really. I'm sure it's from being in the car for so long yesterday. This last month I've noticed that if I sit too long, my back aches."

It was probably true what his mother had told him—that if men had to have the babies, there would be none. He let her lead him over to the bench and he waited until she sat. Then he lowered himself down, making sure their thighs were a foot apart. The *no touching* rule applied here, too.

"At first," she said, "I thought Grandmother was very suspicious and I was just waiting for her to push back, to force me to come clean. But she didn't. When she started asking that we come home for a visit, I came up with all kinds of excuses. You were traveling for work. I was working extra shifts. You had the flu, I had a cold. Then, when I told her I was pregnant, I told her that I just didn't feel good enough to travel."

"She could have come to see you."

"I kept waiting for her to say exactly that. Over the years, she'd been to visit me several times. When she didn't suggest it, I thought it was because she was worried about the vineyard. We had very heavy rains here in late December and early January, to the point that most of the vineyards were under water. Because the vines were dormant, I think most everyone thought they'd come out of it all right but I knew it was still a worry. Now, because I know about the cancer, I think she not only wasn't feeling up to making the trip, she was busy thinking about that."

He studied the fish in the water for a few minutes. "You said that first night on the beach that legitimacy of a child was very important to your grandmother. Why is that?"

She gave him a brief smile. "You've got a good memory, don't you?"

"I guess." He *could* remember things that had happened a hundred plus years ago like it was just yesterday.

"My grandmother and Aunt Genevieve are illegitimate. Their father, my great-grandfather, never married my great-grandmother."

"Were they together but just not wed?"

"No. My great-grandfather Reginald Song was a bit of a

rogue, but evidently an irresistible one. He stopped in every so often but never stayed long."

"Evidently long enough," he said dryly.

She laughed and when she flipped her long hair back, she looked young and carefree. If Reginald Song had been anything like his great-granddaughter, it was no wonder he'd been hard to resist.

"My grandmother was born exactly one day and one year before the big Crash."

"The big crash," he echoed, wishing like hell it was easier to figure out what was going on.

"Right. She was born October 28, 1928. Supposedly after she'd been born, he'd promised my great-grandmother that they'd be married soon. Well, he lost everything like so many others and he evidently felt strongly that Great-Grandmother shouldn't have to marry a poor man."

"But I thought your aunt Genevieve was several years younger than your grandmother."

She nodded. "I did say he was a bit of a rogue. He came back when Grandmother was about two and evidently stayed *just long enough* that nine months later, Aunt Genevieve was born."

"Your great-grandmother never married anyone else?"

"No. Grandmother told me that she thought her mother really believed that one day he'd be back. But a year went by, then another. My grandmother was almost twenty-five when they learned that he was dead, had been dead for four or five years by that time."

"I'm sorry," he said. "For your great-grandmother, for Pearl and Genevieve."

"They grew up without a father, without his name. People laughed at them, at their mother. They said she was a fool, a disgrace."

"That would be difficult for children to hear."

"They've never forgotten it. But in the end, Reginald Song did right by them."

"What do you mean?"

"He'd regained everything he'd lost in the stock market, threefold. He died a rich man. They inherited this land and enough money to go with it to get the vineyard and winery started. Perhaps more important to them, is that they got his name. In his final papers, he acknowledged them as his only living children. I think that's why my grandmother never changed her last name when she got married several years later. She'd waited a long time to be Pearl Song, and she wasn't giving it up."

"So your grandmother and aunt Genevieve share ownership of this property?"

"They did up until the mid nineteen sixties. Aunt Genevieve wanted to travel, to see the world. Grandmother had married by this time and she and my grandfather bought out Aunt Genevieve. She took her half in cash and they didn't hear from her again for almost fifteen years. Then she came home."

"And your grandmother welcomed her back?"

"Of course. They're sisters. Aunt Genevieve doesn't begrudge Grandmother's position—she knows that she got her share. But now," her voice softened with concern, "I worry that when Aunt Tilly inherits the property she might force Aunt Genevieve out."

He wasn't an expert on how property changed hands but he thought she might be missing something important. "Melody, if your mother was still living, she'd share equally with Tilly. Since she's not living, I think her share would come to you."

She didn't look surprised. "That's how it works, usually."

"You and Louis and Tilly would be partners of a sort."

She shook her head. "Can you imagine how horrible

that would be? Years ago, Grandmother and I had this discussion. I told her at that time that she should leave the winery and the vineyard to Tilly and Louis. This has been their home for the past seventeen years. In their own sick way, I think they love the vineyard and frankly, I'm not sure what else they could do."

And she had accused *him* of being too nice. "You're satisfied knowing that you're not going to get your share?"

"Grandmother said at the time that if she left the property to them, that she would make it fair to me."

"What did she mean by that?"

"I have no idea. I imagine she has some other assets, some cash, some jewelry. I have no idea how much and I'm not going to spend time thinking about it. It's too horrible. It's been at least five years since we've spoken about it."

"Do you think Louis and Tilly know?"

"I have no idea. I'm not proud of this, but I sort of hope they don't. In my own sick way," she said, looking a little ashamed, "I like the idea of them losing a little sleep over it."

She stood up and stretched. She was so fair-skinned that even though they'd been out in the sun a short time, her nose was already pink. "Well, I guess I've put this off long enough."

"What?" Damn, but she was a pretty woman.

"Grandmother would like an opportunity to announce our marriage to her friends and neighbors."

She said it matter-of-factly but he could hear the tension in her tone and he wondered if some of her pink nose was from nervousness. "I imagine that is what's done," he said carefully.

"She wants to host a sort-of-formal dinner party. Maybe twenty-five or thirty people. I didn't want to say yes until I'd talked with you."

He'd never been to a sort-of-formal dinner party, but

he'd been dragged to a couple church socials when some well-meaning citizen had deemed it appropriate to expose him to some organized fun. How much worse could a dinner party be? "Is it something you're interested in?"

"I think it would make her very happy."

"And you'd like to do that?"

"Of course."

"Then I think we should tell her yes." He could see the relief in her eyes and knew he'd made the right decision.

"If you'd like, I could ask her to invite Rebecca Fields."

He didn't much care about the guest list. "I suppose that would be all right." He stood up and the two of them started back toward the house.

"She's very pretty, don't you think?"

That stopped him. "She's a handsome-enough woman," he said.

She frowned at him and he wondered if he'd said something wrong. "So, you did like her?" she asked.

He shrugged, wondering just why they were talking about Rebecca Fields. "She's pleasant enough."

Melody waved an impatient hand. "Handsome enough. Pleasant enough. Good grief, George. Is she somebody you'd be interested in?"

He caught up, finally. "Mrs. Johnson," he said, emphasizing the title, "I'm supposed to be married to you."

"I know. But it was pretty obvious that she's attracted to you and, well, maybe she's an opportunity that you're missing."

She looked so serious. This was not a conversation he'd anticipated having and he struggled to find the right words. "I'm thirty-four years old, Melody. I've had my share of *opportunities* and I've made good use of some of them."

Now her cheeks were pink too and he knew that she

understood what he was saying. "Right now," he continued, "I've got no business thinking about opportunities."

Even though she looked as uncomfortable as he felt, she stood her ground. "But sometimes an opportunity squandered is an opportunity lost."

He shook his head. "I imagine you're right. But in this case, it's not that big of a loss."

"Really?"

He'd always been a little slow about things like this but he suddenly realized that Melody was jealous of any attention he'd paid to Rebecca Fields. Which was ridiculous. Even so, he felt flattered, like he'd been paid a great compliment. "She's not the type I favor," he said.

She stared at her toes. "If I might ask, exactly what type is it that you favor?"

That wasn't as easy as deciding which was his favorite flower. Women were more complicated. "I guess I favor those who aren't too hard on the eyes. I like a gentle spirit that allows them to show kindness yet a firm constitution that permits them to be strong when it's called for. I like a woman who laughs easy and makes others around her want to pull up a chair and sit for a spell."

"Oh." She looked up and he saw that she had a dreamy look on her face. "She sounds lovely."

"She is." He started walking again, hoping like hell that she didn't realize the obvious—that he'd just described her.

"I guess we should be getting back," she said. "You haven't had your lunch."

It was as good of a reason as any not to stand in the garden, thinking about things that could never be. He was here just temporarily. The footprints that would lead him home could come at any time. He'd do well to remember that this was a woman who'd lost much already. Her parents, her best friend, and soon her grandmother. She didn't need to be having any crazy ideas that the two of them could be together and then end up losing him, too.

"Yeah," he said. "I think we've wasted enough time here."

He heard her quick inhale of pain and felt like a damn ass. But better she hurt some now, like the gardener with a rose thorn under his nail, than hurt more later, when she'd be left alone to walk in her garden.

TEN

PEARL waited for them on the bench in front of the fountain, her legs extended, her head tilted up to catch the warm sun on her face. She wore loose light green trousers, a blue shirt the color of the sky, and a wide-brimmed straw hat. Pieces of her white hair had escaped, and blew gently around her tan face. When Melody saw her, she stopped.

"Isn't she beautiful?" Melody whispered. "She's always had this uncanny ability to look absolutely at peace with nature, like she's part of the landscape. This is exactly how I want to remember her."

He considered the angle, the light. "Wait here," he said. He walked into the house, up the stairs, and once inside the bedroom, he opened his camera case.

It was a Waterbury, manufactured by the Scovill Manufacturing Company. Hannah had given it to him as a gift for their first wedding anniversary and his picture-taking skill had improved over time. He'd enjoyed it a great deal.

But then after Hannah had died, he'd put his camera

away. He hadn't taken another picture until the one he'd taken of Sarah Tremont and John Beckett—the one that now hung on Melody's bedroom wall.

When he emerged from the house, he was pleased to see that Pearl hadn't moved. Melody had circled around so that she faced her grandmother. When he stood next to her, she pointed and whispered, "That thing actually works?"

If she only knew. He nodded and pointed the camera at Pearl. He widened the bellows to get a good, close shot. Then he pulled the lens cap off, counted to three, and snapped it back in place. "I'll develop it for you later." In his camera case, he'd carried the fluids he needed as well as the paper to transfer the picture to. All he needed was a dark space. He could use their bath.

"Thank you so much," she said. "I'm going to treasure it."

He was glad that he'd made her happy. He couldn't help feeling bad that he'd hurt her feelings back in the garden. "I guess I better get—" he stopped. The dogs bounded out of the house, followed by Genevieve. The door slammed behind her and the noise woke Pearl up from her midday nap.

She stretched and shifted and when she saw them, she smiled. "I swear, I can fall asleep at the drop of a hat," she said. "I didn't realize you were back from the garden." She looked at the camera, which George still held in his hand. "What's that?"

"A camera," he said. "I was just showing Melody." He'd let Melody surprise Pearl with the picture.

She got up to have a closer look. "My gosh. What year was that made?"

His chest started to feel tight. "Mid eighteen eighties, I think."

"It's really in great shape for being so old," Pearl said. "I was at an antique show not too long ago and they had several like it. But that part"—she pointed to the rubber bellows—"was all dried out and looked like it might crack if you tried to bend it. You must have taken very good care of it. Is it a family heirloom?"

Now his chest felt like it might explode. He never should have gotten the camera out of its case. He'd just gotten carried away with the idea of doing something nice for Melody. "You might say that. I guess I better get it put away so that I can catch up with Arturo," he said, hoping to avoid any additional questions.

Genevieve and the dogs had made their way to the fountain. She had two orange feathers behind one ear and she wore a long black dress that hung off her skinny frame. If her sister was at one with nature, a part of the landscape, then she seemed more at one with death, a part of the dark side.

"So? You and Arturo didn't hurt each other?" she asked.

"No, ma'am." The way she asked the question, he wasn't sure which one of them she'd been rooting for.

"Genevieve, you are impossible," Pearl said, her tone loving. She turned back to him. "I want to show you around the place. I was tired yesterday and did a poor job of it. I'd like to make up for that today."

"That's not necessary, Pearl. I can find my way around," he said. This woman had more to think about than playing hostess.

"I've already talked to Arturo and told him I was kidnapping you for a little while. And quite frankly, I'm looking out for my own interests. I can't ask you to step in for Gino and not give you some basic information that will be helpful as you do your job." She put her arm through Melody's. "Plus, I want to spend some time with my granddaughter and her new husband."

George looked at Melody and knew fairly quickly, by the

look of panic in her pretty eyes, that she'd had no part in the plan. Probably was afraid that between the two of them, they'd say or do something that would give them away.

Pearl turned to her sister. "Do you want to come with us?"

Genevieve looked at both George and Melody. "Sure," she said agreeably. "Why the hell not?" She whistled at the dogs and then made some kind of hand motion that had them heading for the porch. Then she reached into her skirt pocket and pulled out a faded, crushed hat, which she pulled low onto her forehead. "What's first?" she asked.

"The cave," Pearl answered. "After all, it is my pride and joy."

He'd never been in any cave that caused him to have much pride or joy. They'd been dark, damp, and generally uncomfortable. He slipped the camera strap over his shoulder and followed Pearl and Melody, who walked arm-in-arm. He walked next to Genevieve, who hummed a little tune under her breath.

They walked past the wine shed, past the cement paddock, and then practically into the side of the hill. Two thoughts hit him at the same time. One, he'd never seen a cave with a door on it and two, it was nicer than most people's houses.

It was brightly lit inside, with electric lights every three or four feet. The floor was a smooth and shiny cement and the walls were a light gray. He rubbed the palm of his hand across them.

"Shotcrete," Pearl said. "It's ten inches of pea gravel, sand, and cement with a coat of paint added in at the end. Come on. There's more to see."

Surely the rest of it could not be so grand.

But it was. In a few minutes, he stood in the middle of a wide circle, with five tunnels leading off in all directions like spokes on a wagon wheel. In each tunnel he could see racks of wine barrels, three or four high, similar to what had been in the wine shed.

"This was Grandfather's dream," Melody said. "He died in 1989, three months after excavation began. Grandmother finished it."

He couldn't tell which grandparent she was prouder of. "It's spectacular," he said. "You use it to store wine?"

Pearl nodded. "Yes. It's an expensive proposition to dig a cave of this size but the payback comes rather quickly. The temperature in here is about fifty-eight degrees year-round. That's really optimal for wine storage. Before we had this, we needed to cool the wine shed to that temperature, and that was a very expensive electric bill to pay each month."

He'd wondered if people had to pay for the power that ran the electric lights. George could hear the sound of men's voices coming from one of the tunnels. He walked over and looked. Pearl joined him. "What are they doing?" he asked.

"Topping off barrels. Even in this natural humidity the wine evaporates and we need to refill the barrels to avoid oxygen getting in and ruining the wine. Each barrel loses about a gallon a year in here. If it was aboveground, it would be more like four gallons. So, that's more payback."

"Amazing," he said. He couldn't think of another word that came close to describing the cave.

Pearl laughed. "It's always a delight to see a person's face the first time they see this. But we should be going. There are other things I want to show you."

He turned to leave the way he'd come in but Pearl, Melody, and Genevieve were headed in the other direction. He followed them and realized quickly that the cave had a back door. They exited less than thirty feet from the cement paddock area behind the wine shed. He figured that was no accident. No doubt the closeness between where they processed the grapes and where they stored the finished product had been by design.

Pearl stopped in front of the machine that Arturo had warned George away from that morning, when he'd said it was reserved for Montai and his father. "There's always work to be done but in September and October, the pace becomes almost frantic. During the crush—that's what we call our harvest—grapes are brought here by the truckload. They are washed and then put in this baby," she said, patting the machine lovingly. "Here they get destemmed and then crushed."

It was starting to make a little sense. "And that's wine?"

"No. Not yet. That's *must*—a mixture of juice, skins, seeds, and pulp. The next steps are a little different depending on whether we're making a white wine, say from Chardonnay grapes, or our Cabernet Sauvignon, which is the red wine you had for dinner last night. With white wine, we press the grapes next. That separates the juice from the rest of the must."

"But it's not the same for red wine?" George asked.

"No, red wine actually gets its color from the clear grape juice having a chance to come in contact with the skin of the red grape. So primary fermentation begins while the juice is still mixed in with the grape skins."

"What's fermentation?"

"Fermentation is nothing more than the process of converting the sugar in the grapes into alcohol and carbon dioxide, which is simply released into the air. It happens when yeast, which is a naturally occurring organism on the skin of grapes, comes in contact with the juice. It's basically a simple chemical process. It does, however, cause heat, and too much heat can be detrimental to the quality of the wine."

Genevieve pulled an orange feather from behind her ear

and handed it to him. "Orange is for clarity of thought. I figure you could use it about now."

"Thank you," he said. He stuck it in his pocket, right next to the purple one that she'd given him this morning. If she was right, he now had clear thoughts and a sense of purpose to carry them out. He walked over to one of the tall silver tanks. There was a ladder, taller than he'd ever seen, leaning up against it. He stepped around it and ran his hand over the dimpled side of the tank. "All that happens inside of here?"

"Yes," Pearl answered. "With red wine, the must rises to the top during fermentation and it's someone's job to punch it down, or mix it all up again, to make sure that there is sufficient contact between the skins and the juice. These extension ladders come in handy. The dimples you see are refrigeration to counteract the heat."

"Speaking of heat," Genevieve said. "It's damn hot out here."

Pearl looked upward and studied the clear sky. "It is, isn't it?" she said, like she'd just suddenly noticed. It was clear that when Pearl Song got a chance to talk about her wine, she took notice of little else. "Are you hot, darling?" she asked Melody.

"Not bad, but I should be getting over to the wine shed. I told Bernard that I'd start the data entry today."

"All right. Lessons are over for today," Pearl said. "Besides, I've kept you from your lunch, George. Go on in the house and Bessie will fix you something. Then, if you want to find Arturo, he said he'd be in Lot C. That's the fifteen acres straight west of here. You can take the four-wheeler or if you prefer, saddle up Brontë. There's a patch of olive trees nearby she can graze under."

He didn't know what a four-wheeler was but if it was anything like a car, it couldn't be good. "That's an easy choice," he said honestly. "I'll take Brontë."

Melody put out her hand. "I can take your camera up-stairs," she said.

He hesitated, then felt stupid. It was just a camera. Even if she pulled it out and looked at it, there was nothing that would make her think it was anything but an old camera in really good shape. He relaxed his shoulder, let the strap fall, and then handed the box to her.

Their fingers met and for one brief moment, they were each connected to the other, and to the camera box. Pearl, Genevieve, even the buildings around them seemed to fade into the background. There was only Melody and him and his camera.

And he could smell the hearty scent of pig roasting on a spit and could hear the gentle murmur of voices in the background. Sarah. John. Fred Goodie and his intended bride, Suzanne. It was all exactly as it had been the night he'd taken the picture of Sarah.

He jerked back and the camera would have dropped to the ground if Melody had not been quick to grab it. "What's wrong?" she asked, wrapping her arms around the sturdy box.

He sniffed the air and listened. Nothing. He looked around. Genevieve and Pearl stood there, their eyes wide with interest but giving no other indication that they'd smelled or heard anything odd.

"George?" Melody asked. Her pretty eyes, more violet today than blue, were filled with concern.

"Nothing," he said. "I'll see you ladies later." He turned away quick, not sure that even he was a good enough liar to carry off this one.

MELODY spent most of the afternoon working in Bernard's small office, at the rear of the wine shed. To get there, she'd walked a bit nervously past the stacks and stacks of oak barrels, half expecting one to jump out of its rightful place and take flight. But they'd all behaved, staying quite still.

She spent the first two hours entering data. Between Bernard and Gino, they tracked everything. Rain amounts, daily temperatures—both the high and the low, sulfur applications, pruning schedules, and everything else in between on an almost acre-by-acre basis. Making great wine wasn't a paint-by-the-numbers kind of activity, but yet, the numbers mattered. When the grapes were ready to harvest, they'd match all the numbers up and try to figure out what worked and what didn't.

She ran out of paper printing off Bernard's reports. She started opening filing-cabinet drawers and was surprised when she came across several drawers that were locked. She couldn't remember them ever having to lock any of the drawers. Nobody came into the office area except family and Bernard and Gino.

She finally found the extra paper in the closet and just as she was finishing her reports, Bernard knocked on the door.

"How's it going?" he asked.

She wiggled her fingers and flexed her wrists. "I'm out of shape. I used to be able to do this all day."

"There's no hurry. It just needs to get done sometime over the next couple weeks."

"I heard some voices earlier. Was that you?"

"Yes. Tilly had one of her tours and there was a man who was insisting that when a wine has a vanilla taste, it's because we're adding vanilla extract."

She pretended to be shocked. "That's not true?"

Bernard rolled his eyes. "You'd have been proud of me. I didn't tell him he was too stupid to live."

"Of course not," she said. "You're much too nice for that."

He snorted. "I hear we're having a party in a couple days."

She wasn't surprised that he knew. Since this was his home, too, Grandmother would not invite thirty friends for dinner without letting him know in advance. "Grandmother seems to think it's the thing to do. I don't want it to wear her out, though."

"If it does," he said, picking up a stack of the papers she'd printed and leafing through them, "it would be a good kind of worn out. The kind that comes from pleasure."

They heard a knock on the door and Tilly stuck her head in. "Bernard, I need you again. I swear, this guy thinks his ten-dollar tasting fee entitles him to twenty questions. He's fascinated by fermentation."

Bernard rolled his eyes but Melody knew it was mostly habit. Grandmother had told her a long time ago that Bernard, like most winemakers, was part artist and part scientist. The artist in him wanted to create his masterpiece in private, to brood over it, to enjoy some anguish awaiting the end product. The scientist in him wanted to finitely examine each element of the process and to discuss it at length, to ponder the implications of varying the process, and to document it to death.

When there were questions from visitors, inevitably the scientist won out over the artist. He'd already followed Tilly out the door before Melody remembered she'd meant to ask him about the locked drawers.

She turned off the computer, cleared her workspace, and stood, absently rubbing her stomach. It made her smile to think of Jingle swimming around, like the fish in Grandmother's pond.

George had liked the pond and she'd thought he'd understood why it and the garden were important to her. But

then he'd seemed almost impatient to leave, had even said
something about wasting time.

Maybe he'd come to his senses and realized that Grandmother's little dinner party was likely to give him indiges-
tion. There'd be well-meaning neighbors and longtime
family friends who'd be naturally curious about the marriage.

He'd do fine. She, on the other hand, if past performance
were truly an indicator of future performance, would be a
mess. She'd stumble over her words and her explanations
would be so circuitous that she'd be lucky if she didn't
strangle herself.

As abrupt as he'd been in the garden, he'd still been
gracious when Grandmother had insisted they tour the
place. He'd asked good questions and his interest had
seemed genuine. Grandmother had loved it and it had been
wonderful to see how excited she'd been to show it all to
George.

She needed to remember to thank him again. And then
she was going to ask for a favor. They needed to rehearse
for the dinner party. Well, fine, *she* needed to rehearse. But
he needed to help her. Tonight, when they *retired for the
evening*, they could make sure they had their story straight.
She was hip-deep in this muck she'd created. If she weren't
careful, it would suck her in, like quicksand in the old horror movies.

Melody left the office and followed the sound of voices.
Bernard stood in the middle of a group of at least ten, with
Tilly off to the side. When Melody got close, she heard him
explaining that their barrels were made out of American
oak and that there was a careful rotation system in place to
ensure that barrels were not used after three or four years;
after that period of time, the ability of the wood to impart
any desirable flavors into the wine would be diminished.

A man wearing a white shirt and bright red shorts that clashed alarmingly with his dark socks and dress shoes, raised his hand. "What happens to the barrels after that?"

"We sell them. Usually to a vineyard that doesn't have the same standard for their rotation or the same high standard for wine production."

It was true but it did sound a little pretentious. The man nodded and began flipping through some sort of pocket wine guidebook. He raised his hand once again when he evidently found the page he wanted.

"Yes, sir?"

"Your 2003 Cabernet received four and one-half stars in *Love Your Wine* magazine. What did it lack that it didn't get a full five stars?"

He'd asked it innocently enough that it was possible the poor man didn't realize those were fighting words. Even Tilly, who had seemed zoned-out to that point, straightened up. No doubt she was concerned that sales in the gift shop, the next stop on the tour, might be hampered if the guests saw the winemaker explode.

Melody knew from past experience that Bernard could easily launch into a two-hour tirade about the ability of so-called experts to rate wine. It would be flavored with adjectives that would shock the woman in the purple-flowered pantsuit and likely leave Red Shorts with a red face.

Melody moved forward, caught Bernard's eye, and winked at him. She knew exactly what the magazine had said about their Cabernet—that it lacked a certain complexity they'd come to expect from Sweet Song of Summer wines. She would bet her last dollar that Bernard knew exactly what the magazine had written.

Bernard smiled at the group. "That's not a publication that I'm familiar with," he said. "Now if you'll excuse me. Please do enjoy the rest of your tour."

Melody caught up with him at the door. "Good job," she whispered.

"That guy would need a guidebook to find his balls," Bernard hissed back. "Sorry," he added.

"No problem. You handled him perfectly. I'm going to take off for the afternoon. I guess I'll see you at dinner."

"Actually, you won't. I've got a date."

"A date!" She said it louder than she'd intended.

He looked irritated. "Yes. A date. With Rebecca Fields."

She wanted to be happy for him. She really did. But there was something too weird about Bernard and the very-thin Ms. Fields dating. "So, where are you going?"

"Dinner at Madeline's in Yountville."

"Very nice." Madeline's was one of the nicer restaurants in an area filled with nice restaurants. "Have fun," she said, feeling bad that she couldn't be genuinely happier for him. "And, Bernard," she said, putting her hand on his arm.

"Yes."

She wanted to tell him to be careful, to protect his heart.

"What is it, Melody?"

She smiled at him. "Whatever you do, don't wear shorts and black socks with your wingtips."

He shook his head. "Do I have asshole written across my forehead?"

WHEN George pulled the saddle off Brontë's back at the end of the workday, he felt like every damn bone in his body hurt. His shirt was sweat-drenched, his pants were dirty, and he could smell himself.

When he walked into the house, Dionysos and Hermes, ever-watchful of intruders, came running. "It's just me," he said, kneeling down, with his hand out. He didn't try to pet them. He just kept his hand still, letting them sniff.

"Is that you, George?"

"It is, Pearl." He'd wanted to go right upstairs but it seemed rude now not to stop in and say hello. He walked toward the piano room, stopping when he got to the door. Both sisters were there.

"Come in, come in," Genevieve beckoned. The cat was once again wrapped around her neck. She leaned over and patted the empty space on the couch.

"I better not," he said. "I've got several layers of dirt on me and one is bound to come off on your furniture."

Pearl smiled at him. "How did the afternoon go?"

He'd sliced a finger with the razor-sharp knife that Arturo had given him and both his heels had blisters. But there'd been no more spats between the men and they'd seemed to accept his presence among them. "Very nice."

"Melody said she mentioned that I'm hosting a dinner party to celebrate your marriage and the baby. It's tomorrow night—you may want to knock off a little early."

"I'll do that. Where is Melody, by the way?"

"We haven't seen her," Pearl said. "I imagine she's out in the shed with Bernard. She should be in shortly to get ready for dinner."

He nodded. "Well, then, if you'll excuse me, ladies, I think I better get cleaned up myself." He walked up the stairs and down the short hallway. He grabbed for the doorknob, pushed the door open, and stopped suddenly when all the air left his lungs.

ELEVEN

HE'D expected the room to be empty. But Melody lay on her bed with barely a stitch on. Her shirt, which had skinny little straps, hugged her full breasts tight and stopped just inches below them. The vee at the top of her legs was covered by an almost transparent little scrap of material and he could see the hair between her legs.

She was lovely. There was no other word for it. And he badly wanted to touch her. To stroke her smooth skin, to brush a hand across her nipples and see them beg for more attention, to spread her legs and taste her sweetness.

He could tell by the gentle rhythm of her breathing that she was sleeping. Her hair looked wet and her pillow damp, like she'd gotten out of the shower, gotten partially dressed, and then stopped to rest. He couldn't stop staring at her stomach. It amazed him to think that as the weeks grew to months, her smooth skin could stretch enough to accommodate her growing child.

In his time, women died giving birth. New babes died, too. If anything had changed in a hundred and eighteen years, he hoped that had. It struck him suddenly that four months was not a terribly long time. Was it possible that he'd still be here? Would he get to see Melody's child? Would he know that she'd seen her way safely through the ordeal? Or was it his destiny to go back to his own time soon and forever wonder what had happened to Melody and her child?

He felt suddenly light-headed, almost sick to his stomach. He couldn't stay in this time. He needed to be where he belonged, in a time he understood.

He *did* know shit about being a sheriff. Not like grapes.

He took a step away from the bed and might have gotten away without her ever knowing he was standing there, staring like a young boy, if she hadn't rolled over and in the process, almost made her plump breasts practically pop out of her little shirt.

"Christ Almighty," he said.

Her eyes flew open and it reminded him of how she'd looked that first night on the beach. Then, she had stared at him, like he was something that had emerged from the sea. Now, she looked less frightened, less wary, but still surprised to see him standing over her bed.

"I didn't know you were in here." He was trying to look everywhere but at her breasts. But he was clearly unsuccessful; she glanced down and quickly shifted, pulling her shirt back into place.

"I'm sorry," he said. "I had no right."

He could see the look of uncertainty in her violet eyes and then they cleared, like she'd come to some decision. "Come here," she said, her voice soft. She held out her hand.

He shook his head. No. He couldn't touch her. Not when

he was feeling so weak. "I'm filthy dirty," he said, grabbing on to the only excuse he could.

"That doesn't matter. Please."

He knew what he should do. But he couldn't walk away. She looked more beautiful than ever—so overwhelmingly female, so lushly ripe with impending motherhood, and his body reacted in what was starting to become a most familiar way.

And he couldn't hide it from her. Her eyes opened wide. "Oh my," she said.

"I'm sorry," he said. *Damn*, he cursed himself.

She scrambled to sit up in bed. "Uh . . . George?"

She was going to tell him to get and not let the door hit his ass on the way out. Disappointment, sharp stabbing points, made his chest hurt. "Yes."

A pink hue rose from her chest, spread up her neck and settled in her cheeks. "Did I do, I mean, cause that?"

Christ. She couldn't expect him to stand here and discuss it. "It won't happen again," he promised, wanting to put an end to the conversation.

"How do you know?" she asked boldly.

He looked at the thick carpet and wished like hell for a hole to swallow him up. "Because I won't let it," he said.

"Oh," she said, her tone considering.

"I've got to get cleaned up," he said.

She stared at him. "Of course," she said. "Please, go ahead." She politely waved her hand at the door to the bath, as if the last five minutes had never happened.

"You're not angry?" he asked. That worried him but what worried him more was that she might be scared of him. He probably had a hundred pounds on her and she no doubt knew that she'd be in no position to defend herself if he chose to force himself on her.

She shook her head. "Angry? No. I guess it's sort of a

compliment. I mean, unless this sort of thing happens to you regularly."

Her voice had trailed off at the end, full of uncertainty. Now what was he supposed to do? He could lie—maybe let her believe that his reaction was nothing special. Would that make her feel any safer?

"Well?" she prompted. "Is it?"

She wasn't going to let it go. Fine. Then maybe the truth was what she needed. "I haven't had a woman in six months, nor have I felt the need for one. But in the last forty-eight hours, I've been hard for you three, no, make that four, times."

She opened her mouth to say something but no words came out.

"I know that's not what you bargained for when you asked me to play the role of your new husband. I know that I don't have the rights of a real husband and I don't want you to be scared that I'm going to take them."

She looked surprised. "Being scared never entered my mind, George Tyler. I haven't known you long but long enough to know that you're one of the most decent men I've ever met. You would not take advantage of me."

He'd stick a knife into his own belly first. "It might be a good idea if you got dressed while I'm getting cleaned up."

She smiled and he thought she looked almost satisfied. "I can do that. Um . . . George, I don't want you to feel bad about . . ." She stopped and waved her hand in the general direction of his unruly cock. "About *that*."

That wasn't getting any better. If truth be told, he had a slim grip on his own control. That by itself, was damn concerning. His whole life, he'd been the type that had planned and then executed, not simply reacted and then jumped. "We shouldn't be having this conversation," he said.

"I'm sorry if I'm making you uncomfortable," she said

and he was fairly confident that she wasn't a bit sorry. She moved, slowly swinging her pretty legs over the side of the bed. He caught a glimpse of her womanhood, barely covered by that piece of lace between her legs.

His face heated up and he felt weak and needy. And when he finally managed to tear his gaze away and look at her face, it almost took him to his knees when he realized she'd done it on purpose.

He backed up a step and held up his hands. It was hard to breathe, hard to think. "Melody? What in God's name are you doing?"

She didn't answer. She simply stood there, her breasts so lush and full, her nipples tight under her little shirt. The skin on her belly was lighter than that on her arms and legs and he put his hands behind his back to keep from reaching out and stroking her.

She took a step forward.

The room felt hot.

Another step. She was close enough that he could smell her scent. Strawberries in cream. Sweet.

Another step. "Melody?"

He sounded like he was begging and he was. Begging her to keep coming forward, begging her to stop? He didn't know.

She reached a hand out and touched his cheek with the tips of her fingers, then ran the soft part of her thumb across his lower lip.

In his head, he heard the distinct snap of his control breaking. He slipped his hand underneath her damp hair and cupped her neck. He leaned forward, careful of her child, and bent his head.

When he kissed her, her mouth was warm and sweet-tasting and he meant to take it slow but reason and intent gave way to an almost-blinding need to possess her. He pressed his lips hard, her mouth opened, and he pushed his tongue inside.

It was everything but not nearly enough and he knew she felt the same when she pressed her warm body against his. He had to touch her, had to know the feel of her breasts in his hands. His mouth still consuming her, he slid his hand under her little shirt and cupped her breast. He stroked his thumb across her nipple, much like she'd stroked his mouth.

Her body jerked in his arms and he captured her groan. Then he felt her yank his shirt free from his trousers and when her hands raced across his bare back, it was he who was groaning.

She tore her mouth away and leaned her head back and he needed no further invitation. He kissed her neck, her collarbone, the valley between her breasts. Her skin was warm, delicious, and so damn tempting that he knew he could not turn away. He was not strong enough.

"Oh, George," she said. "Make love—"

A woman's scream split the quiet afternoon. Almost simultaneously, the dogs started furiously barking. He jerked his hand out from underneath Melody's shirt. He heard doors slamming and voices yelling outside. It was bedlam.

He grabbed Melody firmly by the shoulders. "Stay here," he said.

"That was Grandmother's scream," she said. She reached for the robe at the end of the bed.

He thought she was right. "Please," he begged. "Just stay here until I know it's safe."

She nodded and he ran from the room. He took the steps two at a time. When he got to the bottom, he saw Pearl and Bernard both on their knees, their backs to him. The dogs were still barking and running in circles around them. The front door was wide open. Tilly and Louis stood off to the side, unaware of his presence. They were staring at the woman on the wood floor.

Genevieve. Flat on her back. Three feet away from her, the large lamp that normally sat on the nearby table was on the floor, lying on its side, a ten-inch crack through the glass base.

He scanned the room, thinking that an intruder had somehow gotten in and in the split second it took for him to do that, he knew he would die first before he let anyone in this family be harmed.

"What the hell happened?" he asked.

Pearl looked over her shoulder. Her face was pale and her eyes watery, like she'd been holding back tears. "Genevieve fainted," she said.

It wasn't good but it meant that Melody wasn't in danger. He could feel his breath come a little easier. He took another step toward them and that set the dogs off into an even louder barking frenzy. "Be quiet," he commanded and he made the hand motion he'd seen Genevieve make when she'd given them an order. By some miracle, they stopped barking. He looked them in the eye. "I'm not going to hurt her," he said.

The two dogs crowded together, their ears up, their teeth bared. But they let him pass. When he got to Genevieve's side, he saw that someone had put a pillow under her head. Her skin was pale and there was a fine sheen of sweat on her forehead. Her lips were absolutely colorless and one orange feather was half-crumpled under her shoulder.

He squatted next to her and reached for her hand. Her skin was cool and felt thin on her bones. She opened her eyes and regarded him solemnly. He forced a smile. "Genevieve?" he asked, hoping like hell she still knew her own name.

It took her a moment to answer. Finally she licked her

lips and said, "You'd think none of them have ever seen an old woman fall before."

He felt the relief all the way through him. He reached and gently pulled the feather out from beneath her. He started to smooth down the edges but stopped when he heard footsteps on the stairs. A second later, he saw Melody. She stopped when she saw them, her hand over her mouth.

He stood up, moving fast. "It's all right," he said. He got close enough to put his hand under her elbow. "Your aunt fell but she's fine."

Melody broke away from his gentle hold, ran to her aunt, and dropped to her knees. "Are you all right? Did you hit your head?" She looked up. "Did someone call an ambulance?"

Call *what*? George looked at Pearl and Bernard but they were shaking their heads. "She won't let us," Bernard said.

Genevieve turned her head toward Bernard. "Quit talking about me like I'm not here. It makes me think I might be dead after all."

That made Pearl smile. "Do you want to try to sit in a chair?" she asked her sister.

Genevieve nodded. "If my choices are that or lie here all day, I think I'll take the chair. Help me up, George, will you?"

He squatted next to her and put one arm under her shoulders. He helped her sit up and when he saw that she was steady, he helped her get to her feet. Once there, she stretched out her hands and both dogs immediately came to her side. Several seconds later her cat, which had obviously been hiding somewhere close by, ran up and rubbed itself against her ankles.

George gave them all a moment and then he wrapped an arm around her thin shoulders. The closest place to sit was the piano room so he led her in there and got her settled in the middle of the couch. Pearl immediately sat on one side, Melody on the other. The dogs plopped down at Genevieve's feet and the cat, not to be outdone, jumped up into her lap.

"What happened?" Melody asked again.

George kept his eyes on Genevieve, unwilling to look at Melody. He'd seen that she'd put the robe on but he knew exactly what she had on underneath, and it wouldn't do him any good thinking about that.

Genevieve turned to her niece. "I was going upstairs to get ready for dinner. I got dizzy and suddenly knew I was going to fall. I think I tried to grab hold of the table in the foyer and managed to knock the lamp off in the process."

Pearl leaned forward. "I heard the lamp hit the wood and by the time I got there, Genevieve was already on the floor. I think I may have screamed."

"You did." That was Tilly jumping into the conversation. She and Louis had taken chairs across from the couch. "That's what caused me to come." She looked at Genevieve. "I thought you'd had a heart attack so I ran outside to find Louis. He and Bernard were both in the wine shed."

Genevieve's pale face took on just a hint of color. "I guess I caused some commotion."

Pearl shook her head. "That doesn't matter. As long as you're all right. Are you sure you don't want to see your doctor?"

"Very sure." Genevieve looked at the timepiece on her wrist. "Dinner is in a half hour. What I'd like is to enjoy a cup of tea now and then have my meal. Can we do that? Can we just forget this last half hour?"

Melody stood up. "I'll make your tea," she said. She left the room.

Bernard, who'd been quiet up until now, looked at Louis. "Perhaps we could finish our discussion?"

George saw something flash in Louis's eyes and it

resembled the look he'd seen often enough in men's eyes right before the cell door slammed shut. It was arrogance tinged with fright. But Louis didn't say a word. He simply nodded and the two men left.

Tilly, a puzzled look on her face, stood very still and watched them go. Then she walked over to the small table in the corner. With one hand, she grabbed a bottle of wine and the contraption they used to open it. With the other hand, a glass.

"Tilly," Pearl said, her tone hesitant.

Tilly shook her head and gave her mother a brief smile. "Worry about Genevieve, Mother. Not about me." Her hands full, she left the room without another word.

Once she was gone, it left just George, Pearl, and Genevieve. He handed Genevieve the orange feather that he still had in his hand. "For clarity of thought," he said.

"My thoughts were clear," she said, her voice serious. "Just unhappy."

That confused him. He looked to Pearl for explanation. She reached out her arm and patted her sister's hand. It struck George once again how similar their hands were and how similar they were to the hand that had helped Hannah pull him to this time.

He desperately wanted to ask them, wanted to be brave enough to know the truth. But now wasn't the time. A question like that could cause all kinds of other questions and soon enough, he'd have both of them dropping to the floor.

"Genevieve and I were having a discussion about . . ." Pearl's voice trailed off and she looked at her sister.

"Go ahead. I'm not going to slip off this couch," Genevieve said, looking irritated.

"We were discussing how I want things handled once I'm gone. You know, my funeral and all the other things that come after that."

He'd had to organize Hannah's funeral and well-meaning people had asked him about music and prayers and what she should wear to be buried in. It had been horrible. He'd been ill-prepared and he'd worried that he was making choices that Hannah wouldn't have wanted.

"I guess it's good to have those kinds of conversations," he said, careful with his words. He looked at Pearl. "Probably puts your mind at ease now." He switched his gaze to Genevieve. "And will no doubt help you when the time comes to make those decisions."

Genevieve frowned at him. "I generally like you, George, but not when you're so damn reasonable."

He smiled at her. "I generally like you, too."

They sat is silence for a few minutes and then Melody returned with the tea. Steam rose from the two cups she placed in front of her grandmother and in front of her aunt. It smelled like the tea Hannah had loved.

Melody leaned forward and kissed each woman on the cheek. "I'm glad you're both okay," she said.

"We're fine," Genevieve said. "And unless you're planning on wearing your robe to dinner, I suggest you leave us old women alone."

"You're sure?"

Both Pearl and Genevieve nodded. Melody looked over her shoulder at George. "I guess we should finish getting ready for dinner."

Well, okay. But that wasn't exactly what they'd been in the middle of. Unless *getting ready for dinner* was the modern way to say he'd been just about to bed her. He motioned for her to start up the stairs and he followed her. He shut the bedroom door behind them.

She stood three feet away from him, looking young and sweet. She ran her fingers across the edge of her robe. "Well? This is sort of awkward, huh?"

Fifteen minutes ago he'd had his hand wrapped around her breast, his fingers stroking her nipple. Yeah, he guessed awkward was as good a word as any. "I'm sorry, Melody. I should not have been so forward."

"Forward?" She shook her head. "You weren't doing anything that I didn't want you to do. I mean, I think I was pretty clear. I wanted you to—"

"Please, stop," he interrupted her. They should not be having this conversation. "It's done. It's over."

"I don't understand," she said. She looked absolutely miserable and he knew it was his fault.

"We're too . . . different," he said. It wasn't a good enough reason but the best he had.

She backed up a step. "So we're just going to pretend it never happened?"

The hurt in her voice almost undid him. He'd rather have taken a bullet in the back than hear that kind of pain. "Melody, you are a beautiful woman. And I would be a fool not to want you. But you know that I'm only here for a short time. It wouldn't be right for me to start something with you."

Her bottom lip trembled. "So you're doing this to protect me?"

Her. Him. No one would be spared the pain. "Yes."

She stepped forward, closing the gap between them. She poked him in the chest with her finger. "What if I said that I don't need protecting? That I'm capable of looking out for myself."

"I would tell you that I know you're one of the strongest, most capable women I know. But that doesn't change anything. A man makes choices, Melody. He can choose to do the right thing or the wrong thing. And while taking you to my bed would undoubtedly be a good thing, a great thing I suspect, it would be wrong and I won't do it."

She let out a loud sigh and let her hand fall back to her side. "I know this sounds crazy but I sort of wish you were a little less principled."

He'd spent the last six months hunting down men, with full intent to kill them. He didn't think that was what a highly principled man might do. "Don't make me out to be a saint, Melody. I'm not."

"Whatever." He could hear the frustration in her voice and she wouldn't look at him. She walked over to the dresser and pulled open a drawer. She yanked out something that looked like a shirt, then wadded it up and threw it back in the drawer. She pulled out a second one and then did the same thing. It was like she needed something to do with her hands. "Look," she said, giving him a quick glance over one shoulder, "you need to get cleaned up and while you're doing that, I'm going to get dressed and go on downstairs."

In other words, she wanted to get as far away from him as fast as she could. He felt sick to his stomach. "That's probably a good idea," he said.

"By the way, the dinner party is tomorrow night." She sounded as happy about that as a man who'd been told he was going to hang before sunset.

"Your grandmother told me."

"I've got a doctor's appointment in Napa but should be back in time."

"You'll drive yourself there?"

She nodded.

"Be careful," he said.

She turned to look at him. Her eyes were dark and her lips pale. "You do care, don't you, George?"

He wouldn't lie. "I do, Melody. More than I've got a right to." He walked past her and went into the bath. He shut the door behind him and then leaned his weary body against the door.

Yes, he cared. And he wanted. Neither of those things mattered. Not when the footprints that would take him home could come at any moment. He had to stay ready.

And he knew that if he took Melody Song to his bed, he might never be ready again.

TWELVE

BY the time George came downstairs for dinner, Melody had a plan. She was going to seduce him.

Now, given that she was five months pregnant, it was a fairly grand plan. But since the other alternative was going to the hardware store and buying lumber and nails and all kinds of other stuff, it seemed like the only logical plan.

Because without a wall, she was doomed.

She was no trembling virgin. Obviously. But neither was she terribly experienced. What she needed was another woman to talk to. She had Grandmother and Aunt Genevieve, of course. But given that they thought she was married to George, they'd have more questions than answers. Tilly didn't count. That left her alone.

Which meant that she really needed to go to the place where she never felt lonely. She looked at her watch. It was another fifteen minutes before dinner. Plenty of time. She walked out the front door, past the length of the house, and turned the corner to get to the garden. She walked with purpose through the vine-covered arbor, past the colored stepping-stones, and didn't stop until she reached her destination.

It was cooler than it had been at lunchtime, and the shadows were gathering. She could hear the frogs in the pond and could both hear and see the small yellow bees that jumped from flower to flower. The hour or two before sunset was absolutely the best time to be in the garden and she wished she had more time to relax and simply draw it in.

But she hadn't come to relax. She'd come to confess and perhaps seek a little absolution. She sat down on the bench. "I think I love him," she whispered. It seemed a fitting way to start the conversation. "He's smart and funny and very kind. And he's gorgeous and doesn't even seem to realize it."

She dug the toe of her sandal into the soft dirt. She needed to be honest. "He hasn't said anything about staying. I don't think he's planning on it."

She reached down, grabbed a handful of pebbles out of the dirt, and one by one, sent them skipping across the surface of the pond. "I'm not asking him to make promises that he can't keep. I guess all I'm asking for is now."

She could feel the wind pick up. The black-eyed Susans leaned to the right and the fresh scent of Russian sage traveled in the breeze. "Be happy for me, Momma. I know what I'm doing."

The wind suddenly changed direction and she could have sworn that she heard the gentle call of a seagull. But she knew that was impossible.

She sat for a few more minutes before she wandered back to the house. She reached for the front door just as it swung open. George stood there, a worried look on his face.

"We were about to sit down to dinner. Where were you?" he asked.

"I just needed a walk," she said. "To clear my head."

She started to move past him and he reached out. He plucked at her sleeve and then handed her a small sprig of wisteria. "I don't want to be the cause of your concerns," he said.

"I'm not concerned," she said honestly. She'd come to a decision. It felt peaceful. If George, on the other hand, knew what was in store for him, he'd be running for the next county.

She led him into the dining room. Grandmother was already seated as were Tilly and Louis. Across the table, Aunt Genevieve was just taking her chair. George pulled out Melody's chair and she took her seat. Once he was seated, she scooted her chair in.

And a little to the right.

A few minutes later, when she leaned to reach for the rolls, she took some pleasure in hearing his breath catch when her bare leg brushed up against his pants. And she could barely keep a smile off her face when Grandmother had to repeat her question twice before George seemed to realize that she was talking to him.

"I'm sorry, ma'am," he said. "What was that you asked?"

"I wondered if there was anyone whom you wanted me to invite to our celebration?"

He shook his head.

"No family in the area?" she asked.

"No, ma'am."

"Friends?"

He shook his head.

Uncle Louis laid down his fork and leaned forward. "Just where is it that you come from, George?"

George took his time cutting a piece of meat. "North Dakota," he said finally.

Melody moved her leg away. George didn't need her

messing with his mind, not when Louis looked like he was just beginning.

"So you two met when Melody was in college?"

"Yes, that's right," George said.

Melody let out her breath. So far so good. But she tensed again when Louis opened his mouth. Before he could speak, she jumped in. "We . . . uh . . . met again . . . uh . . . late this fall and—"

George laid his hand on her arm. "Let me, darling. I love telling this story." He turned back to Louis. "I met your niece on a beach and I knew right away that she was something special. But I was a younger man then, full of ambition and dreams of faraway places. I let her get away and regretted it. When our paths crossed again, I knew I wouldn't make the same mistake twice."

She made a conscious effort to close her mouth. The man made it look so easy. And if she had any knack in reading the faces around the table, they were buying it hook, line, and sinker.

Grandmother and Aunt Genevieve were smiling. Bernard was nodding his head. Tilly looked a little misty-eyed. Louis was dry-eyed but he had settled back in his chair.

Her grandmother raised her wineglass in the air and said, "To the happy couple."

"Hear, hear," Aunt Genevieve chimed in. Everyone at the table reached for their wineglasses. Melody picked up her water glass and drained it.

They'd missed a bullet and it was because George had pushed her out of the way. If he had let her talk, she'd have painted a target on their backs.

"Grandmother, whomever you want to invite will be fine," Melody said, doing what she could to keep the conversation from coming back to George. "How about the menu?" she asked.

The ensuing discussion of possible appetizers and main courses and desserts got them all the way through that night's dinner and dessert. Within seconds of finishing her apple pie, Melody put down her fork. "I've got a book I've started that's calling my name. Will you all excuse me?"

She didn't wait for an answer. She pushed back her chair but George, as usual, beat her to the punch. He was already standing with a hand out to help her up. He followed her up the stairs.

"You were amazing," she said, as soon as he'd closed the door behind them. "How do you do it?"

He looked uncomfortable with her praise. "All I did was tell them the truth."

"What?"

"Everything I said was true. I just left out the part that it all happened in a span of less than twelve hours."

What was it he'd said? That he knew she was something special? Her heart started to beat too fast and Jingle, having been sort of quiet during dinner, did a flutter kick. "So you meant everything you said?" she asked.

He ran a hand through his thick hair. "Melody, do we need to talk about this?"

His meaning was clear. Nothing had changed. He still wasn't going to act upon any attraction that he might feel for her.

The hell with that.

But there was no need for him to know about the Plan. "Of course not. I'm sure we're both tired. How about we get some sleep?"

She undressed in the bathroom and when she opened the door, George was in his usual spot, the quilt pulled up to his shoulders. She climbed into bed and turned away from him. Two minutes later, she rolled to her back. Five minutes later, to her other side. This time she let out a sigh. It was soft but definitely audible.

Five minutes later, she rolled back onto her back. Finally, with what she hoped was the appropriate note of apology in her voice, she said, "George?"

"Yes."

"I hate to ask but my back is killing me. Do you think you could rub it?"

She heard the sound of him throwing back the quilt. With her back toward him, she edged toward the middle of the bed. "Have a seat," she said.

She felt the mattress tip as he sat next to her. "Where does it hurt?" he asked.

"In the middle," she said.

His hands were hot on her skin and his touch tentative. "Here?" he asked.

"Yeah, that's good," she said. And it was. She tried not to feel guilty. Practically every book she'd picked up on the subject of pregnancy said a good backrub did wonders.

She knew exactly what else would do wonders, too. Maybe even bring a glow to her skin. Heck. She was just practicing good health. It was sort of like watching her cholesterol.

"Better?" he asked, sounding hopeful. She could feel his weight shift, like he was getting ready to spring off the bed, back to the safety of his quilt.

No way. He was not getting off the hook that easy. "Just a little bit lower," she said.

He paused, then she felt his hands inch down the length of her back and finally settle at the base of her spine. "That's it," she said.

He kneaded her muscles with his thumbs and in the process, his fingers spread across the rise of her buttocks. Feeling bold, she arched her back. His hands stilled.

"Melody?" he asked. His voice sounded hoarse.

"Yes."

"What in God's name are you doing?"

She was glad that she couldn't see his face. "Stretching?" she replied.

He made some kind of noise. It wasn't a laugh or a groan but some odd combination of the two. "You've no shame, do you?" he asked. He didn't sound mad, just resigned.

She flipped over onto her back and looked at him. There was just a hint of light in the room coming from the bathroom light, which always stayed on. He was shaking his head at her.

"So this is your new way to torment me?" he asked.

"What?"

"It takes everything I have to lie on this floor, to know that you're just feet away from me. But I could do it because I could tell myself that we both knew it was wrong. But now, you expect me to lie here, my wanting only increased by the knowledge that you'd have me without protest. That you'd take me into your body, and have my heat warm you, and my sweat touch your skin. You would have me, all of me."

Oh brother. Her lungs felt like she'd been running a marathon and moisture gathered between her legs. "George?" she whispered.

"Don't look at me like that," he said. He sounded weary. "I'm not that strong."

She reached up and touched his face. "Take me to bed, George."

His whole body shook and she thought that just maybe she had convinced him. Then he reached up, wrapped his hand around her wrist, and gently lowered her arm back to her side. "No."

He stood up and gathered his pillow and quilt up off the floor. He placed the pillow next to her and laid the quilt at the end of the bed. Then he walked toward the door.

"Where are you going?" she asked.

He put his hand on the doorknob. "I'll sleep downstairs, in the piano room."

She pressed two fingers to the bridge of her nose, willing herself not to cry. "It doesn't have to be this way."

"Yes, actually it does," he said. He opened the door and walked out, closing the door softly behind him.

The room seemed suddenly empty and very quiet and she felt very alone. She rolled onto her side and pushed her body up. Then she walked over to the dresser, gently picked up the Raggedy Ann doll, and returned to bed.

Even so, it took a very long time to fall asleep.

AT noon the next day, when George showed up for lunch, he had grease up to his elbows. Arturo didn't look much better. Melody, who'd just finished her own lunch, sat on the front porch with her grandmother. She been enjoying watching the dogs play in the yard. They were now sunning themselves on the front step of the porch.

"What happened to you two?" Grandmother asked.

"Irrigation pump stopped working," George said.

That wasn't good. Grapes needed water, not too much, but definitely not too little, either. "Do you have the parts to fix it?" Melody asked, knowing that Gino kept reserve parts for almost everything.

"We've got everything but an extra pulley," Arturo said, sounding disgusted. "I called around and Peterson's Plumbing in Napa has one."

"Then it's your lucky day. I'm going that way," Melody said. "I could pick it up for you."

Arturo shook his head. "It weighs at least fifty pounds. There's no guarantee there will be anybody there to help you lift it."

She stood up. "I'm sure they have a cart or something."

Grandmother shook her head. "You'll still need help getting it into your car. Why doesn't George just go with you?"

It was a reasonable question. One that should have been easy to answer. But how could she tell her grandmother that her "husband" had slept on the couch last night because he was unwilling or afraid or maybe a combination of both, to make love to her.

She didn't risk a look at George. The thought of being in a car with her probably had him turning green around the gills. After all, in such a small space, he might actually brush up against her, actually have to touch her.

He didn't want that. He couldn't be much clearer. And the last thing she wanted was to make him uncomfortable.

Right?

"Well?" her grandmother prompted.

Melody looked at her new husband. Who was she kidding? She had almost lost her waist, her thighs felt flabbier every day, and if the pregnancy books told the truth, her breasts were minutes away from starting to sag.

But he had liked what he saw. He'd been turned on.

How cool was that?

Cool enough to make her warm in places that hadn't been warmed by anybody in a long time. Cool enough that she'd walked around with a silly smile on her face for most of the morning even though she'd been flatly rejected last night.

Cool enough that she was willing to try again.

"Maybe Peterson's Plumbing could deliver it?" George said, sounding hopeful.

Arturo shook his head. "For what it costs, you'd think they would."

"You could pick it up," George said, looking at Arturo.

"I could. But the vines are growing like a son of a gun in Lot E and we need to get those trellis wires raised."

"Then you need to be here," George said. His tone had an air of finality, as if it was midnight and carriages were going to start turning into pumpkins and horses into mice. "I'll go with Melody," he said.

She felt like the ugly stepsister. "Don't bother," she said. The words popped out, like pulp out of a squashed grape.

Her grandmother frowned at her.

George didn't make eye contact. "Just give me a few minutes to get cleaned up and we can go." He walked into the house, shutting the door quietly behind him. Arturo went in the other direction, toward the wine shed.

Her grandmother reached out and brushed the pad of her thumb across Melody's cheek. "Are you feeling all right, sweetheart?"

She felt small and petty and very needy. "Maybe a little tired," she said.

"Of course."

Melody was grateful that her grandmother didn't push it. Five minutes later, when George emerged, his face and arms were clean and he'd changed his shirt. He was holding a paper sack.

"What's that?" she asked.

"When Bessie found out I was leaving, she made me a sack lunch."

Proof that George, with his quiet ways and good manners, had wormed his way into the cook's heart. She resisted the urge to roll her eyes.

Melody gave her grandmother a kiss and walked down

the steps. When they got to the car, she yanked open the driver's side. George waited until she got in and pulled her seat belt tight, then he carefully shut the door. He walked around to his own side and got in with considerably more grace than the first time he'd ridden in her car.

She took deep breaths as she negotiated her way back to the highway. Getting to her grandmother's from the main road was tricky. Getting back to the main road from her grandmother's was downright dangerous. The decline and the sharp curves were nothing to mess with. It didn't help that Dionysos and Hermes ran alongside the car for most of the way, making her even more nervous.

"Damn dogs," she said under her breath.

"You won't hit them," he said. "They know how to stay out of the way."

"I know you're right, but Aunt Genevieve would be crushed so I don't want to tempt fate. You'd think given that they're named after Greek gods, they'd be a little smarter."

"Greek gods?"

"Yes. Although I could never quite figure it out. Dionysos was the Greek god of wine, mysteries, and the theater, so I guess his name makes some sense. Hermes was the Greek god of merchants and we are in the business of making money, so I can buy that."

"What can't you figure out?"

"Dionysos and Hermes were part of a trio. The missing one is Aphrodite, the Greek goddess of love and beauty."

"Trio?" he repeated, sounding suddenly hoarse.

"Uh-huh." She negotiated the last turn and eased her car onto the road to Napa. The dogs fell back, evidently intending to return home.

"But there's never been a third dog?" George asked. "You're sure?"

"I'm pretty sure. Aunt Genevieve just showed up with them one day, said she got them from the pound. I think if there had been a third dog, he'd have come home with her, too. Is something wrong, George? Have the dogs been bothering you?"

"No. I like dogs," he said, rather absently. "I do."

He was acting odd, but she couldn't really blame him. He'd had very little choice about coming with her. "I'm sorry," she said. "I know you don't want to do this."

"It's fine. We need the pulley."

So he was going to pretend that he didn't know what she meant. Fine. Two could play at that game. "I suppose when the pump stopped working you learned some Spanish that can't be repeated in mixed company."

That got her a small smile. "How did you know?" he asked.

"I've spent more than one harvest working side by side with Arturo. There's nothing like having a truckload of grapes ready and the crusher stops working to get the old vocabulary going. The air practically turns blue."

George turned his head to look out the window. "There's more to growing grapes than a person might think," he said.

She flipped on her turn signal and took the Napa exit. "It can make a sane person crazy. First of all, there's the climate. It's either raining too much or not enough. Too sunny or not sunny enough. Then there's the soil—is it fertile or not? Is there too much slope or not enough? What about drainage and erosion? The list is endless."

He turned to look at her. "I'll never look at a grape the same way again."

"You know the French have a word for it. *Terroir*. It's that unique magical combination of natural factors that makes every vineyard different. Our grapes are different from our neighbor's grapes. That's what makes our wine different."

She pulled up behind a line of cars that were waiting to make a turn at the light. She looked at her watch. "Peterson's Plumbing is on the far-east side of Napa and my doctor's office is just a few blocks north. It took a little longer than I thought to get here. Do you mind if we do my appointment first?"

"That's fine."

She watched the road carefully. "I'm sure there's a McDonald's or something around here. You can eat your lunch there and grab a cup of coffee and some fries to go with it."

When he didn't respond, she looked over. "Okay?" she asked.

"Don't worry about me," he said. "Just watch these cars."

Melody handed him a slip of paper that she'd stuck in the empty cup-holder. "I wrote the building address down. Can you read it off to me?"

He did and she drove another block. "There," she said. "It's got to be one of those four buildings."

"You don't know where you're going?" George asked, sounding concerned.

"I sort of know," she said. She pulled into a lot between two of the buildings and parked her car. "And you're in luck. The golden arches are almost just across the street. I'll come get you when I'm done."

She opened her door and got out. She started walking toward the building. He caught up with her in a few steps. "If it's all the same to you," he said, "I'll stay with you until you've found the place."

There he went again—taking care of her. It should have

been confining and overwhelming but it felt sweet. "This is a good neighborhood, George," she felt compelled to explain. "I'm not going to get mugged."

He didn't answer. He simply fell into step next to her and she was surprised at how natural it felt—like they'd been walking side by side for years.

When they got inside the first building, she consulted the directory on the wall. "I was right," she said. "Fourth floor." She pushed the elevator button and the silver doors slid open.

It startled her when she heard a sound come out of George's mouth—like someone had punched him in the stomach. "Are you all right?" she asked, as she stepped into the elevator.

"Oh, sure."

He didn't sound very convincing and he looked like he was about to be ill. And for a man who just minutes before didn't seem to want to leave her side, he now seemed rooted to the spot. "Coming?" she asked.

He took a giant step over the threshold of the elevator.

"Step on a crack, break your mother's back," she teased.

He didn't laugh. Instead, when the elevator doors closed and it started to move, he sort of threw himself into the corner and braced his hands on the walls on both sides.

Oh good grief. Was the man afraid of heights? Had she found his Achilles' heel?

When the door opened, she stepped out. He followed without a word. Just a few steps down the hall, she located the doctor's office door and opened it. There was a receptionist at the front desk.

"Melody Song for Dr. Thacker," Melody said.

The young woman entered the information into her computer. "First appointment," she confirmed.

"Yes."

"Excellent." She held out a clipboard with a stack of papers attached. "Fill these out. And I'm glad to see that you brought your husband. Dr. Thacker likes to have a conversation with Dad."

"Oh, he's not—" Melody stammered.

THIRTEEN

"STAYING?" George interrupted. "Of course I will." His smile took in both Melody and the receptionist and he took the paperwork from the receptionist's outstretched arm. "Much obliged, ma'am," he said. He walked over to a set of purple chairs at the far side of the room.

She followed, feeling like some kind of sad puppy. A sad, fat, puppy whose thighs were starting to rub together. "I didn't know," she said. "They never said anything about you being here when I scheduled the appointment."

He handed her the clipboard and then picked up a magazine off the table next to her. "If we're going to pretend that we're married and this baby is mine, then we stick to the story. At all times."

He was right. She felt sophomoric and careless. For all she knew, the receptionist and her grandmother got their hair done at the same place and she'd be outed during a wash and blow-dry.

Could this get much worse?

She realized it could when George flipped the page and the article was titled *Pregnancy and Constipation.* She grabbed it out of his hand, ignoring his startled look. She turned to the index, scanned it, and turned to page 73. "Here."

She desperately tried to ignore him while he dutifully started reading about pregnancy and the benefits of a good walk. She worked her way diligently through the stack of papers and had barely finished when the nurse called her name.

The young woman in the pale yellow smock dotted with cute little ripe strawberries and matching red pants led them down a hallway. They stopped in front of a scale and Melody dutifully stepped on and tried not to cringe when she saw the number. Then they continued on until they reached a small room. The nurse motioned for Melody to take a seat on the exam table and for George to take the chair in the corner. Then she took Melody's temperature and her blood pressure. She was still making notes in the chart when there was a discreet knock on the door and an older man, probably close to sixty, wearing a light blue coat, entered.

"I'm Dr. Thacker." The man extended his hand. "It's nice to meet you, Mrs. Johnson."

It was the first time someone other than George had referred to her as Mrs. Johnson. It startled her. Her first thought was *Who is Mrs. Johnson?* and then, as the words seemed to hang in the air, her second thought was, *Whew, thank goodness it was Mrs. Johnson who'd now gained a total of twelve pounds and not her.*

"It's nice to meet you," she said, finally recovering. "Uh . . . this is my husband, George Johnson."

George stood and the two men shook. Then the doctor picked up her file and looked through it. After a minute, he said, "I appreciate you having Dr. Jetille forward on your records. That always makes it a little easier."

She nodded.

"It looks like you've had a pretty uneventful pregnancy so far. Still having the morning sickness?"

She stopped to think. "You know what, I haven't thrown up in three days." She looked at George and he smiled at her.

"Good. That's the way it works sometimes. It's like somebody flips a switch." Dr. Thacker motioned for her to lie back on the table. "Why don't we have a look?" he said.

She saw George start to move to the door. Dr. Thacker looked up and smiled. "You don't want to miss this, Dad. Have a seat."

She could see the indecision in George's eyes but he nodded and returned to his chair. Then Dr. Thacker helped her lie back and lifted up her shirt. The doctor took a tape measure and measured both the length and width of her stomach. "Looks fine," he said. "Let's have a listen." He took a tube, squeezed out some clear gel, spread it across her stomach, and then placed the transducer on her belly. And suddenly, as plain as day, amidst the gurgles and slurps of her stomach, was the unmistakable sound of Jingle's heart.

She thought her own heart might burst with joy. She heard George's chair scrape the tile and suddenly he was there, standing beside her. He was pale and his eyes were suspiciously bright, like he might have blinked away tears.

She reached for his hand and she felt the calluses on his palm. Together, they listened.

And all felt very right with the world.

After a minute or so, the doctor stepped away. "Sounds good but I think it would probably be a good idea if we took an ultrasound today."

Her other doctor had never even mentioned an ultrasound. "Is something wrong?" she asked, before turning her head to look at George.

He squeezed her hand.

The doctor shook his head. "I have no reason to think so. Ultrasounds are perfectly routine and just give us a more accurate way to assess the baby's development."

"Will it be painful for her, this ultra sound?" George asked, saying it like it was two words.

"Absolutely painless for both mom and baby. Actually, it's sort of fun. Come on, I'll show you."

Fifteen minutes later, she and George got their first glimpse of Jingle. He or she was curled in a ball. "There's the spine," the doctor said. "And that's the heart. Look, you can see all four chambers."

It positively took her breath away. "Can you tell if it's a boy or a girl?" she whispered.

The doctor looked at her. "Do you want to know?"

Melody looked at George. A bead of sweat was working its way down the side of his jaw. He smiled at her and when he swallowed, she could see the muscles in his throat work.

"What do you think, George?"

"Well, I never was all that fond of the name Jingle," he said.

Melody sucked in a deep breath and turned to her doctor. "Tell me."

Dr. Thacker shrugged. "Let me preface this by saying that you're only about twenty weeks along and that's just the point where we feel pretty confident making these kinds of predictions. That said, if I was a betting man, I'd say you've got yourself a little girl."

A daughter. She was going to have a daughter. "And she's okay?" Melody managed to ask.

The doctor nodded. Then he fiddled with the machine and some measurements flickered across the screen. "All the data matches up with the early September due date that Dr. Jetille established." He held out a hand to help Melody sit up. "Do either of you have any questions for me?"

"She's been having some leg cramps at night," George said. "Should we be concerned about that?"

She was amazed that he'd remembered and it was a good reminder that George Tyler didn't miss much.

"Fairly common, I'm afraid," Dr. Thacker said. He picked up her chart and wrote something down. "Avoid sitting with your legs crossed or in one position for too long a time. Take a short walk every day. Also, sometimes a warm shower or bath before bed can help." He made another entry into her chart. "There's an old saying that the leg cramps and the frequent need to urinate at night are nature's way of preparing both Mom and Dad for the sleep disruptions that are coming their way once the baby is born."

There was no *Mom and Dad*. She and George wouldn't be sharing midnight feedings. There'd be no gentle arguments over whose turn it was. He'd have returned to his old life, a few dollars in his pocket, and that would be the end of it. His sleep would be undisturbed. A year from now, if he happened to wake up in the middle of the night, would he even remember her?

Would she ever forget him?

Dr. Thacker stopped writing, closed her chart, and reached for the door. It was now or never.

"I have a question," she said.

Dr. Thacker stopped. "Yes."

"What about sex? As in having sex?"

George made the same sound he'd made when the elevator doors had opened. Melody kept her eyes on the doctor.

"Continuing to have sexual intercourse is perfectly acceptable."

There was no *continuing* here. It wasn't a marathon that

she'd been training for. This would be the first time in a while that she put on her running shoes. "We . . . uh . . . haven't exactly been having much sex," she said. "I didn't feel all that great," she added. "So it would sort of be like starting up again. Does that make a difference?"

Dr. Thacker shook his head. "It's not that unusual, especially when you're experiencing typical morning sickness symptoms, to temporarily lose interest in sex. Many couples in the middle stages of pregnancy find great satisfaction in resuming a normal sex life. From a practical perspective, as you get bigger, you may find that it's more comfortable if you're on top."

She made the mistake of looking at George. He was staring at her. The tip of his nose was pink and his eyes were big, the pupils very dark.

She couldn't look away. Her throat felt dry and it seemed hard to breathe. Energy, barely contained, seemed to sizzle around them and her skin felt hot. Her nipples hardened and pushed against her thin bra and shirt.

Dr. Thacker cleared his throat, causing both her and George to jump. "Generally," he said, looking amused, "we like for our patients to wait until they get home."

WHEN Melody parked in front of Peterson's Plumbing, George could hardly remember why they were there. There was no room in his head for rational thought. One, he'd just seen a child *inside* her mother's womb. No one in his time had even conceived of such a notion. The picture had been so clear that Melody now knew she was having a daughter. It was staggering.

Then, on top of that, Melody had asked the doctor about sex. She'd been bold as could be and if not for the chair that he'd grabbed onto the back of, he'd have slumped to the floor and cracked his damn head open and Dr. Thacker would have had a second patient.

Christ, if all the women were as bold as Melody, why weren't all the men walking—no, make that strutting—around with big smiles on their faces? He knew the answer. It was no doubt because men hadn't changed all that much in a hundred-plus years and they still weren't sure what to do when a woman came sniffing in their general vicinity.

Men were dumb when it came to women. Maybe because all the blood pooled in their cocks, leaving their poor brains to muddle along without fuel.

"George?"

And now she had the nerve to act like what she'd asked the doctor was of no consequence. As if she'd begged for a tonic to soothe a sore throat.

"Are you getting out?" she asked.

He stared at her. "You're good with the questions today, aren't you?"

Her eyes widened at his tone. It made him feel bad but he couldn't stop, not when what he had to say needed to be said and he wasn't sure he was a strong enough man to say it later if a sheet was the only thing that separated them.

She shrugged. "Dr. Thacker asked if I had any questions. I did. I figured it was the time to ask."

"You might have given me a little warning."

"Look, George, I'm sorry if I embarrassed you. It's not that big of a deal."

Now that made him mad. "Oh, really."

She sighed. "He said I *could* do it, not that I *had* to. And by the way, nobody is holding a gun to your head."

But she had his balls in the palm of her hand. "It would be a mistake," he said.

"Why?"

Because I'm waiting for the footprints to take me home. Who knew how much time he had left here? He'd known many men who could spend the night in a woman's arms and move on in the morning without a backward glance. He'd never been one of them. And even though it had only been a few days, he felt fairly confident that she'd be the type to be devastated if they were intimate and then he up and deserted her.

"Well?" she prompted.

"Because it wouldn't be right." He grabbed the door handle.

"Says who?"

Christ, she needed to let this go. "Says anyone with half a brain in their head." He opened the door. "Let's go."

She shook her head. "I'd rather not."

It had to be ninety in the shade but there was severe frost all around. "Come inside. It's too hot for you to stay out here."

She didn't look impressed with his logic. She pointedly looked at her watch. "You'd better hurry. Maybe you've forgotten that Grandmother is celebrating our marriage tonight."

"Damn it, Melody," he said. "This is not my fault. It's not yours either," he added hastily when he saw the storm clouds gathering in her pretty violet eyes. "But it's the way it is." He swung his legs out of the car.

"Because you're not staying?" she accused, stopping him. "You're going back to North Dakota?"

That and more. He belonged in 1888, in Bluemont. "That's right."

She pressed her lips together. "You don't have to go," she said, her voice tight.

He could perhaps leave his position and his time but he couldn't forsake the promise that he'd made when he'd stood over Hannah's grave. He'd promised her that the men who'd taken her from him would pay. Two were dead. A third still roamed free. And while George had no way of knowing who that man was or where he lived, it didn't mean that at some point, there might not be another clue, something that would lead him to the bastard. But how could he explain all that to Melody?

"I do have to go," he said. He got out and looked up and down the street. "I don't like the idea of leaving you out here by yourself."

She stuck her nose in the air. "Don't worry about me. I'm used to being alone and that doesn't look like its going to change anytime soon."

"Melody," he said, trying to convince her to be reasonable.

She waved a hand, cutting him off. "You know what really gets me?" she asked. "It's your ego. You've turned me down now a couple times. I've gotten the message. So, maybe, just maybe, when I asked the question about sex, I wasn't even thinking about you."

He wiped the back of his hand across his sweating forehead. He could feel the sandwiches Bessie had made for him turn in his stomach. "What?"

She shrugged. "Maybe there are other people who might not be as picky."

The thought of her with another man made him see red around the edge of his vision. "Last time I checked, Mrs. Johnson," he said, "you were married to me."

She rolled her eyes. "For now," she said, dismissing him. She stared at the door. "Can we please just get this part and go home?"

He got out. "Lock the doors," he said.

She let out a sigh. But she did it.

"I'll be back as soon as I can."

She didn't answer. He was fairly certain she didn't care if he ever came back.

SHE was a shrew. A rip-roaring bitch. An evil, needy, clingy, little woman. She was . . . oh, just face it, pathetic. That was really the best adjective to describe her.

As soon as George got inside the building, Melody rolled down her window and let some air into the hot car. Given the way her mouth had been going, she figured it was a toss-up as to whether there was more hot air outside or inside the vehicle.

George wasn't the bad guy here. She'd hired him to do a job. She should probably appreciate that he wasn't the kind of man to sleep with his female boss. It was admirable. Frustrating as hell, but admirable.

When she'd decided to seduce him, she hadn't factored in a will of pure steel. She'd given up gracefully the night before but today, his *just say no* attitude had put her in a tailspin. Maybe it was because of what had happened in the doctor's office. He'd been holding her hand when she'd gotten her first glimpse of Jingle. They'd been connected, the three of them. And maybe for just a minute she let herself believe that they really were a family.

But it wasn't true. He was leaving soon—with her threats of sleeping with someone else ringing in his ears. Earlier she'd felt sophomoric. Well, this was worse. She'd been deliberately hurtful.

It wasn't how she wanted him to remember her. She owed him an apology. She'd had every right to invite him to her bed, but he also had every right to turn her down. It hurt but she couldn't argue that she was getting anything worse than she deserved.

Ten minutes later, she saw him exit Peterson's Plumbing,

his arms wrapped around a large box. She pressed the trunk release and felt the back end of the car sink down when he loaded it. He opened the door. "Here," he said and handed her a plastic cup. "I put it in my pocket but I spilled a little on the way."

He'd brought her water.

She felt the hot rush of tears and she blinked hard.

He got in the car and reached for the cup. "Melody, you don't have to drink it," he said, his voice thick with concern.

She hung onto the cup with both hands. "I'm sorry," she said. "Look, I was an idiot earlier and I'm being an idiot now. I'd like to blame my hormones or the swelling in my ankles but I can't."

She stopped and waited for a response. He didn't say anything.

She started the car and pressed on the gas, pretending to be totally focused on pulling out onto the street. After a minute, she risked a quick look at him. George was studying her, frowning.

She returned her focus to the road—it was so much easier not looking at him. "There's a strip mall a mile or so up the road," she said, changing subjects. "We should probably stop there. We didn't buy you anything the other day that will be appropriate for Grandmother's dinner party. You'll need pants for sure. Maybe a jacket. I don't know about a tie."

My God, she was babbling. But since there was only silence from his side of the car, somebody needed to fill it. "That sound okay to you?" she asked and forced herself not to cringe. She sounded like an overanxious used car salesperson trying to convince somebody to buy a lemon. *That sound okay to you that it only gets seven miles to the gallon? That sound okay to you that it only starts about half the time?*

"Melody," he said finally, his voice soft.

"Yes."

"It's not that I don't want you."

She bit the inside of her mouth. She would not cry. She would not. She gripped the steering wheel and took a sharp left. She took her time looking for a parking spot, then busied herself shutting off the car and putting her keys into her purse.

Without looking at him, she opened her door. She started to get out but he gently grabbed her wrist. "Melody," he said.

She was so not going to have any more conversation about this. There wasn't enough tea in China. She turned toward him and gave him a big, if not sincere, smile. "Great. Glad we could clear that up. Now, let's get those pants."

For a minute she thought he was going to push the issue but then he got out and followed her across the parking lot. She was relieved. Maybe he'd realized how close to the edge she was, how slim her handle on control was, and had decided that he didn't want to risk a full-fledged meltdown in the mall parking lot.

Once inside the store, she let the overattentive salesman take charge and in less than fifteen minutes, they were back in the car with a new pair of charcoal-gray dress pants and a blue dress shirt.

"I want to pay for my own clothes," George said.

She'd seen the set of his jaw when she'd handed over her credit card to pay for his clothes and figured that it galled him to be so dependent upon her. "I owe you money, anyway. Just think of it as an advance against your salary."

"Fine. Don't forget about what you bought the other day at the Target store."

That was clear enough. He didn't intend to be indebted to her. Fine. After all, this was business.

It's not that I don't want you.

She gripped the steering wheel. It had stopped being business a long time ago. Now, it was very, very personal. She started the car and pulled out of the lot. She needed to get home and get away from him. Before she did something really stupid—like start begging.

She reached over and turned on the radio. George sat forward in his seat and stared at the dashboard. "I hope you like talk radio," she said. Because if he didn't, it was too damn bad. She was done talking.

He nodded and from the look in his eye, he was intrigued with the discussion about home rule and the impact that recent noise legislation might have on the fall harvest. Fifteen minutes later, she parked her car in her grandmother's driveway and turned it off, once again blasting them into silence. She frowned at George when he ran his hand across the dash. What was he doing?

"Look, I think people will begin to arrive by five or so," she said. Oh Lord, how was she going to pull this off?

"I'll be ready," he promised. He touched her hand. Gently. "It'll be fine, Melody. We can do this."

No. She didn't think so. He wanted her. But it didn't matter because for some crazy reason, that wasn't enough. "You better get that pulley down to the shed," she said briskly, hoping to change the subject. "I imagine Arturo's back by now and chomping at the bit to get it installed."

"I'll take it to him now," he said.

Great. That meant he'd be out of the room. She pushed the trunk-release button with a renewed sense of confidence. Maybe it would be okay. She'd get herself under control and he'd never know that with seven simple words, he'd rocked her world.

It's not that I don't want you.

She reached into the backseat for the sacks. "I'll take these in for you." She opened her door at exactly the same moment the front door opened and Tilly came out of the house. She was wearing a low-cut, tight, yellow sweater, even tighter white pants, and when she walked toward the car, on ridiculously high-heeled white sandals, she wobbled as if she might have gotten into the wine early.

Melody expected George to grab the pulley and run but he calmly got out and stood by her side. "Hello, Tilly," she said.

Her aunt eyed the packages. "I thought you had a doctor's appointment."

"I did. We did a little shopping afterward."

Tilly swayed toward George. "I love to shop," she declared, then she giggled.

Oh, brother. As she had suspected, the woman was drunk or close to it. "Where's Grandmother?" Melody asked.

Tilly rolled her eyes. "Killing the fatted calf in your honor."

So she and George weren't the only ones not crazy about the idea of a dinner party to celebrate their marriage. "I should probably check on her," Melody said to George.

"I'll be happy to keep your husband company," Tilly announced.

George's face never even changed expressions. "I've got to get this pulley to the shed."

"I'll walk with you," Tilly said.

"Ma'am, with all due respect," he said in a tone that made it clear that he didn't think much respect was due, "you don't look all that steady in those shoes. I think you better go on inside."

He'd said he could handle Tilly and gosh darn, he could. It was sweetly satisfying to see her aunt's face turn red.

"I've got better things to do anyway," Tilly said, tossing her hair. "Maybe I won't even come to this damn party."

Then she hiccuped, ruining the effect of outrage. "For once," Tilly added, "Genevieve seems to have beaten me to the punch."

"What?" Melody asked.

"Your great-aunt has disappeared into her room again."

Melody knew Tilly wasn't lying. Dionysos and Hermes hadn't bounded out of the house when they'd pulled in. If she'd have been thinking, she'd have realized how odd that was. It could only mean that they'd taken their positions outside the door of Aunt Genevieve's room.

Melody wanted to tell Tilly not to bother to come, that it wouldn't be any skin off her back, but she held her tongue. No doubt her grandmother would be upset with Genevieve's behavior but she'd be even more devastated if Tilly and Louis weren't there for the party. There'd be too many questions from the neighbors, too many explanations to have to make.

"I've got to go check on Grandmother," Melody said.

George nodded, grabbed the box out of the trunk, and took off for the shed.

When Melody got to the house, she turned around to look. Tilly still stood next to the car, looking angrier than Melody had ever seen her.

FOURTEEN

WHEN George walked down the stairs, he realized that guests had already started to arrive. Melody, standing near the front door, talked with a man and woman who looked to be in their early sixties. George ignored them and focused on his wife.

She was lovely. She'd put her long hair up on top of her head and she had on a black dress that hugged her belly and ended at her ankles. She'd taken off the shoes that showed her pink toenails and put on some flat-heeled, shiny black shoes with ribbons on them.

She was the most delicately made woman. And he desperately wanted to bed her.

She looked up and caught him staring at her. Her eyes widened and he knew that he had been too slow, that he hadn't been able to wipe the longing off his face.

Christ, now what? Nothing had changed from this afternoon. He couldn't take her and then leave. He just needed to somehow, someway, get through this night.

She motioned for him to join her. When he got close, she said, "George, this is Margaret and Donald Trippert. They own the next property north of here." She turned to the older couple. "This is my husband, George Johnson."

"It's a pleasure," George said, shaking their hands.

"Oh, it's our pleasure," Margaret said. "Melody has practically been like a daughter to us. In fact," she added, smiling, "we always hoped she and our son Mark would pair up. You know, they dated all through high school. He'll be disappointed to know that he's out of the race."

"Mark is such a great guy," Melody said.

What the hell did she mean by that? Was she just being nice?

Mrs. Trippert beamed. "You know, he's coming home in September for the class reunion. Maybe the two of you can get together, catch up on old times."

"I'd love that," Melody said.

George kept a smile on his face even though he suddenly wanted to kill the faceless Mark. Maybe it was Mark who Melody had been thinking of when she'd asked the doctor if she could have sex?

Would it be Mark who raised Melody's child? Would Baby Girl Jingle call this man Father?

He tugged on Melody's hand. "I think your grandmother wants us in there," he said, nodding toward the dining room.

Melody motioned for the Tripperts to precede them. "Oh, God," she murmured.

His heart stopped. "The baby?"

"No. Rebecca Fields is here. I bet she's Bernard's date."

He searched the crowd. It wasn't hard to find Rebecca. She wore a bright red dress that ended more than six inches above her knee and she had on gold shoes that had at least a three-inch heel.

"She really is beautiful," Melody said, her tone almost wistful.

She was, he supposed, but all he could think about was that Rebecca's bare knees did nothing for him while Melody's made him want to pant like a rabid dog. It wasn't fair.

Maybe Mark Trippert liked Melody's knees, too. "So, how come you haven't mentioned this Mark Trippert?"

She shrugged. "I don't know. Probably because I haven't thought about him in years."

"It sounds like you were close. Maybe he'd have liked the opportunity to play husband?" he whispered, feeling the need to vent a little of his frustration.

She laughed and leaned closer to his ear. Her breath was warm and sweet and her skin smelled like summer flowers. "Mark Trippert is an incredibly sweet, handsome man who, last I heard, was living with his boyfriend in San Francisco. I'm not sure if his parents don't know or simply pretend to not know."

In his time, there'd been men who preferred men, too. He'd never understood it but never judged either. Now it just made him incredibly happy.

They'd reached the arched doorway leading to the piano room. The double doors were open to the balcony outside and he could see a woman in a long dress in the far corner playing a harp. There were candles everywhere, flowers poured from vases, and there were platters and platters of food scattered around the room.

It made him think about Tilly and her comment that Pearl was killing the fatted calf. He glanced around the room and found both Tilly and Louis at the edge of the gathering. Each had a drink in hand and bored looks on their faces.

Bernard sat next to Rebecca Fields, but her attention

seemed to be focused on the two younger men who hung on her other side. She was trouble, and he hoped Bernard soon tired of waiting on her.

"There you are," Pearl said. She leaned forward and gave Melody a kiss on the cheek. "You look lovely, dear. How are you feeling?"

"Fine. Grandmother, this is a wonderful party. I . . . uh, we weren't expecting all this. You shouldn't have gone to all this trouble."

"Nonsense. It's my pleasure to be able to celebrate your marriage and the impending birth of my great-grandchild." She turned around and with a flourish clapped her hands several times. "May I have your attention, please. May I have your attention."

It took a moment for the room to quiet down but soon enough all eyes were on them. He hoped like hell he'd remembered to pull up the zipper on his trousers.

"My friends know that I'm not one for speeches," Pearl said. "But there are some occasions in life that simply call for it." She paused and the crowd waited.

"I'm a blessed woman. I have my home, and all of you as my friends, and my dear family. I have lived a life of great joy. But little gives me more happiness than to be able to present my granddaughter, Melody, and her new husband, George."

The crowd clapped and he could feel Melody start to shake. "Speech, speech," someone cried out.

Christ. If she started to talk, she'd probably blurt out the truth. *Aw, shucks, we're not really married.*

It might be the thing to get Tilly and Louis to perk up. Maybe even get Aunt Genevieve out of her room. George stepped forward. "I suspect I'm even less for speeches than Pearl Song," he said. The folks in the room smiled at him. It didn't make him any less nervous.

He glanced at Melody and she was smiling at him, suddenly looking relaxed, as if she were confident that he could handle this. He stood up straighter. "My wife and I are grateful to have all of you here tonight to help us celebrate, and I am thankful for the chance to meet all of you who are important to her."

He stepped back and everyone in the room clapped. Everyone except Tilly. She drained her glass and reached for the bottle.

Pearl looked pleased. "Thank you, George. We're delighted to have you as part of the family. Now, if you'll all follow me, we'll have dinner."

The next hour went fairly smoothly. Melody was to his right and Bernard to his left. Bernard generally ignored him except to pass a dish—his attention being solely focused on Rebecca Fields, who entertained their end of the table with stories of mishaps on her television show. George now understood the whole television thing, having witnessed Pearl watching the news.

It had startled the hell out of him that first time, thinking that there were small people inside the screen, but he'd figured it out soon enough and understood it was some kind of electric signal.

There was much about the future that he liked. The food was tastier, the choices more. There was almost immediate access to information, either in the form of a newspaper, television, or radio. The clothes were softer and the carpet on the floor as thick as some beds he'd slept in.

Melody leaned toward him just as dessert was being served. "You handled the speech thing beautifully. Thank you." She sounded tired.

"How do you feel?"

"Fine. I guess I'm hoping people have the good sense to go home early."

But Pearl had other ideas. Ten minutes after the dessert plates and the fancy coffee cups were cleared, she rose from her place at the head of the table. Within seconds, the chatter ceased. "I hope you've enjoyed your meal," she said. "Now, if you'll join me in the living room, the bride and groom will have the first dance."

Chairs were pushed back and napkins thrown on the table. Men loosened their ties and their wives slipped their shoes back on. Everyone seemed to be in motion. Everyone but him. He couldn't move.

Hannah had loved to dance. And whether it was a crowded Friday night social, a noisy Saturday afternoon chivaree, or an intimate evening in their own home, he'd indulged her.

He felt too warm, like he couldn't breathe. There was noise all around him but he wasn't part of it. He danced with Hannah. Only Hannah.

"George?" Melody said. She stood next to him, her violet eyes filled with concern. "What's wrong?"

He opened his mouth but it felt like his throat had closed. He could feel fresh sweat on the back of his neck. "I'm sorry," he managed.

"It's all right," she rushed to assure him. "Whatever it is, it's all right. I'll make our excuses to Grandmother," she said. She turned quickly and walked away.

He barely caught up with her by the time she'd reached the piano room. "Wait," he said. He extended his hand to her. "I . . ." He stopped. There was nothing he could explain, nothing that would not leave her with doubts and concerns and more questions than he could ever answer. The past was better left in the past. "We shouldn't disappoint your grandmother. May I . . . have this dance?" he asked.

She hesitated and then suddenly she was in his arms and they were dancing. She smelled sweet and fragrant, like a new rose, and her skin was warm and very soft. And with each calming breath that he took, the room slowly came back into focus. Pearl had dimmed the lights and the woman who'd been playing the harp had moved to the piano. The double doors leading to the back porch were still open, letting in a warm, night breeze.

The others had taken their places at the edge of the room, watching, offering smiles and gentle nods of approval. He and Melody were the center of attention but he felt strangely detached from all of it. It was as if they were alone, separate from the rest of the world.

It was just her. And him. And while he knew it was weak of him, he gave into the need to hold her. He pulled her close enough that she was pressed up against him and the top of her head just brushed the underside of his jaw.

They danced that song and another and at some point, he wasn't sure when, others left their spots next to the wall, took the hands of their partners, and joined them. The room was full of people dancing. Bernard and Rebecca, the Tripperts, even Bessie had shed her apron and was enjoying the company of a man.

He knew that for a man who had sworn off touching, he was doing a poor job of keeping his promises. And as he might have predicted, his body was beginning to ache with what was becoming a most common response. He shifted, hoping to hide his need. He knew the decent thing to do would be pull away, but having Melody in his arms felt too good, too right.

Melody's slight stumble and the tap on his back came almost simultaneously. It was Bernard, with Rebecca on his arm. "It's time for my dance with the groom," she said.

Oh, Christ. He couldn't dance with someone else. "I . . . uh . . . I can't—"

"He can't because I'm getting a little tired and he's going

to walk me to our room," Melody said, smiling sweetly at Rebecca. She had her fingernails pressed hard into the palm of his hand. Heat flooded his face. She knew exactly how the dancing had affected him.

"Bernard," she said, "would you be a dear and let Grandmother know. Tell her I'm fine, just a little tired."

Bernard nodded, evidently relieved not to have to let Rebecca free to dance with another man. Melody pulled on George's arm and before he knew it they were in the foyer, up the stairs, and behind closed doors in their bedroom. She walked directly to the bed and sat. He leaned his body against the solid wood door.

"Thank you," he said. There was, after all, no sense ignoring what had just happened. He'd been poking into her and there was no excusing that away.

"My pleasure," she said. She didn't sound angry. She got up off the bed and walked with purpose toward him.

"Don't," he begged, shaking his head.

She didn't listen. She got close and then leaned forward and gently kissed his lips. He willed his body to stay still, to endure, but the collar of his shirt felt too tight around his neck and when he tried to swallow, it was like his throat had forgotten how. She ran her tongue across his lips and he curled his hands into a fist. She suckled on the very edge of his bottom lip. It was a light touch, barely there, and yet it seemed to pull on his body, to where he thought he might just break through his own skin.

"Melody," he said. She had to stop.

"Open your mouth, George," she whispered.

And like a greedy fool, he did. And then her tongue was inside. He felt the pull all the way to his wanting cock.

He gripped her arms, near her shoulders, and gently set her away from him. "You're dangerous," he said.

She smiled and undid the top button of his shirt. Then the second and third.

He knew he had to stop her now. But the need and the want of her were too powerful, too much for him to deny.

When all the buttons were undone, she pulled his shirt open and off his shoulders. He pulled his arms out and let the fine garment drop to the floor. His naked skin felt hot, then cold, and when she bent her head and took his flat nipple in her mouth, it was pleasure and pain and he knew that he'd passed a point of reason.

"I want to—" He stopped. Oh, Christ, her hand was pressed against his cock. He moved his hips forward, straining against her. Her head jerked up and he knew at that moment, she'd realized he was a lost man.

He wrapped one hand in her hair and kissed her with untamed urgency. They consumed each other with lips and tongue and heat.

"I want to lay with you," he said, his breath coming in spurts.

"Yes, yes. Take me," she begged and he knew that she was as far gone as he.

He shifted his arms and lifted her up. She let her head drop back and pieces of her hair, long since pulled from her fancy clip, hung over his arm. She was wantonly needy and the urge to service her, to make her his own, to have her cling to him in madness, made his blood hot.

He wanted to howl at the moon.

He wanted to possess her.

"I'll be careful," he promised. He would hold back, no matter what it cost him. "We'll take it slow," he said, depositing her gently on the bed.

She smiled, shook her head, and reached for his belt buckle.

"Have mercy, Melody," he begged. Christ, he was seeing stars.

And they were exploding in his head and—

Jesus. It wasn't the stars exploding, somebody was pounding like hell on the door.

"George, it's Arturo. Open the door. I need your help."

Melody yanked her hand away and he staggered back, practically falling on his ass. What the hell? He looked at Melody but she was busy pulling down her dress.

He whipped the door open and one look at the man told him that something was very, very wrong.

"What happened?"

"The woman who Pedro spent last night with, she is married. He swears he didn't know." Arturo was speaking fast, using his hands. "I believe him. After the fight with Rafael, he told me that he would not have been with her if he'd known about her and Rafael. I know he would never take another man's wife."

This had trouble written all over it. "The husband knows?"

"*Sí.* He has called Pedro out."

"Called him out?" George repeated.

"Challenged him. They're to meet at the quarry. Pedro's got some crazy idea that he loves this woman, even after all this, so he's already on his way."

He heard Melody moving behind him. She grabbed his arm. "It's a rock quarry, about five miles straight east. Arturo, did he go by car?"

"Yes."

She looked at George. "You can get there much faster by horse."

He looked at Arturo. "Can you ride?"

"Of course."

"I'll call the police," Melody said.

Arturo shook his head violently. "No. Her husband is white, a businessman in town." He turned to George. "It'll be his word against Pedro's. You have to know I took a chance coming to you."

George wished like hell he had his gun. But none of that could be helped. He turned to Melody and put his hand on her arm. "Wait. If your police need to be called, then I'll do it. But let us go now."

She kissed him. A hard, bruising smack on the lips. "Be careful," she hissed. "If you do something stupid, I swear to God, I'll kill you myself."

George grabbed his shirt off the floor and buttoned it as Arturo led him down a set of backstairs George hadn't even known were there. Then they ran across the yard, saddled the horses quickly, and rode east.

It reminded him of how he'd ridden with John Beckett and Fred Goodie. Only that night, he'd been hell-bent to kill a man and now he was hoping like hell he wasn't too late to stop one man from killing another.

Arturo's horse was no match for Brontë, but he handled it well and it didn't slow them much. George understood why Melody had said it would be easier on a horse. The ground was rocky and rough with weeds so tall they brushed against his boots.

The sky was dark with only a few stars and the air was sticky and heavy. Both horses and men were breathing hard by the time they got close to the quarry and it didn't help their hearts any when the ringing echo of a gunshot split the quiet night.

The son of a bitch was shooting at them.

In one smooth motion, George slid from the saddle and took cover behind a big rock. Arturo dropped in beside him. "George, where the hell did that come from?" he whispered.

"A hundred yards up, at the edge of that stand of trees."

George shifted, just far enough that he could see around the edge of the rock. The shooter had taken cover. But George had gotten a good enough look to know it wasn't Pedro.

"Mister," George called out. "We mean you no harm. Put your gun down."

Silence. Finally, there was a stirring from the trees. "Who the hell are you?" the man asked.

"I'm George Tyler," George answered automatically, then cursed himself when he realized that he'd used his own name. He didn't look at Arturo, could only hope that the man hadn't noticed.

"This isn't any of your business," the man said.

"Well," George said, "if you're gunning for a man who works at Pearl Song's ranch, then I think I might have to debate that. I would, however, prefer not to do it over a rifle barrel."

There was no response. George closed his eyes and listened. The man was moving, circling around to George's left.

Damn. Why wasn't this ever easy? George motioned for Arturo to stay behind the rock and he moved, melting into the trees behind him.

George waited and listened, judging the man's progress. He heard the snap of a twig, just close enough, and he rushed him. They went down in a tangle of arms and legs and the man's rifle flew. It was no contest. Within seconds the man was flat on his stomach, his face in the dirt, with George's booted foot resting solidly in the middle of his back.

There was just enough light that George saw Arturo scramble and pick up the man's gun. He offered it to George but George waved it away. They needed to settle this without anybody taking any shots.

"Calm down," George said to the man.

"You son of a bitch," the man said.

George lifted his foot, bent down, grabbed the man's coat, and flipped him over to his back. Then he planted his foot once again, inches away from the man's throat. "My patience is wearing thin, mister. First you shoot at me and now you're swearing at me. You need to understand something. I'm not going to let you hurt one of my men."

"Bastard slept with my wife."

George nodded. "And that was wrong. But he says he didn't know."

The man squirmed under George's foot. "He's lying."

George did not want to have to tell this man that Pedro wasn't the only man his wife had been entertaining while she should have been working. That was not the kind of news a man told to a stranger, even when that stranger had been shooting at you. "Is that what your wife told you?" George asked carefully.

"She . . . she . . ." The man shut his eyes and dug his fingers into the hard dirt under his body. A minute passed before he let out a sigh. His body relaxed, almost seeming to sag into the ground.

"Damn her," the man said, all trace of fight gone from his voice. "Damn her to hell. She says she leaving me. That she loves him."

George heard the sound of a car off to his left and he motioned for Arturo to go intercept whoever was arriving. Then he lifted his foot and stepped back. "Killing my man won't make her stay," he said. "It will only make more trouble for you."

The man rubbed his hand across his face. "Do you think I don't know that?" he said, his voice heavy with pain. "I should have known it would never work with her. We're too different."

Sort of like him and Melody. Couldn't be more different.

They hadn't even been born in the same century. Just what the hell had he been thinking when he'd stuck his tongue in her mouth and his hand up her dress?

The man on the ground shifted. "What are you going to do about this?" he asked.

George figured he ought to get down on the ground and kiss the man's feet. If Arturo hadn't knocked on the door, he'd have bedded Melody. That would have been a terrible mistake.

"Depends," George said. "What—" He stopped when he once again heard the sound of a car engine. Perhaps Arturo had convinced Pedro to leave altogether rather than just stopping him from coming farther. "What do *you* want to do?"

The man looked surprised. "What I want to do is go home. She's already cleared her stuff out."

"Then what?" George asked.

The man thought for a minute. "I don't think I have much choice," he said, sounding resigned. "I guess I'll go about my life and pretend that everything's fine."

George understood that pretending was sometimes the only defense a man had. "Then go."

George could see suspicion war with hope. "Just like that?" the man asked. "I took a shot at you."

"I haven't forgotten," George said, offering the man his hand to help him up. He waited until the man was standing and then looked him in the eye. "Understand this. If you come after me or one of mine, you won't walk away a second time."

The man took a step back. "I don't suppose I'm getting my gun back?"

George shook his head.

The man didn't argue. He just walked away, in the opposite direction of where Arturo had gone.

George whistled for the horses and both ambled up. He swung up on Brontë and grabbed the reins of Arturo's mount. When he got over the hill, he pulled up tight.

There were two cars parked there. One he didn't recognize, so he assumed it was Pedro's. The other one was Melody's. She was standing next to the car, talking with Arturo and Pedro. She'd left the car door open and light from the interior illuminated her backside.

She'd pulled all the pins out of her hair and it lay in soft waves to the middle of her back. She had her party dress on still but she'd pulled an old shirt over it, obviously more concerned about haste than fashion. From the back, she didn't even look like she was carrying a child. She was slim-hipped and sexy as hell.

She must have heard the horses because she turned and when she saw him, her face lit up. When he got close enough for conversation, she asked, "Are you all right?"

She sounded sort of breathless, like she had in the bedroom, right before she'd said, *Take me.*

"Are you all right?" she repeated.

How the hell could he be? She was driving him crazy. One look at her and he was ready to forget all his good intentions. "What are you doing here?" he asked.

She jerked back. "I was worried," she said, sounding hurt.

He knew he'd been harsher than necessary. But he didn't want her waiting for him to come home, worrying about him. That was the thing someone did when they cared, and he didn't want her caring about him. He sure as hell didn't want to care about her.

"It's late," he said, looking past her. "Go home and get some sleep."

She stiffened. "In a minute. Where's the other man, the one the rifle belongs to?"

She needed to get the hell out of here. Her shirt didn't button in the front and from his vantage point on the horse, he could look down her dress. Her breasts, her plump, full breasts, were there for the taking. "That's none of your business."

She didn't say anything for a long minute. When she did, her voice was hard. "That's where you're wrong. It's my family's business, my family's ranch, my family's everything."

The message was clear. He wasn't family. Fine. That's the way he wanted it. "He's on his way home. I don't think he'll bother Pedro or *your family* again."

She turned on her heel, like she was a queen or something, effectively dismissing him. She spoke quietly to Arturo and Pedro, then she got in her car, and drove away.

Arturo approached with Pedro trailing behind. "It's done," George said. He looked at Pedro, who now stood awkwardly, his hat in his hand, at Arturo's side, "I don't think he'll bother you again."

"I am sorry for the trouble I bring to the family," Pedro said.

There was that *family* word again. George stared at him. "I want the truth. Did you know she was married?"

Pedro shook his head back and forth, violently. "No. On my mother's grave, I swear to you, I did not know."

"If that's true, she lied to you."

"Yes." Pedro looked miserable.

Arturo swung his body toward the younger man. "I've told him not to have anything else to do with her but he won't listen."

Pedro shrugged. "I love her," he said simply. "If you want me to go, I'll leave tonight."

George shook his head. "If you'd have known she was married, you'd already be on your way. Now get in your car, go home, get some sleep, and be at work on time to-morrow."

Arturo and George watched the young man drive away. Arturo grabbed the horn of his saddle and swung up. "He's a fool."

George didn't argue. He just nudged his horse in the ribs and they took off for home. Pedro was a fool. But that's what a woman did to a man. Even now that Melody had told him in no uncertain terms that he was nothing, he hungered for her.

FIFTEEN

SHE pretended to be asleep when he came into the bedroom. She heard him open the bathroom door, heard the sounds of water running, and then he came out and took his place on the floor.

He could sleep outside with the horses for all she cared.

Right. Who was she kidding? She wanted him in her bed, inside of her. And then she wanted him to do it again. And then maybe a third time. That might just get her through the night.

They'd been so close. Then Arturo had knocked on the door and everything had changed. At the rock quarry, George had acted like she was nothing but a bother, a little girl who'd tagged after him.

She hated—really hated—that feeling. It brought back every feeling of inadequacy she'd had as a child when she'd come to live at her grandmother's ranch. She'd lain in her bed, her arms clutched around the Raggedy Ann doll, and sworn that she wouldn't be a burden, that she wouldn't be any trouble at all. Then nobody would have a reason to want her to go.

She lay motionless for what seemed like an eternity but what was probably only forty-five minutes or an hour, at most. When she was sure he was asleep, she very quietly pushed back the sheet and blanket and swung her legs over the side of the bed. She walked past him, her feet making no sound on the thick carpet. She put her hand on the door and silently twisted the knob. The door—

"Are you ill?" he asked.

Well, yeah, he'd just made her heart thump and grind. That couldn't be good for her. "No."

"Do you need water?"

"No."

He sighed. "Melody, I'm sorry. I was cross earlier and . . . you don't deserve that."

This wasn't helping her heart. She flipped on the light and they both blinked. He slept with his clothes on. It didn't matter. She knew now how beautifully made he was, with wide shoulders and sleek muscles. She swallowed hard. "I guess I am a little thirsty," she said, grasping for something to say.

"You were right, you know," he said, ignoring her attempts to change the conversation. "I made decisions tonight that were probably yours to make. I overstepped my bounds and I'm sorry. It won't happen again."

She shook her head. "You did exactly what my grandmother would have expected you to do when you're filling in for Gino. You took care of the situation. You protected her interests. I should have been thanking you, instead I was a . . . bitch about it."

He smiled and shook his head. "Melody, on your worst day, you couldn't be that."

It wasn't the slickest compliment she'd ever heard but she thought it might be the nicest. "I can't sleep," she said.

"I thought I might go down and get a sandwich. Jingle's hungry."

"Jingle?" Now he was frowning. "You're not really going to name your daughter Jingle, are you?"

"No. But I don't have another name picked out yet so I'm sticking with it. Do you—" She stopped. She'd almost asked him if he had any favorite girl names. She didn't want to make him so uncomfortable that he shut her out. It was nice talking with him, having conversation. She'd been alone for a very long time. "Do you want to join me for a sandwich?" she asked.

She thought he was going to refuse. But then he nodded. "That would be nice," he said. He got up and they walked down the hallway in silence. They passed the stairs that led to the third floor. It made her think of Genevieve.

It must have done the same for George, because he asked, "So, how long does she stay in her room normally?"

"Not usually more than a couple days. When I was younger, I was worried she would starve but then Grandmother told me that she's got a small refrigerator and a hot plate in there."

They walked down the steps. He put his hand just under her elbow, not touching her, but close enough that he could catch her if she slipped. It made her want to swoon.

He was just so darn nice.

And sexy.

And clearly not interested in taking up where they'd left off. He'd apologized, she'd accepted, and now they were back to acting like business associates.

Except she didn't want to go to a meeting with him or trade emails. She wanted to screw him.

They walked into the kitchen and she opened the refrigerator door. "Looks like there's leftover roast beef or some sliced turkey or"—she stopped and lifted a lid—"egg salad. What's your preference?"

"Turkey is fine," he said.

"Me too." She pulled it out of the refrigerator and started to reach for the bread.

"Let me," he said. "You've got to be tired. I'll make the sandwiches."

It was so silly and she was sure it was her darn hormones again, but she started to cry.

He dropped the bread onto the counter. "What? Jesus. Honey, I'm sorry. You can make your own sandwich."

She cried harder. And suddenly his arms were around her and her face was pressed next to his chest and he was patting her back like one might do for a small child.

"Now, now," he muttered. "It's going to be fine. Just stop crying."

And finally she did. But then she got the hiccups.

"Hold your breath," he said. "No, wait. Don't do that. That might not be good for the baby. Maybe you should sit down," he said, sounding a little stressed.

The man could evidently handle tears but hiccups put him over the edge. It made her smile.

"Can we go outside?" she asked. "You know, get away from the sandwiches."

That made *him* smile. "That's probably a good idea." He wrapped one arm around her shoulder and used his free hand to snag a thick blanket from the back of the couch as they walked through the family room. When they got outside, he wrapped the blanket around her shoulders and then they sat down on the porch swing. It was a very dark night and the yard light that generally burned bright was out. It seemed like they had slipped into a black hole. She could feel the wood under her legs but she couldn't even see the swing. She could feel the solid warmth of his big body next to her but she couldn't see his hand.

"Better?" he whispered.

"Yes." Aware that others in the house could have their windows open, she kept her own voice low, too. "I'm sorry I fell apart in there."

"It's been a big night, Melody. You're entitled to a few tears."

She was silent for a few minutes, debating her next words. But finally she could only think of one way to say it. "George?"

"Yes."

He sounded peaceful. She had a feeling she was about to rip that away from him. "Before Arturo came to our door earlier, we were sort of *involved.* What happened to change your mind? I mean, I thought you were . . . uh . . . interested."

He didn't say a word and she wondered if she had shocked him. She felt him shift and then heard a soft sigh. "Melody, I was interested. Very. But then I had a chance to think about what we were doing and I knew it was wrong."

She gritted her back teeth. She refused to cry again. "What's so wrong about it?" she asked, when she felt she had it under control.

"I told you I was married."

"Yes," she said, trying hard to understand. "I guess I don't know how long ago you were divorced. I mean, I know it can take time to get over—"

"I'm not divorced," he interrupted, his voice hard. "My wife died. She was taken against her will by three men and then they killed her."

A chill spread fast, from her toes to the top of her head, and she clutched the blanket tighter around her. She'd been raped and murdered. Oh, the poor woman. Poor George.

She felt her stomach churn and she thought she might

be sick. "I had no idea," she said. "Oh, George, I'm sorry. I know that's inadequate but it's all I can think of."

He was silent. After a moment, he spoke again. "We were married for three short years. Hannah had just found out a few weeks before her death that she was carrying our first child. I came home for a meal and found her dead."

She had thought it couldn't get any worse. "Oh, George," she said again and felt bad. She should think of something to say, something that would comfort him, but her mind was blank.

"I loved her, Melody, and losing her almost killed me. I don't intend to ever love another woman and I couldn't take you to my bed under false pretenses."

She was definitely going to get sick. Thoughts and emotions swirled in her head, making her light-headed. She thought of Hannah and the terror that had ended her life. And she knew that any woman George had loved was the kind of woman who would have done every single thing she could to protect her child and stay alive.

She thought of George and the absolute horror of finding his wife brutalized and dead. He was the kind of man who handled things and this would have been something way out of his control.

And she thought of herself. She'd waited twenty-eight years to fall in love with a man and she'd fallen for a man who'd been so deeply wounded that he'd sworn to never love again.

They rocked back and forth on the swing, neither talking nor touching. Finally, when she felt she had the strength, she stretched her legs to stop the momentum of the swing. "I'm glad you told me," she whispered. "I am so dreadfully sorry for your loss."

"You, maybe more than some, know how difficult it is to lose someone you love."

She did. It made her feel awful that she had tried to trick him into her bed. "I pushed you. I hope you can forgive that," she said.

She heard him sigh. "I'm a man, Melody. A man more than capable of making his own decisions. You didn't push me into anything. I don't want you feeling bad."

She felt horrible. And lost. And alone. "I'm okay," she lied. "Maybe we should go back—"

The front door of the tasting room opened and light spilled out into the dark night. She hardly even felt George move but suddenly his finger was up against her lips, telling her to be quiet.

Two men, both wearing dark suits, came out. The men walked directly over to an SUV that was parked next to the building. Melody realized it had been there the whole time but she'd missed it because of the darkness. The men got in, started the car, and pulled out of the drive, not turning on their lights until they reached the gate.

Seconds later, Louis filled the open doorway, once again almost blocking out the light. He stood there, staring off toward the fading taillights. There was just enough light that Melody could see that he looked very serious. He stood there a full minute after the lights could no longer be seen. Then he stepped back into the tasting room and shut the door behind him.

George didn't waste any time. "Let's get inside," he whispered. He got up and helped Melody to her feet. Once inside he pulled the blanket off her shoulders and put it back on the couch, just the way it had been. Then he motioned for her to go upstairs. "I'm going to clean up our sandwich mess," he said. "Go upstairs. Don't turn on or off any lights."

"What do you think that was all about?"

He shook his head. "We'll talk later. Go now. He could come inside any minute."

Melody went upstairs; she'd barely gotten into bed when George came in. The bathroom light had been on when they left with the door cracked just a hair. It gave off enough light that she could make out his shape as he sat on the empty side of the bed.

"Did you know those men?" he asked.

"I don't think so. I mean, that's not unusual. I haven't been living here for many years so there are lots of Louis's friends that I don't know."

"They didn't look all that friendly."

"I know," she said. "And it's sort of late for a wine-tasting event. Although I suppose they could be buyers."

"At this time of night?"

"I know it sounds weird but the wine business is very competitive. Especially in the restaurant market. Good placement on the wine list at a popular restaurant can make or break a vintage. If you can get the wine steward to recommend your wine, all the better."

"I'm not sure I understand," George said.

"Deals get made. Wine brokers, the people who are in a position to influence those kinds of things, sometimes enjoy the finer things in life, compliments of the winning winery."

"Bribery."

"Yes. Grandmother is adamantly opposed but I wouldn't put it past Tilly or Louis."

George rubbed his chin in contemplation. "I guess it's possible. Would you want to tell your grandmother?"

"I'm not sure what I'd tell her. It's all just speculation on my part." It was frustrating that things were going on and she had no reasonable explanation for them. But she couldn't accuse Louis of something unless she had proof. He was family. She had to give him the benefit of the doubt. "Maybe they were playing cards? Or maybe it was like a Mary Kay party for men and they were getting facials?"

"Mary Kay? Facials?"

"Cosmetics. Pink cars," she added.

"What?"

Oh for goodness's sake. "Never mind."

He stood up. "We both need some sleep." He laid down on the carpet, with his shirt on this time. He didn't bother with the quilt.

Ten minutes later, she sat up in bed. "There are two locked drawers in the wine shed," she said. "There have never been locked drawers before. Do you think that has anything to do with what we saw tonight?"

"I don't know," he said. "I didn't think Louis used that office."

She lay back in bed. "You're right. It's probably nothing."

It was a good five minutes later when he said, "I didn't say it was nothing, Melody. Do me a favor, okay? Keep an eye out for trouble and don't take any unnecessary chances."

"George, don't you think you're overreacting?"

"There is no such thing when it comes to either yours or your child's safety."

The words hung in the air, then floated down, until they lay heavy on her heart. He cared. Damn him, he cared. But he'd loved and lost and he was afraid to love again. If there was anything she understood, it was that.

She'd loved her parents and lost them. She'd loved both Sarah and Miguel and they, too, had been taken. But to lose a spouse, to lose the one person that completes you? She pressed her hand against her belly. To lose a child before it ever even had a chance to live?

It was horrible and her soul ached for him. He was a good man and it hurt to think that he'd suffered so.

"George," she said.

"Yes." He sounded sleepy.

"Thank you for telling me about your wife and your baby."

He was silent for a long minute and she wondered if he'd fallen asleep. Finally, he said, "I wanted you to know. Not so that you'd feel sorry for me but that maybe you'd understand me a little better."

She understood all right. He'd loved and lost and he'd have no part in causing that kind of pain for somebody else.

She closed her eyes and willed herself not to cry. He didn't know it was too late. She'd already fallen in love with him. But that would stay her secret. He didn't need her adding to his already heavy load.

GEORGE waited until he was sure that Melody was asleep. Then he carefully folded back his quilt and stood up. Something was bothering him and he couldn't sleep until he'd put it to rest.

He walked out into the hallway and up the stairs to the third floor. As he expected, the two dogs lay in front of Genevieve's door. He took a step forward and their ears went up and they growled menacingly. Based on Melody's story about how they'd reacted to Louis when he'd gotten too close, he figured if he took another step, he'd be lucky to get away with all his toes.

Plus, everyone in the house would be wide awake. He needed to find another way.

He walked down the three flights of stairs. On his way out the front door, he detoured through the dining room and grabbed one of the candles that had been burning earlier. He walked over to the sideboard and opened the top drawer. He felt around, stopping when his hand came upon matches.

It wouldn't be as good as a lantern but better than nothing. He couldn't take a chance and turn on any of the electric lights. He put the candle and the matches in his pocket and walked out the front door. It was so dark outside that if he hadn't known where he was going, it would have made for some difficult travel. As it was, he walked slower than usual, making sure that he didn't trip over any unexpected obstacles.

When he reached the cement paddock, it took him a minute to find the ladder that was now leaning up against the wall, half the height it had been earlier.

He grabbed it and shifted it horizontal. Now he was thankful for the thick cover of darkness. He didn't need anybody looking outside and seeing what he was up to. He carried the ladder around the side of the house and through the arbor. When he judged that he was close to the right spot, he set the legs of the ladder on the most even ground he could find.

It was a damn big house and the lines of the roof, where the second and third floor jutted out from the main part of the house, had a steep slope. He knew from studying the house in the daytime that the roof of the first floor had to be at least thirty feet in the air. It took him a minute to figure out how to extend the ladder but once he did, he took a deep breath and started climbing. It was so dark that each step felt like he was sliding into a deep well.

By the time he reached a spot where he could step off onto the roof, he was hot and generally irritated that he had to go to such extreme measures. The ladder went on another five or so feet but it wasn't enough to get him to the roof of the second floor.

It took him less than five minutes to figure out that his best chance was crawling up the outside of the chimney.

There were just deep enough crevices between the bricks to provide for hand- and footholds.

He held his breath the whole way, hoping like hell he didn't dislodge some brick and send it cascading across the shingles, only to have it bounce onto the driveway. But everything held solid and soon he was standing on the roof of the second floor. It had an even steeper pitch, and he dropped to his knees to keep his balance.

He crawled over to where the third story jutted up into the black night. It was flatter here so he stood and felt his way around the structure until he found the window he was looking for.

His heart was beating fast in his chest. This was a crazy thing to be doing but he'd come too far to stop now. He had to know. Had to start putting some explanations to the things that he didn't understand.

He put the heel of one hand against the wooden frame and pushed. It made a soft noise as it slid up and he waited to hear something from inside the room, something that would tell him that he'd been discovered.

But it was quiet. He pushed it up farther and stuck his head inside. It was pitch-black inside. "Genevieve," he whispered.

No response. "Genevieve," he said again.

He waited through another minute of silence before climbing in the window. Once inside, he pulled the candle and matches out of his pocket and on the second try, got the candle lit. He held it up.

It was a big messy room. He guessed it to be twenty-by-twenty, and there wasn't a square foot of clear space. There were stacks and stacks of papers, piles of clothes, and dirty dishes everywhere.

There was a hell of a lot in the room but not what he was

looking for. There was no Genevieve. The bed was empty. He walked past it and looked in the bath. He felt the towels that were hanging from the hook. They were dry.

He wanted to be surprised but in his heart, from the minute Tilly had told him and Melody that Genevieve had disappeared into her room again, he'd known that something was wrong. And he hadn't been able to shake the feeling that it had something to do with him.

Where the hell was she? An old woman couldn't just disappear.

His knees felt weak and he sat down on the edge of the bed. Wax dripped down the side of the candle, burning his hand, but he ignored it and tried to figure out what to do next. Should he wait? How could he? Melody had said before that sometimes her aunt disappeared for days. He couldn't hide out in this room for that length of time.

No. He had to go about his business and simply wait for her to come back. He stood up and walked over to the chest of drawers on the side of the room. There was a jumble of feathers, all sorts of colors. He picked out the most distinctive one, a bright green one with a band of orange near the base, and he carefully stuck it in his shirt pocket.

He blew out the candle and left the room the same way he'd entered it. Within minutes he was back on the ground, the ladder under his arm. He put it back where it belonged and then returned to the house. Too keyed up to sleep, he sat down on the swing that he and Melody had shared earlier. He lifted his legs and braced his feet against the strong wooden railing.

Midnight visitors. Locked drawers. A missing old woman. Was it happenstance? Or was there some twisted connection?

He didn't know but he damn well planned to find out. Because whatever it was, he wouldn't let it touch Melody or her child. He'd failed once to protect the woman he loved. He wouldn't fail a second time.

His feet slipped and his boots hit the wood floor. The sound seemed to vibrate in the quiet night air. It sort of matched the sound his heart was making.

The woman he loved. Christ. He didn't want to love another woman. And Melody sure as hell deserved to be with somebody from her own time, somebody who belonged, somebody who didn't need to go home and take care of unfinished business.

He owed Hannah. Not that it was a debt she'd asked for or maybe even one she'd appreciate. He remembered that after Dority's death, he'd been wallowing in self-pity that he hadn't been able to question the man, that he hadn't gotten information that would lead him to the third and final killer. He'd sworn that in the wind, he'd heard his sweet Hannah tell him that vengeance would not heal the pain. Had been so sure of what he heard that he'd told John Beckett about it.

She'd been right. Vengeance didn't heal the pain. But she'd been wrong, too. Because she hadn't understood that it was the need for vengeance that had gotten him up every morning, gotten him through the day, and most important, had gotten him through the long, lonely nights.

In George's time, a killer and a violator of women walked free. He couldn't turn his back on that. He owed Hannah, whether she wanted the debt repaid or not.

SIXTEEN

GEORGE stayed in the swing all night. He dozed off once or twice but mostly, he'd just stared out into the dark night. When dawn was still just a hint, he eased his body out of the swing and walked inside the house.

Wanting to avoid Melody, he washed up in the downstairs bath and then made his way to the kitchen. It was too early for Bessie to have the coffee going so he made do with cold cereal. He ate it standing up in front of the sink.

He finished and then washed out his bowl. Then he quietly left the house and headed straight to the barn. As he made his way down the length of the building, he spent a moment with each of the horses, giving them a word and a friendly rub on the head. When he got to Brontë's stall, he wasted no time in saddling up the horse. Then he led her outside and swung a leg over the saddle.

And everything felt a little more right with the world. He walked her, then they trotted, and finally, when he nudged her in the ribs, she took off into a full gallop.

They ran hard until he pulled back on the reins and slowed her down. The sun was cresting the horizon and it was a beautiful sight. In the distance, grapevines sparkled and hungry birds chirped. He could smell the sweet scent of the grass. It was perfect. So perfect that when he heard the sound of a car approaching, his first thought was annoyance. Then he realized that it was a car coming up Pearl's long lane, and given that it was awfully early for someone to be calling, he quickly pulled Brontë back into the shadow of the olive trees.

He had a good view of the road and it wasn't hard to see that it was Bernard driving the car. He was alone. Something or someone had obviously kept the winemaker away for the night.

If George had been a betting man, he'd have put two bits on Rebecca Fields. Was it possible that the two of them were really in love? Or was the woman stringing Bernard along for some reason?

George waited until Bernard had parked his car and gone into the wine shed. Then he nudged Brontë in the ribs and guided the horse as quietly as possible back to the barn.

Ten minutes later, he opened the door of the wine shed and walked down the cement corridor. He didn't see Bernard but he heard his voice coming from the office area. He got close enough to see that Bernard faced the window. He was leaning forward slightly, one hand holding the telephone up to his ear, the other hand braced against the glass.

It dawned on George that the man was probably exhausted after being out all night. He was clearly too old for such shenanigans. And now he was working before the rest of the world had drunk their coffee. And based on what George was overhearing, the person at the other end of the telephone was feeling the wrath of Bernard's tiredness.

"I've paid you good money," Bernard said. "You said your contacts had what I needed."

George moved off to the side, so that even if Bernard turned, he wouldn't see him. There was silence and George assumed Bernard was listening.

"Just get me the other photos," Bernard said. "Now."

George heard the telephone slam down and then movement in the office, like Bernard had pulled out his desk chair. George moved quickly, silently. In less than a minute he reached the side door and was outside the wine shed.

What the hell? Should he tell Melody what he'd heard?

He discounted the idea right away. If all he had was questions and no answers, he wasn't going to say anything to Melody and worry her needlessly.

He walked over to the bunkhouse and sat on the bench outside the building. It was still too early for Arturo to have arrived. He sat and stared at the rows and rows of grapevines. He was still staring at them when Arturo drove up ten minutes later. Arturo opened the truck door and stepped out. "I was sort of hoping you might sleep late," he said.

"Why?" George asked.

Arturo dug the point of his work boot into the dirt. "I interrupted your marriage celebration last night. I'm sorry about that. And then when Melody came to the rock quarry, I could not help but overhear. I didn't mean to cause trouble for you and I . . . I guess I hoped that the two of you had made up."

They had, he guessed. Not that it made any difference.

"You don't need to worry," he assured Arturo. "Melody and I understand each other."

WHEN Arturo and George pulled into the yard at lunchtime, Pearl and Melody were walking toward Melody's car. Melody wore a yellow dress that buttoned down the front and fell just inches shy of her ankles. The wind made it swirl around her legs.

He knew he was a goner when he found himself hoping for a peek of her knees.

"Hi," she said, waving to him as he got out of the truck.

She had her hair pulled back into a braid and it was tied with a yellow-and-white ribbon. She looked fresh and clean and pure, and a great longing filled his soul. When he had to leave her, he hoped that he would remember her just like she looked today. "Hello," he said. "Where are you going?"

"Grandmother has an appointment with her oncologist. I'm going to drive her. I mentioned this to Tilly, but I should probably tell you, too; if she's not too tired afterward, we may have dinner in Yountville."

That meant it would be Louis, Tilly, Bernard, and him at dinner unless, of course, Genevieve decided to make a surprise reappearance. He wasn't worried about Tilly—she'd be busy buttering her bread. Bernard and Louis could be a problem. Maybe he'd talk to Bessie in advance and have her remove all the sharp objects from the table.

Melody opened the car door for her grandmother and closed it gently once the woman was seated. George beat Melody to her side of the car and opened the door for her. She smiled at him and slid in behind the wheel.

"Be careful," he said, unable to quell his own uneasiness.

She looked surprised, like she wasn't used to having anyone look after her. "It's just to Napa and then maybe dinner," she said.

Still. He'd avoided more than one bullet by paying attention to the hairs on the back of his neck and right now, they were up, wanting to be noticed.

"I'll call you if we're going to be late," she said.

"Call?"

She reached her hand into her purse and pulled out the machine she'd used in the car—the one that had allowed them to talk to Tilly.

"On my cell," she said. "Grandmother's number is the first one in my telephone book. I press one and I've got you."

Of course. "Right. You do that. Call me," he added, like a man who'd lost his senses. Hoping to avoid further embarrassment, he turned and started walking. Near the bunkhouse, he ran into Bernard. "Morning," George said.

"Good morning," Bernard answered. He looked toward the gate where Melody's car was just making the turn onto the road. "Is that Pearl and Melody?"

"Yes."

"Everything okay?"

"Appointment for Pearl and maybe an early dinner."

"Good for them. They need to be spending their days together."

MELODY drove home, her speed carefully controlled. Her emotions were another thing altogether.

They hadn't gone to dinner. Grandmother had felt good enough after her appointment with the oncologist to do a little shopping in Napa but had confessed afterward that she was too tired to stay out for dinner. Melody had walked her back to the car, one hand under her elbow, the other hand busy with a shopping bag. It held at least ten sleepers for the baby in all shades of pink.

"I'm sorry about dinner," Grandmother said. Her face was turned toward the window.

"Another time," Melody said.

Out of the corner of her eye, she could see her grandmother turn toward her. "We shouldn't wait too long," she said.

The silence hung in the air. "Definitely not," Melody said, once she could speak. She knew her tone was too bright, too much, but it was the best she could do. "I won't be eating out much after the baby is born."

Her grandmother smiled. "Of course not," she said, choosing to let it go. They drove in silence for several miles before her grandmother spoke again. "I like George."

Me too. "I'm glad."

"It's wonderful that you could both come for a visit and now with Gino's news, I'm very grateful for George's help."

"He's happy to do it." At least she hoped he was. It *did* get him away from Tilly and Louis.

"Will the two of you keep living in Los Angeles?"

Melody kept her eyes on the road. "We haven't talked about it," she said. He, no doubt, wanted to get a few dollars in his pocket and then go home. When he'd said he was from North Dakota, she'd heard a real sense of longing in his voice.

"Maybe the two of you would consider settling here?"

Melody flipped on her turn signal and turned off the main road. They'd be at her grandmother's house in less than ten minutes. "I'm not sure that would work," she said. She had some savings but not enough to pay George to stay for a really long-term assignment.

"Why?"

It wasn't like her grandmother to push an issue. Melody gave her the only explanation that she could. "Well, I don't think that Tilly or Louis would be thrilled about it." She negotiated a hairpin turn.

"Tilly's an unhappy woman," Grandmother said, her voice heavy. "It's difficult for me to see that. To know that's how I'm leaving her."

Melody gripped the wheel and gave her grandmother a glance. "You have enough to worry about without stressing out over why Tilly is in a perpetual funk. Leave that to her massage therapist, her manicurist, or her personal shopper."

The minute she said it, she felt bad. It wasn't her business if Grandmother wanted to look at Tilly with rose-colored glasses. Heck, maybe she'd do the same for Jingle one day. Parents loved their children. Totally. Which meant loving their cracks and holes, too. It was the way it was meant to be. "I'm sorry, Grandmother."

She leaned over and patted Melody's leg. "It's all right, darling."

Melody looked down, looked at the familiar hand that had guided her through adolescence and beyond, and sorrow filled her heart. She was losing her best friend. Could it get much worse?

She looked up, saw the old blue pickup that was barreling toward them on their side of the narrow road, and realized that it could.

Oh, Jingle.

It was her last thought before she whipped the wheel to the side.

ON top of the rise, where they often came to play, two black-and-brown dogs stopped, sniffed the air, and looked down at the road below, just in time to see a green-colored car plummet over the hill and a blue-colored pickup truck speed off.

Running like the wind, they went home.

GEORGE had just set the water jug back onto the bed of the truck when a huge car rounded the corner at a speed that had him jumping to the side. Somehow the great beast got stopped just inches from where his legs had been.

The door opened and Aunt Genevieve leaned her body halfway out. Her feathers were pink and sticking straight out from her head. "Get in," she ordered.

She acted like she had every right to suddenly appear and order him around. The woman had some explaining to do. "Beg pardon?" he said, as politely as he could.

She shook her head, looking impatient. "No time for long explanations. Melody and Pearl have been in a car accident."

He reached the car in three strides, wrenched open the door, and threw his body inside. His butt was barely in the seat when Aunt Genevieve backed the car up with such speed that it knocked his head back. "Where are they?" he demanded.

"On their way to the hospital. In an ambulance."

Ambulance. There was that word again. Now he knew what it meant. He'd read it in the newspaper last night. A child who had fallen into a swimming pool had been rushed to the hospital by ambulance. But the child had still died. Fear made his insides turn to water.

"Is Melody dead?" he asked.

"No." Aunt Genevieve turned the wheel to the left and swerved around one car, then another, before getting back on her side of the road.

"What happened?"

"Some idiot in a blue pickup truck ran them off the road. They went over the edge, down a hillside, and the car ended up on its side."

He'd seen more than one wagon do the same. The lucky ones were thrown clear before the wagon came to a jarring stop. The unlucky were crushed.

It seemed like it was very hard to breathe, like the air in the car had all been sucked up. He figured that was why it took him a minute to realize what she'd said. "Ran them off the road?" he repeated. "On purpose?"

She didn't answer. She passed another car and then took a quick turn onto a road marked with a sign reading NAPA. "Five more minutes," she said, "and we'll be there."

"I asked if it was on purpose," he said. He said it hard, wanting her to know that he wouldn't be put off.

"Yes, on purpose," she said, giving him a cross look. "And don't ask me any more questions," she said. "I don't know anything else."

He didn't need anything else. He'd find out who. He'd been a lawman for the past ten years. He knew how to find a clue and follow it, unraveling the threads as he went. *Who* wasn't hard. The *why* was generally tougher. Sometimes there was a reason for such hatefulness. But often enough, he'd dealt with men and women, too, for that matter, who had harmed others without provocation.

Aunt Genevieve turned the wheel sharply and pulled into an area filled with cars. A big brick building, several stories high, loomed in front of them.

They ran to the door. It gave him pause when they got close and the door slid open, like it was magic. The room they entered was brightly lit, with chairs all around the edge. About half were full. There was a baby crying and it scared him, thinking that it might be Melody's baby born too soon. But then he saw the woman holding it, with a man pacing behind her chair, and knew these strangers had their own worries.

There was a young girl sitting behind a desk. Aunt Genevieve walked straight to her. "My name is Genevieve Song. My sister and great-niece were in a car accident and brought to this emergency room by ambulance."

The girl did not look overly concerned, and George wondered if there were so many accidents with cars that one more was not anything to warrant notice. "Names, please?" she asked, pleasant enough.

"Pearl Song and Melody Song," George said. "Are they here?"

The woman pressed her fingers to some machine that had all the letters of the alphabet as she stared at the lighted box in front of her. Finally, she looked up.

"Are you both family?"

"Yes," he answered. "Are they here?" he repeated.

"I show that a Pearl Song arrived by ambulance about a half hour ago. I have no record of a Melody Song."

She was dead. A heavy, crushing weight, settled on his chest, making it hard to breathe. His vision turned gray.

"Melody Johnson," he heard Genevieve say. "Check for Melody Johnson."

"Yes. She's here. I'll let the nurse know that family has arrived."

The woman paused and he knew she was looking at him, had perhaps even heard him gulping for air. "Sir," she said, "perhaps you should have a seat. You don't look so good."

He wasn't sure he'd have made it to the chairs if Genevieve hadn't grabbed his hand and pulled him in that direction. Once there, he sank down onto the hard plastic.

Genevieve patted his hand. "They're both going to be fine. Just keep thinking that."

There was a clock mounted on the wall and George watched the seconds tick into minutes. He focused his attention on it, on the strict rhythm, and tried to sort out his chaotic thoughts.

She wasn't dead. That's all that mattered. Whatever else, they would handle.

He knew that he wouldn't be any good to Melody if he couldn't think, couldn't reason. As her husband, would he be expected to make medical decisions for her? In his time, that's how it went. Husbands turned to wives, wives turned to husbands. Children turned to parents.

He had no right to make decisions for Melody and her child. He'd known her just days. It made him feel woefully inadequate. But if not him, then who?

An older woman, her hair short and gray, approached and stood in front of Genevieve. "Ms. Song?"

Genevieve nodded. "Yes, I'm Genevieve Song. Pearl Song is my sister. This is George Johnson. Melody Johnson's husband."

George tried to read the nurse's face, to know whether it was good or bad news, to prepare himself. But it told him nothing. He reached for Genevieve's hand and squeezed it gently.

The nurse spoke to Genevieve. "Your sister has some bruises and a badly sprained knee. She's going to need some help getting around for a few weeks."

It was good news. "My wife?" he asked.

The woman turned to him and smiled. "She's bruised, but other than that, fine."

"The child?" he managed.

"Everything looks very normal."

He was grateful that he was sitting down because if he'd have been standing, his legs would have surely crumpled.

"Ms. Song should be done shortly and can go home. They are admitting your wife for observation. She'll need to spend the night."

He felt the blood drain out of his head. She couldn't be fine if they wouldn't let her go home.

"It's strictly a precaution," she added.

"For her? For the child?" He had a thousand questions.

"For both of them. I'll check and see if they've been assigned to a room yet." She took a step away, then stopped. "Mr. Johnson, are you all right? You look sort of pale. Maybe you should put your head between your knees for just a minute."

He felt ashamed. The last thing Melody needed was a husband who took to fainting. "I'm fine," he said, sucking in a breath to clear his head. "I'd just like to see my wife."

SHE was asleep and he was grateful, because he knew he couldn't hide his fear when he saw the scrape on her cheek or the one that started at her elbow and went almost to her wrist. They'd put her in a faded blue nightdress that tied around the neck. She had a white sheet pulled up almost to her breasts and her hands rested on her stomach.

He lowered himself into the chair beside her bed. That's when he noticed the needle in her hand and the clear small tube running up to a bag of clear fluid, which hung from a tall silver post with hooks.

And he knew. He was going to find the bastard who'd caused this and make him pay.

He must have made a sound because she opened her eyes. She blinked, then smiled. "Hi."

"You're going to be fine," he assured her. "Jingle, too."

"They told me," she said. Tears filled her eyes. "I was scared. All the way to the hospital in the ambulance, Jingle didn't move. They kept telling me that they had a heartbeat but I wanted . . . needed . . . to feel her."

It made him crazy that she'd felt even a moment of worry.

"And then, right as they were wheeling us in, Jingle started doing cartwheels, like she somehow knew that I needed to know."

He reached out and took her hand, the one without the needle. Her skin was warm and soft and very alive and he wondered if God would think him too much of a hypocrite if he were to say thank you. "Already watching out for her momma."

"Did you talk to Grandmother?" she asked.

"No. Aunt Genevieve is with her. She's going to drive her home. Your grandmother is going to be fine. You know that, don't you?"

"I wouldn't come up to a room until I got to see her. I knew Aunt Genevieve would be so worried but I didn't want to call until I knew Grandmother was fine."

For a minute he was angry that Genevieve hadn't said that she'd spoken to Melody. He'd still have been worried but it might have taken the edge off.

"Then when I got the answering machine, I . . ."

She stopped and looked at the clock on the wall. "How did you get here so quickly?" She checked the timepiece she wore on her wrist. "I left a message less than fifteen minutes ago. You must have been at the house, practically in the car, to make it here that fast."

He'd been a good fifteen minutes from the house, they'd driven for another fifteen, and then he and Aunt Genevieve had sat for another ten before the nurse had come to talk to them. What the hell was going on?

He'd worry about that later. He had more important things on his mind. "Your aunt said a blue pickup truck ran you off the road."

She looked startled and he felt bad, like maybe he shouldn't be reminding her of it. "If you don't want to talk about it right now," he said, "I understand."

"I never told Aunt Genevieve about a truck."

Seventeen

MELODY'S great-aunt had some explaining to do when he got home. She had better be wearing feathers that prompted truthfulness. But first things first. "Well, she must have talked to someone. I just want to know if that's what happened?"

"I think so. I mean, it happened so fast. I looked down for just a second, I know it was just a second, and then, when I looked up, the truck was coming toward me." She paused, like she wasn't sure she should go on. Then, she licked her lips and said, "I could see the driver. He was looking right at me. He could have gotten back in his lane but he didn't."

"Describe him to me."

It was like he hadn't spoken. "Maybe he had a heart attack," she said. "I thought he was looking at me but maybe he was really in pain, out of his mind. Maybe he's an epileptic and he had a seizure."

Maybe he was some selfish bastard who got his kicks out

of scaring women. "Why he did it is a matter for the law to decide."

"I know," she said, rolling her eyes. "That's why I already gave a report to the police."

"Good. Now tell me what he looked like."

"Why?"

Because I'm going to kill him. "I told you that I used to be a sheriff. I'm just one more set of eyes and ears. If I know everything you told your police, then I can help them."

She stared at him. "You're sure that's the only reason."

"I'm waiting."

"He was about thirty and dark-skinned. Maybe Hispanic. He had a very round face and his hair was dark and very short."

"Anything else?"

"Not that I recall. I only saw him for a second or two. But I'm generally good with faces."

He was, too. And the face she described didn't match any of the men he'd met. "Tell me about the truck."

"It was an old one, like from the sixties. It was big and I knew if it hit me, I was in trouble. It was light blue but when I took the other lane, I think I saw some darker blue, like maybe a fender was a different color."

She was a good witness. Some people panicked and couldn't remember anything. "You said you took the other lane. What happened?"

"I would have been okay. There was just enough room for me to get by."

"What happened?" he repeated.

She chewed on her lip. "I think what happened is when he saw what I was trying to do, he edged over."

"If that's true," he said, trying to keep his voice even, "he literally ran you off the road."

"That's why I told the police. I wanted to excuse it away as an accident but I couldn't." Her eyes filled with tears. "Why would someone do that to me?"

He reached for her hand. "Could it be the father of your baby? Is it possible that he doesn't want you to have this child?"

"I thought of that. But it's too crazy. I don't think he cares one way or another about this baby. Look, I should have probably told you before but I was embarrassed that I'd used such poor judgment. Alexander is married, with two children."

"That bastard."

She waved off his comment. "I haven't seen or heard from him for five months. Why would he come now? If he wanted to harm me, it would have made more sense to do it before I came home."

It was quite a speech. But it made sense. "If it was deliberate," he said, "it had to have been someone who knew that Pearl and you would be on that road, around that time." As he said it, he remembered the conversation between himself and Bernard. He was about to tell Melody but knew that she'd dismiss his suspicions right away. And even to him, it seemed crazy. Bernard treated Melody like a daughter.

"I hate to even say it," she said, "but after last night and seeing those strange men, do you think it could possibly be Louis or Tilly? Are they that crazy?"

"I don't know," he said. He couldn't dismiss what he'd overheard Louis and Tilly saying the night Melody had almost been killed in the wine shed. But Tilly loved her mother. There was no question about that. If they were trying to hurt Melody, he didn't think they'd do it with Pearl in the car.

Melody went to push her hair back from her face and

paused when she saw the scrape on her arm. "I can't worry about—"

She stopped when the door opened. A man wearing a white coat entered. He extended his hand to George. "Mr. Johnson, I presume. I'm Dr. Lacardi. Your wife and I met briefly in the emergency room. While she's here, I'll be supervising her care."

"She tells me everything is fine."

"It is," he said. "The most serious concern we have after a pregnant woman is in a car accident is placental abruption. That's when the placenta pulls away from wall of the uterus. That can happen when there's been a sudden trauma to the abdomen."

"Placental abruption." Melody repeated the harsh words. "I read about that. Wouldn't I be in a lot of pain?"

"Yes. So it's a good sign that you're not. The ultrasound we did in the ER looks fine so I'm feeling pretty confident that you're going to be fine."

George thought he might be sick but he willed himself to be strong for Melody. "What else do we need to know?" he asked.

"Other than that, I'm a little concerned about her blood pressure. It may just be up from the stress of the accident but it's important to watch it."

She'd been so confident that everything was fine that he'd stopped worrying. Now, it seemed like he'd been a little too carefree. "Is it dangerous, this blood pressure?"

"It can be. And certainly as her pregnancy advances, it becomes all the more important to keep it in check. She needs to watch the usual things, like making sure she's eating healthy, getting a little moderate exercise every day, and trying to avoid sudden shocks or stressful situations."

She shouldn't be worrying about somebody trying to kill her. "I'll make sure those things happen," he said.

"Hello. I'm in the room." Melody waved her hand.

The doctor shrugged his shoulders. "When it comes to the safety of a pregnant woman and her unborn child, I'm not above enlisting the help of a spouse." He turned to George and smiled. "That's your job, right? Looking out for your wife?"

His job had been to be a pretend husband. But that was before he'd realized that somebody might be trying to harm her. "That's right," he said, looking at Melody. "It's my job and I damn well intend to do it."

WHEN Melody woke up just before sunrise, George reached for her hand. Her skin was cool and soft. "Do you want the nurse?" he asked.

She shook her head. "Some water, perhaps?"

He held the plastic glass for her and she sipped out of the straw. "Thanks," she said. She looked at the big wall clock across the small room. "I can't believe you spent the whole night in that chair, George. Your back has got to be killing you. Have you had any sleep?"

None. Every time he'd closed his eyes, he'd thought about her car rolling in the ditch. "Don't worry about me," he said.

"I have to," she said. "You're obviously not worrying about yourself. You haven't even had anything to eat since last night."

He hadn't had anything since yesterday's lunch. But when the nurses had come the evening before to care for Melody, he'd excused himself. On the way out of her room, he'd pulled her cell phone out of her purse and after some fiddling had figured out how to call the house. Bessie had answered and he assured her that Melody was doing fine. Then he'd asked her to find Arturo. He'd waited for what seemed like hours but was probably only minutes when the young man answered.

George didn't waste any time. He told him what had happened to Melody, about the blue truck with the darker blue fender, and gave him the description of the man. Arturo had not known immediately who the man might be but had promised that he would check around. George had warned him to be careful, to keep his inquiries general. After all, he didn't want to scare the bastard off but neither did he want the trail to grow cold while he was with Melody.

And he wasn't leaving her unprotected in the hospital. If someone had been desperate enough to run her off the road, would they be crazy enough to try to finish the job while she lay helpless in her bed? He wouldn't take that chance.

When he'd finished talking to Arturo, he'd returned to the room and when she'd assumed that he'd left to find something to eat, he'd let her believe it. He'd sat by her bed and they'd watched television for a short time until she'd grown tired and fallen asleep.

Now she looked rested, although the scrapes on her face and arm had turned into dark bruises. When she suddenly placed her hand on her stomach, his heart thumped in his chest.

Placental abruption. Those were horrible-sounding words.

"I'll get the doctor," he said, already rising.

She grabbed at his hand. "I'm fine," she said. "Jingle's just waking up."

And he knew that if he hadn't believed in miracles before, he did now. "She's an early riser," he said. "Not like her mother," he teased.

Melody rolled her eyes and he was grateful to see some of her spirit coming back. "I know. It's so unfair. I see a whole lot of five o'clock feedings in my future. I just hope I don't fall asleep and drop her."

She wouldn't. Melody would stick pins in her eyes if that was what it took to stay awake. But that wouldn't be necessary. He'd had a lot of time to think during the night, a lot of time to decide what was right. "I'm generally awake early," he said. "Maybe I could be of some help."

She jerked her hand out of his. "What are you saying, George?"

He could feel the back of his shirt get damp with his own sweat. "What I'm saying is that I'd like to help you with your daughter."

He'd hoped that she would be happy. Had at least expected that she'd be grateful. He wasn't prepared when she narrowed her eyes at him. "I don't have that much money," she said, her voice flat. "I can't afford to pay you to stay."

He felt the fresh rush of anger and maybe if he'd had any sleep, he'd have been able to handle it. But that wasn't the case. He stood up, his movements jerky. "The hell with your money," he said. "Damn you. I'm not offering myself up for sale."

She pushed herself up in the bed, almost to the point of sitting up. Her eyes flashed with annoyance. "Just what the hell are you offering, George?"

Everything he had. Which wasn't much. He sat down hard on the chair. "The truth is Melody, that I don't have a lot to offer you. And I wouldn't blame you for telling me that you're holding out for a better proposition." He closed his eyes and took three deep breaths. When he opened them, she was staring at him like he was some kind of crazy person.

It would have been easy to stop but he'd started this and

he damned well planned to finish it. "But if you'll have me, I'd like to stay on as your husband. I'd like to help you raise your daughter."

She made some kind of noise, like a small squeak. But she didn't say anything. He reached for her hand but she pulled her arm back.

And he felt his heart break. She didn't want him. "Melody," he said. "Please—"

"Why?" she interrupted. "Why do you want to stay now when you've been so determined to go?"

It wasn't an easy answer. He'd had hours to think about what it would mean if he stayed. He'd be giving up everything that he knew and living in a time that was still so very strange to him. But then he'd thought about what he'd told John Beckett when John was being bullheaded about loving Sarah. He'd told him that he'd give anything to have another day with Hannah.

That wasn't to be and he'd come to accept it. But it had dawned on him during the middle of the night that he was making the same mistake twice. And while he'd never been a great book learner, he'd always figured he had some common sense, so the knowledge of what he was doing hit him hard.

He was giving up days. Days that could be shared with Melody. Days that could be filled with love. Days that could lead into a lifetime.

"I asked you why," she said, startling him out of his thoughts.

He couldn't tell her everything. Not when the doctor had warned them about her blood pressure, that she should avoid sudden shocks or stresses. Learning that he had traveled from 1888 would certainly qualify.

He'd tell her soon, right after the baby was born. For

now, he'd tell her the one thing that he could. "I love you," he said.

She opened her mouth.

"I didn't plan on it, I didn't want to," he continued. "But I do. And I hope in time that you'll come to love me back and that we'll raise our daughter and maybe give her a brother or a sister."

She started to cry. Big, fat tears rolled down her smooth cheeks.

"Please, no," he begged. He didn't want her upset. That's what he was trying to avoid. "We can talk about this later. Or never, if that's what you want."

"Come here," she said.

He scooted his chair closer. She shook her head and then moved in her bed so that she was hugging the side. She patted the empty space in the bed next to her. "No. Here."

What was she thinking? Nurses had been coming in and out all night without warning. "I can't get into bed with you."

Her lips trembled. "I just want you to hold me."

Oh, hell. He lowered the railing on the bed, the way he'd seen the nurse do it. Then he carefully climbed in next to her. He lay on his side and he slipped his arm under her shoulder and gently pulled her close. "Like this?" he asked.

"Perfect," she said, sounding happy for the first time.

It was. And he told himself that if she never learned to love him but she at least wanted his touch, that it would have to be enough.

After several minutes, she lifted her head. "What time is it?"

The question surprised him but he turned his head to see the clock. "Just before five. Why?"

"Because there's been enough time."

He was confused. "What?"

"You said that in time you hoped I would come to love you. Well, I do. Very much."

And he wasn't too tired to realize that she'd played him perfectly. He'd said once that she was sunshine and sugar and a hot drink on a cold day. She was also laughter and joy, the things that made life good. "You're going to be a handful," he said.

"You're right," she agreed and snuggled closer to him. "You better rest up."

He closed his eyes and let the sleep come.

MELODY looked out the car window, grateful to be going home. However, if George didn't stop treating her like she was some kind of fragile glass that was about to break at any minute, she was going to scream.

When she'd awoken in the hospital shortly after eight in the morning, his side of the bed had been empty. But he'd been sitting in his chair. He'd stood up, leaned over her bed, and given her a brief kiss.

It had been wholly unsatisfying.

Then there'd been hours filled with nurses coming in, then the doctor, then the person in charge of getting her dressed to go home had appeared. By a little after ten, she'd been wheeled down to the lobby and had gone from sitting in the wheelchair to sitting in the back of her grandmother's car. Arturo was driving and George sat next to her.

But he hadn't touched her in two hours. Had barely looked at her.

When Arturo pulled into her grandmother's driveway, she leaned forward in her seat. "Thank you for coming to get us," she said.

"I'm happy to do it," Arturo replied, looking in the rearview mirror. He stopped the car. "I have been looking for—"

"Let's get you upstairs," George said to her, interrupting Arturo. He got out on his side and practically ran around the car to open her door. Then the house door opened and Grandmother, Aunt Genevieve, and Tilly came out.

Her grandmother walked with crutches, with Tilly close to her side. "Don't try the steps," Melody called out. "I'll come to you."

She hugged each one in turn, even Tilly. "How are you?" she asked her grandmother.

Her grandmother's eyes were warm. "Fine. Now that you're home and I can see for myself that you're all right." She turned to George who'd followed her up the stairs. "I imagine you could use some sleep," she said.

"I got a couple hours," he said.

He had. He'd fallen asleep almost immediately after crawling into that narrow hospital bed with her. She'd lain there, staying awake as long as she could, and watched him sleep. "I think I'm going to go upstairs for a nap," she said. "Maybe I can convince him to take one, too."

Aunt Genevieve looked at Grandmother. "Maybe you can do the same now that she's here."

Grandmother smiled at her sister. "I've been driving them crazy all morning. All right. Come on. We'll all take naps."

Melody was going upstairs but she didn't plan on sleeping.

"I'll walk you upstairs," George said.

Great. As long as she got him there.

When they got upstairs, George walked immediately over to the bed and pulled back the sheet and blanket. Then he fluffed up her pillow. That was the straw that broke the camel's back. "Oh for goodness's sake, George. I thought the job you signed on for this morning was husband, not maid. I swear, if you have chocolate mints in your pocket, I'm going for your throat."

He looked at her like he expected her to start foaming at the mouth.

She was close. But really, how much was a woman expected to take?

"You're tired," he said, valiantly trying to excuse her behavior. "You should get some rest."

She took a step forward. He took a step backward.

Great. Now, she'd had him running. "Stay here with me," she pleaded.

He shook his head. "I have to talk to Arturo. It's important."

It didn't take a genius to have figured out that George had enlisted Arturo's help in trying to identify the man who'd run her off the road. She had to admit that it was a smart move. Knowing George, she doubted he could think of anything else until he got the full report. "Fine. But come back. I need to tell you something," she said. "It's important."

"Tell me now," he said. "I've got time if it's that important."

He did not have nearly enough time for what she had in mind. "No. It can wait." Barely. "Just come back as soon as you can."

The door was hardly shut behind him before she started taking off her clothes. She walked into the bathroom, turned the shower on, stepped in, and took one of the fastest showers of her life. She did slow down when she shaved her legs because she thought it might put a damper on things if she nicked a major artery.

She got out, dried off, put lotion on, and then pulled back the sheet and blanket even farther. Then she lay down on the bed, as naked as the day she was born. She was practically panting with the exertion.

Ten minutes later, when the door opened and George walked in, the look on his face was worth the effort.

"Mother of God," he said. He stared at her, stunned. After a long minute, where the temperature in the room seemed to heat up fast, he had the presence of mind to shut the door behind him.

"Are you feeling all right?" he asked. He spoke softly, calmly, like he didn't want to startle her. It was more of the same of what she'd been enduring for the last two hours. He was being careful with her.

She wanted to hurt someone. Badly. "Yes," she said, her voice just as calm.

"Maybe you should get dressed, then."

It was like he was talking to a small child. And he still hadn't moved.

She was done trying to make this easy for him.

She spread her legs. And then she touched herself. Delicately. Deliberately.

She smiled when he made a sound just shy of pain. "Stop that," he said. He sounded breathless and needy.

It was all the encouragement she needed. She did it again.

This time there was no sound. But she could see his face. The man wasn't doing well. He was pale and he'd leaned back against the door, like he perhaps needed something to keep him braced up.

She went for the goal shot. "If you're not going to be of any assistance, then I think I'm going to have to take care of matters myself," she said. "But you can watch," she added.

She took her hands, cupped a breast in each, and rubbed the pad of her thumb across the nipple.

He closed his eyes and looked up to the ceiling, like he

was appealing to a higher power. "From the minute I dragged her out of the ocean, I knew she was going to be trouble," he muttered.

She'd been a cakewalk up to this point. "What's it going to be, George?" she prodded. "Are you a watcher or a doer?"

EIGHTEEN

HE covered the distance between the door to the bed fast enough but once he was there, he took his time. He stood over her and looked down. He started with her face, then almost inch by inch, his gaze traveled her naked body.

And it dawned on her that the balance of power had shifted. She forced herself to lie still, her hands at her side.

It was the most intimate thing she'd ever experienced. It was the middle of the day, the room was bursting with sunshine, and she was watching the man she loved devour her with his eyes.

Her breasts felt tight and moisture gathered between her legs. Her skin felt super-sensitive, like she could feel every thread in the sheet that she lay on.

He was so quiet that she wasn't sure he was even breathing. Finally, he licked his dry lips. "You are the most beautiful woman."

She realized that he'd always made her feel beautiful, that his eyes had always told her how much he desired her.

"But I am afraid," he added.

His honesty touched her heart and she knew if she hadn't loved him before, that would have done it. She reached for his hand. His skin was warm and the light dusting of hair tickled her palm. She laced her fingers with his. "I know. But you don't need to be. I won't break."

"I don't want to hurt you or your child."

"We'll take it slow," she promised and pulled him to the bed.

WHEN George woke up, the afternoon sun was well over to the west. He looked at the clock on the bedside table and saw that it was just after five.

He'd spent the afternoon making love to Melody. She'd lied to him. They hadn't taken it slow. It might have started that way, as they'd learned each other's bodies, as they'd discovered the little touches that delighted the other, but in the end, he'd lain on his back and she'd settled her warmth on him and he'd been a lost man.

The second time had been much the same and then finally, the third time, she'd let him watch. Until, of course, he'd been compelled to take over at the end.

He couldn't remember being happier. She'd been generous and giving and even now, as she lay sleeping in his arms, her back pressed up to his front, he felt himself stiffen.

Would there ever be a time when he didn't want her desperately? But he knew she was tired, knew that her body had to be craving rest.

He slipped his arm from underneath her and rolled to the side of the bed. Then he walked toward the bath, picking up the clothes he'd tossed earlier.

"What time is it?" she asked.

He turned around. Her eyes were open but she hadn't

moved. "It's after five," he said. "I'm going to get cleaned up and go downstairs." Earlier Arturo had had no news for him but the man had intended to spend the afternoon in town. George had wanted to go, too, but Arturo had explained that he would be at places that would welcome him but would only consider George an outsider. People would scatter, leads would vanish.

"I don't think I'm going to make dinner," she said. "Will you make my excuses to Grandmother?" She stretched and the sheet fell below her breasts.

They were lovely and he couldn't help staring.

She shook her head. "Don't get used to these. They're almost a size bigger than normal."

He couldn't resist teasing her. "So after you have your child, it will be like making love to a different woman?"

She reached over, grabbed his pillow off the bed, and threw it at him. "You're lucky I'm too tired to get out of this bed," she said.

He was lucky. Damn lucky. He'd turned his back on love but she'd managed to find a way into his heart. "I'll tell your grandmother that you're still sleeping," he said.

She smiled. "Why don't you tell her the truth? That you spent the afternoon ravishing my body?" She sat up suddenly, causing the sheet to fall below her very sexy stomach. "No, wait," she said. "Save that for Tilly. But wait until I'm there to see her reaction."

She was something. "I've said it before but it's never been more true: You've no shame."

She winked at him. "You weren't complaining earlier."

"I'm not stupid, Melody."

She looked very satisfied and she lay back in the bed. But then her expression changed and she looked serious. She turned toward him and propped her body up on one elbow. "I suppose it's a little late to ask but there's nothing

I need to know about you, right? I mean, I told you about Alexander and how he sort of just forgot to tell me about his wife and two children. I can't make that mistake again."

This was his chance. He could tell her everything. About Sarah and the footprints. That he'd been born in 1854.

She should avoid sudden shocks or other stressful situations.

It was as if the doctor was in the room, standing at his shoulder. How could he tell her the truth? Her life. Her child's life. They both hung in the balance.

He looked her in the eye. "You know everything about me that's important to know," he said.

Her pretty violet eyes cleared. She settled back on the pillow. He walked into the bath and had almost closed the door when he heard her say, "I know one thing you never mentioned. You've got a very nice ass."

ARTURO'S news was unsettling. There was talk of a man, recently arrived from Mexico who had been bragging in one of the saloons that he was soon going to be rich. That he'd met a gringo who needed some business taken care of. They told Arturo that they'd seen this man driving a light blue truck with a darker blue side panel.

Nobody claimed to have seen the truck or the man for several days. Arturo had left word that they should call him if the man showed again.

It was nothing more than what the police already knew, so George did not feel compelled to tell them. Plus, he knew that if the authorities started snooping around at the saloon, Arturo's sources would dry up faster than a creek in July. Arturo had trusted him once. Now he needed to trust that Arturo knew what he was doing.

Dinner was a quiet affair. Bernard was absent again and Louis and Tilly hardly said a word to anyone. Both of them drank several glass of wine, and he noticed that Tilly especially looked very tired. Pearl accepted without question the news that Melody was sleeping and made pleasant conversation with him throughout the meal.

If possible, Genevieve was even odder than usual. Several times he looked up from his steak to find her staring at him. When dinner was over, she practically ran from the table, the dogs on her heels.

He excused himself equally fast and caught her on the stairs to her room.

"May I have a word with you?" he asked, edging in front of her. Both dogs growled at him.

"I'm tired," she said and tried to step around him.

"I'll be quick," he said, blocking her way. Dionysos bared his teeth and gathered his muscles, like he was ready to spring.

She made the familiar hand motion. "That's enough," she said. Both immediately stopped growling but George swore they were still glaring at him.

He was grateful for her intercession. Melody had been appreciative of certain parts and he'd have been sorely pressed to tell her that they'd been bitten off.

"Follow me," Genevieve said. They walked past her bedroom and she motioned for the dogs to lie down. Then she led him to a small room that was next to her bedroom. There were three chairs in the room but nothing else. She sat and he followed her lead. The room was hot and even though there was a window open, the air seemed heavy.

"I hear there's supposed to be a hell of a storm tomorrow night," she said.

He wasn't here to talk about the weather. "I want to know how you knew about the accident," he said.

She shrugged. "Melody called and left a message on the machine. I'd let you listen to it but I think I deleted it."

"I know she left that message long after you and I were already on the road to Napa."

She didn't even look rattled. "That's impossible."

"Bullshit," he said.

She had the nerve to look amused. He stood up and undid the button on his shirt pocket. He pulled out the bright green feather with the orange ring around the bottom. He handed it to her. She didn't look amused any longer. "Where did you get that?"

"From your dresser. Look, you and I both know you weren't in your room the night of the party. I want to know where the hell you were."

She shrugged. "Traveling."

"Where?"

"Wherever I like," she said smugly. "I've had a certain fondness for eighteenth-century Paris lately. Last year it was fifteenth-century Scotland. I can be fickle like that."

It felt like all the air in the room had been sucked up. His vision started to grow gray at the edges. "You know where I came from, don't you?" he managed to ask.

She smiled. "Where and when."

"You brought me here?"

She shook her head. "Oh, no. That's not true."

He didn't think she was lying. She'd said it with conviction. But how could that be?

"Then who did?"

"I don't know," she said.

Damn. He had no more answers than he did before. Suddenly, it dawned on him that he hadn't asked the most important question. "Could you take me back?"

"No." She got up and opened the door. "I'm tired, George."

"I want to know how you knew about the accident."

She considered him. "Dionysos and Hermes told me."

It should have shocked him but it didn't. Maybe he was way past ever being shocked again. "Stay away from Melody," he said.

She poked him in the chest with a long, bony finger. "Don't be an idiot, George. I love my niece. You can't actually think I'd ever do anything to hurt her."

He knew better. Had known even when he made the crazy demand. But he was getting tired of things happening that he couldn't explain or connect. "I don't know what kind of game you're playing."

He was out the door and halfway down the hall before she spoke again. "It's not a game, George. It never was."

He turned. Just what the hell did she mean by that?

But she'd already gone into her room and closed the door behind her.

GEORGE was not expecting to look up and see Pearl Song making her way down the narrow, long row that separated the grapevines. It scared him at first, thinking that there must be something wrong with Melody but then he realized that she didn't walk with the purpose of a woman needing help, but rather she wandered with the abandon of a woman enjoying a morning stroll.

Although the sky was overcast with threatening black clouds in the distance, she wore a big hat. Her loose trousers and shirt looked as if they'd seen their share of wash days. "Morning, Pearl," he said.

"Good morning, George. It's warmer than I expected."

It was damn hot. And the air was so heavy it was hard to breathe. The wind had changed directions four or five times since early morning when he'd arrived in the vineyard.

Genevieve had predicted a hell of a storm and it looked like she was going to be right.

He and Arturo had begun their day by checking the pump to make sure it was still working and then had started irrigation in the far-western patch of grapes.

Then they'd gotten in Arturo's truck and driven around to check the progress of the workers. There were three teams of four men each working in different areas of Pearl Song's two-hundred-acre vineyard. While they were driving, he'd insisted that Arturo again go over what each person at the saloon had told him. At the end of their drive, George hadn't known anything more than he'd known to start with.

What he did know was that he was going to figure out who'd tried to harm Melody. For the last hour, he'd been walking up and down the rows, his sickle swinging side to side as he mowed down the mustard plants that grew between the rows. With each swing, he'd vowed that he was going to make sure that whoever had tried, never had another chance.

Pearl reached out a hand and touched his arm, which was slick with sweat. "Be careful in heat like this, George. I've had it sneak up on me." She looked rather longingly at the grapevines, which crawled up the hillsides. "There was a time when I would spend all day out here, doing exactly what you're doing now. I loved it. It was the best kind of tired in the world, the kind where your muscles ache but your mind is clear and worry-free."

He obviously needed to work harder. Most of the morning his mind was cluttered up with images of Melody's naked body and the two times they'd lain together last night after he'd left Genevieve's room. He hadn't been with a woman for six months, and yesterday he'd spilled his seed five times. No wonder he was tired and he had an ache or two. But he didn't think it would be all that helpful to explain it to Melody's grandmother.

She tilted her hat back on her head and looked up at him. "But now I think I'm a bit like a child whose eyes are bigger than her stomach and she's taken a piece of cake she can never manage. Will you walk me back, George? We're starting blending trials today and Bernard will be fluttering around like a mad bird if I delay the process."

He took off his leather gloves, stuffed them in his pocket, and leaned the sickle up against the wire that ran between the vines. He put his arm out and she looped her arm through his. They started to make their way down the row. "What's a blending trial?" he asked.

She laughed and it reminded him of the sound of Melody's laugh—so sweet, so natural. "First of all, it's a terribly terrifying time of year for most everyone here because Bernard and I totally lose our sense of humor."

"I'm not sure I understand."

"Let me try to paint the picture. Each year, several times a year, Bernard and I take our places around a table and we more or less, taste-test for about two days. Our goal is to determine what is going to be the perfect blend to produce the ultimate bottle of Sweet Song of Summer wine."

"So you drink wine for two days straight?" No wonder they were surly at the end of it. In the days following Hannah's death, he'd done that a time or two with whisky and he'd been mean as a bear.

"Drink, no. Taste, yes. We let the blend settle in our mouths and then we ask our tongues to distinguish a myriad of characteristics. In the end we don't swallow it—we spit it out, clean our palates with water, and then taste the next blend."

He tried to imagine Pearl Song spitting out wine like men spit out snuff but it was too difficult. He figured she would somehow manage to make even that look refined and elegant. They'd reached the end of the row and could see the roof of the wine shed over the next hill. He slowed the pace even more because he could hear her breathing becoming heavier.

"What we're looking for," she continued, "is whether the blend has balance, meaning that it's neither too harsh or too sweet. Does it have length, meaning can you taste it all the way back on your tongue? If you can, that's good. Many of our competitors are happy producing a wine that has a big impact up front on the palate but little staying power as the wine flows over the tongue. It needs to have good depth, or in other words, layers of taste to enjoy. Quality wines will have both length and depth."

George was very grateful that Gino had not had a role in the blending trial process. It would have been damn difficult to fill in for the man in that capacity. "Melody told me that you said that Bernard was part scientist and part artist. Maybe the same goes for you?"

"Maybe. But I know my limitations. I know ultimately what product I can be happy with but I have always relied upon Bernard to determine the combinations that will lead us to that ultimate product."

"Combinations?"

"Yes. For example, we grow Cabernet grapes in three locations on our property. Each of those locations has a unique microclimate and thus, the same grape ends up producing a different juice."

He supposed that could be true. He'd seen the same kind of seed corn produce very different types of ears based on where it was planted. "So you don't just take all the juice that was collected from the grapes and mix it together."

"Oh, heavens no. I'm grateful Bernard didn't hear that," she said, her tone teasing. "He'd have a heart attack. Not only do we have to determine the exact mix between the same grapes grown in different locations, we have to determine whether or not we're going to add in another different kind of grape altogether. It's a law that if we want to label our wine as a Cabernet, that 75 percent of the end product must be made up of Cabernet grapes. The other 25 percent is up for grabs."

He shook his head. He'd thought growing the grapes was complicated. Hell, that was the easy part. "How do you know what the right combination is?"

"Experience. Knowledge. Grapes have certain tendencies. We know that Merlot grapes are generally low tannic and carry a smooth, chocolatelike aroma. So if we're trying to even out a Cabernet, which is very tannic and full-bodied, we'll maybe do an 80–20 mix, with 80 percent being Cabernet and 20 percent being Merlot."

They'd reached the peak of the hill. From this angle, they were approaching the back of the wine shed. It was less than two hundred yards away. "So that's another reason why your Cabernet tastes different than your neighbors, because they don't have exactly the same mix."

"You've got it. Are you sure you weren't a winemaker in a past life, George?"

He almost stumbled and caught himself in time to avoid taking her down with him. He didn't have a past life. He had two very different *now* lives.

What the heck had prompted that question? He risked a sideways glance at her but she didn't seem overly interested in him. She was watching the ground, making sure she didn't stumble.

"I'm especially excited about this year's blending trials," she said.

"Why is that?" he asked, grateful to be back on a safe subject.

"We're blending our 2004 Cabernet harvest. We've been barrel-aging it, but it's ready now. We'll want to bottle before the fall crush to make room for the new harvest. It's exciting because 2004 was an exceptionally fine growing year."

"Lot of grapes?" he asked.

"Yes, but more than that. We had a very early bud break and then many months of simply ideal weather. Then Mother Nature threw us a curve and we had intense heat toward the end of the growing cycle. It spurred an early harvest, perhaps the earliest I'd seen in thirty some years. But the end result was a grape that was extraordinary in flavor and even shortly after harvest, when the wine was in its early fermentation process, the aromas were robust. It could be one of our best vintages ever."

He heard something in her voice that hadn't been there before and he realized that Pearl Song had accepted that this year's blending trials would be her last. This would be her final wine—her legacy. They walked the last hundred yards in silence. When they rounded the corner of the shed, Pearl stopped suddenly, pulling on his arm. With alarm, he looked down at her.

"Oh, Lord," she hissed between clenched teeth. "Just what do you think *she's* doing here?"

He followed her gaze. About halfway between the house and the wine shed, near the fountain in the front yard, stood Rebecca Fields and Bernard. "Maybe she's here for the blending trials," he suggested.

"That's not possible," she said, sounding shocked. "All this time, it's only ever been Bernard and me. I'm not ready for that to change."

Not yet. She didn't have to say it for him to understand it. "Maybe she's just leaving?" he offered hopefully.

She looked at him like he was dense. Given that Bernard

and Rebecca had arms and legs practically draped over each other, it did seem sort of dumb.

"I have to handle this carefully," she muttered, practically under her breath. She glanced at him. "I can't have Bernard in a snit during the blending trials. We'll end up with something resembling vinegar under our label."

Suddenly she pulled at his arm. "George, you have to help me. Go find Melody and between the two of you, you need to do something with her. If she goes willingly with you, that's a whole lot better than me sending her away."

"But—"

"Please, George. You know I wouldn't ask if it wasn't important."

He knew that. Just as he knew that Melody would do most anything for her grandmother and she'd expect him to do the same. "I'll be back in ten minutes," he said.

He found Melody in the piano room. She was sitting in a chair, her back to him, reading a magazine. Likely in deference to the heat, she'd piled her hair on top of her head and the shirt she wore dipped low in the back. He could see the delicate shape of her neck, the slope of her feminine shoulders, the straight line of her upper spine.

She was exquisitely beautiful.

"Melody," he said, his voice soft. Still, the magazine flew.

She looked at her watch. "Did something happen? Did somebody get hurt?"

"No," he assured her. He didn't want her to worry. "But your grandmother has asked us to entertain Rebecca Fields."

"Huh?"

She had a right to be confused. "Bernard and your grandmother are doing blending trials today."

She cocked her head. "I thought you didn't know anything about wine-making."

He smiled. "Your grandmother explained it to me.

Anyway, Rebecca is here and Pearl doesn't want that. She doesn't want to order her off, though, thinking it will make Bernard angry."

"So we're babysitting her?" Melody said.

It wasn't a word he'd have used but it likely fit well enough. "Yes. Any ideas?"

Melody shook her head. "The woman only has two interests—cooking and men."

George considered the information. "She's got a fair-sized ego as well." He learned that firsthand when she'd spent most of that first dinner whispering in his ear. "Ask her to teach you how to cook something," he said.

"What? Are you crazy?"

"No. She likes being regarded as an expert. She told me she loves it when people literally beg her to teach them something."

She raised an eyebrow. "Are you sure she was talking about *food*?"

Her meaning hit him as if he'd taken a jab in the stomach with the blunt end of an ax. He felt heat crawl up his body and he knew his face was probably red. "I am no expert on women but I think I know when one is offering *that*."

She studied him. "I suppose you did catch on fairly quick last night. But anyway, trust me on this, if I ask her to teach me how to cook something, she's not going to jump at the opportunity."

"Your grandmother is expecting us to come up with something."

Melody ran a hand through her hair. "I really wish Bernard had picked a different time to have a midlife crisis," she said. "But that's obviously well out of our control. It'll have to be you," she added, with a note of finality.

"Me?"

"Yes. If you ask her to help you, she won't be able to make it to the stove fast enough."

Could it work? Hannah had handled the cooking in their house. He wouldn't be pretending if he said he needed help. No, she'd believe that readily enough when she witnessed his abilities. But wouldn't she question his sudden interest? "We need a reason why. I can't just have woken up this morning with a sudden yearning to cook."

She nodded, looking very thoughtful. Then she got up, wincing when she did.

"Are you ill?" he asked, all thoughts of Rebecca gone.

She shook her head. "My back aches." She smiled at him. "For real. I'm not just trying to get you in a compromising position."

She would not have to work very hard. "Do you want me to rub it?"

She waved a hand. "I'll be fine." She walked over to the window, and looked out. "Oh, lord," she said.

She sounded so much like her grandmother that it gave him a start. "What?"

"Look at that!"

He joined her at the window. Rebecca and Bernard had their backs to the house. They were walking toward the wine shed, hip to hip. Bernard had his arm around Rebecca's shoulder and she had her arm around his waist. Pearl stood in the same place as when he'd left her, her hands on her slim hips, looking over her shoulder, back toward the house.

Melody turned to him. "We have to do this. Here's the deal. When we went to see my doctor the other day, did you see that poster in the elevator? The one about the YOU'RE INVITED event that's coming up in a couple weeks?"

No. He'd been too busy waiting for the crate to drop out of the sky and send him straight to hell. He shook his head.

"It's a fund-raising event for one of the homeless shelters in Napa," she explained. "People donate all the ingredients and they prepare and serve their favorite dish. The attendees pay a hundred dollars a plate. We'll tell her that you're participating in the event and you need her to teach you how to make the food."

"Will she believe it?"

"It's the best story I can come up with on short notice. It'll have to do. Let's go."

NINETEEN

BY the time they got to the wine shed, Grandmother had already followed Rebecca and Bernard inside. They found all three of them in the far corner of the building, sitting at a big round table. There was nothing in front of Rebecca, but the places in front of Bernard and Grandmother were identical. There were at least fifteen wineglasses, a pad of writing paper, a pen, and a small silver urn. The spittoon, he imagined.

In the middle, there were four pitchers of what looked to be red wine and there had to be at least twenty tall, absolutely straight measuring glasses. He was grateful that Pearl had explained the process or else he was sure he'd have been absolutely dumbfounded.

"Melody, George," Pearl said, smiling brightly. "What can we do for you?"

Melody looked at him and he knew the burden rested firmly on his shoulders. "I'm sorry to bother you," he said, "but I wanted to try to interrupt before you got started.

Rebecca, we . . . uh . . . I was wondering if you might be available to assist me?"

Rebecca leaned forward in her chair. Bernard frowned at her and said, "Rebecca, we're just about to get started here. You said you'd never witnessed a blending trial."

"I wouldn't ask if I wasn't plum desperate," George said. At least that much was honest. "But I've gotten myself into a jam by volunteering at a charity event."

"The You're Invited fund-raiser in Napa this coming weekend," Melody added, finally jumping in.

Rebecca pushed her chair back and stood up. "And you need me to teach you how to make something."

Bernard put his hand on her arm. "Maybe Bessie could help him?"

Rebecca did a deliberate shudder. "The woman tries, Bernard, but really. He's got to have something special. After all, George is representing the Sweet Song of Summer brand."

"But you were looking so forward to this," Bernard said. "And given that this is our special day, I thought we'd spend it together."

"Special day?" Pearl asked.

"Rebecca and I are engaged to be married," Bernard said, in a rather matter-of-fact manner. He did not sound like a man wildly in love.

George looked at Melody. She had her mouth open but no sound was coming out.

George extended his hand to Bernard. "Congratulations."

Pearl was the next to come around. "Yes, of course, my congratulations to you both."

Rebecca waved her hand in front of Melody and Pearl. George didn't know much about diamonds but it looked big to him and if the look on Melody's and Pearl's faces were any indication, Bernard had done right by his woman.

Rebecca leaned down and gave him a brush of her lips across his cheek. "I know this is our special day, Snookums. But this is your area of expertise and I'm needed in my own."

Bernard didn't answer.

Melody pressed her lips together. George figured it was easy enough, however, to ignore the fact that Rebecca was acting like she'd been called to serve some kind of noble cause, when he could see the satisfied look on Pearl Song's face.

Rebecca looped her arm through George's. "What is it that you want to make?" she asked.

He had no idea. He looked at Melody. She stared at Rebecca and said, "Tarts."

Rebecca did a pronounced shiver. "Oh, excellent. I've got the most wonderful recipe for a cinnamon, raisin, walnut, and apple tart."

They'd reached the door of the wine shed. A heavy rain had started to fall and the wind was picking up even more. "We'll have to make a run for it," Rebecca said.

"You go ahead," he said, dislodging her arm. "I'll help Melody. I don't want her to slip."

Rebecca looked at Melody. "I didn't realize you were coming," she said.

Melody gave her a big smile. "I wouldn't miss this for the world."

George waited until Rebecca had taken off running toward the house. Then he turned to Melody. "I don't see anything good coming from this," he said. "Do not leave me alone with her."

"Do I look crazy?" she said. She stood on her tiptoes and kissed him. It was short, barely a brush against his lips. Then she patted his chest in a comforting gesture. "Just a word of warning, George. If she asks if she can pinch your buns, run like hell."

Once inside the house, Melody was relieved to see that the kitchen was empty. She hadn't been looking forward to cajoling Bessie into abandoning her kingdom. The long-time cook came in early and fixed breakfast for whoever wanted it. Then she'd prepare sandwiches for the field workers to have for lunch as well as get the evening meal prepared. After that, she always took a couple hours off to visit her sister who lived in a nursing home in Napa and then returned to put the finishing touches on dinner.

If everything went according to plan, they'd be in and out before the woman ever came back. If not, well, then she'd let George explain it.

Rebecca surveyed the kitchen with something short of disdain and turned to George with a hopeful look on her face. "I'd so much rather be doing this in my studio."

Melody could have predicted the next line.

"Maybe we should go there," Rebecca said. "I have my car here. Of course," she said, looking at Melody, "it's just a two-seater."

Melody started to see red.

George didn't miss a beat. "I'm sorry," he said, "but since I'm filling in for Gino, I need to stay close. In case I'm needed."

Rebecca reached over, grabbed his hand, and rubbed the top of it, like one might scratch the top of a cat's head. "Oh, what's not to like about a man who takes his responsibilities so seriously?"

Melody squatted down, pulled some stainless-steel bowls and tart pans out of the cupboard, and banged them down on the counter. "I think we ought to get started."

"This is Chanel," Rebecca said, motioning to her pantsuit. "I hope you have an apron."

Melody pulled three out of the drawer. George looked

at his with a raised eyebrow but he put it on. It had little butterflies on it and what would have reached Bessie's knees, barely covered his waist.

"Cute," Melody whispered as she brushed past him.

He frowned at her.

Rebecca opened the refrigerator, leaning so far over that her suit jacket pulled up and the top of her blue thong, resting above her low-rise pants, was clearly visible. She looked over her shoulder at George but he'd suddenly developed an interest in his shoes.

Looking frustrated, she turned back to the refrigerator. She hauled out butter, a sack of apples, and the egg carton. She handed the sack of apples to Melody. "Perhaps you could start on these," she said.

George pulled out her chair for her. When she sat down, she leaned very close to his ear and said, "She's making a mistake if she gives me a sharp knife."

"George, you can help me with the crust," Rebecca said. She handed him two sticks of butter. "Be a dear and melt this in the microwave."

It was the closest thing to panic that she'd ever seen on George's face. He stood motionless.

Melody pointed to the built-in microwave that was above the stove. He walked over, studied it for a moment, and then finally opened the door. He laid the butter sticks inside and closed the door.

"Uh, George," Melody said. "You're going to want to put those in a dish of some kind. Otherwise, Bessie is going to kill you when she opens the door and there's melted butter everywhere."

His face turned pink and he didn't look at her as he pulled a dish out of the cupboard and placed the sticks in it. Once he'd shut the microwave door again, he simply stood there.

Fortunately, Rebecca was rummaging around in the cupboards pulling out sugar and flour and she wasn't paying attention. Melody pushed her chair back, walked over, punched in thirty seconds, and pushed the start button. How had the man managed to be in his thirties and never used a microwave?

"You never made much popcorn at the sheriff's office, right?"

He shook his head. When the buzzer rang on the microwave, he opened the door, and started to reach for the bowl. "It'll be hot," she warned.

He nodded and carefully grabbed for the edges of the bowl. He sat it down next to Rebecca, looking every bit like a man about ready to run for the nearest exit.

"Excellent," she said, smiling at him. She handed him a sack of walnuts. "Chop these up in the food processor."

His sigh was silent but Melody could see his chest fall. She pushed her chair back again. "I'll show you where Bessie keeps it," she said.

She pulled the appliance out of the cupboard, plugged it in, set the blade at the right level, dumped the bag of walnuts in, and stepped back. All he had to do was turn the switch on, which he did in an able fashion.

"Thank you," he said.

"No problem." She dumped the almost-crushed walnuts into a bowl and pushed it toward him. "I'll just be over here with my apples." She went back and sat down.

Rebecca had mixed the ingredients for the crust and dumped the ball of dough into the center of the tart pan. "Come here," she said to George. "You look like a man who's good with his hands."

Oh, good grief. The woman was as transparent as plastic wrap. Melody heard the telephone ring. And continue ringing. Where the heck was Tilly? She was the one always racing to answer the phone lately. On the fifth ring, Melody shoved her chair back yet again.

She walked to the kitchen door but before she opened it, she made a point to catch George's eye. She switched her gaze deliberately to the knife she'd left on the table, then back to him, this time focusing on the area right below his belt. "Behave," she mouthed and walked out.

She picked up the phone on what had to be the tenth ring. "Hello."

"Pearl Song, please."

It was a man. Not that that was so unusual. Any number of male friends and neighbors regularly contacted her grandmother. But she knew her grandmother would not want to be bothered during the blending trials.

"I'm sorry. She's unavailable right now. May I take a message?"

"Who am I speaking with?" he asked.

"This is Melody Song. Song-Johnson," she added. "I'm—"

"Pearl's granddaughter. Of course. This is William Beagle. I'm your—"

"Grandmother's attorney," she said, finishing his sentence. William Beagle had taken over his father's law practice some years ago and Grandmother liked to refer to him as Young Will Beagle, her handsome legal eagle.

"Yes, that's right. I really need to talk with your grandmother. It's very important."

She didn't want to take the chance that her grandmother had been waiting for this call. "If you hold for a moment, I'll get her," she said.

She put his call on hold and pressed the intercom button that would allow her to page the wine shed. They'd installed the technology several years ago and had the same capability with the gift shop and tasting room. "Grandmother," she said, "you have a telephone call on line one."

She half expected her grandmother to demand who had the audacity to interrupt her at a time like this but instead, what she heard was, "Thank you, I'll pick it up."

Melody turned off the intercom and watched to see that the blinking red light on the phone turned to a solid red, indicating that the line had been answered.

She went back to the kitchen. George was patting dough into baking dishes and Rebecca was watching him. He stood on one side of the counter and she was on the other. She had her arms braced on the countertop and was leaning forward.

The woman had opened another button. George, if he chose to look, had a very nice view.

This was getting ridiculous. The woman had no shame. She was openly flirting with him while his pregnant wife was right there.

"How's it going?" she asked.

George looked up and she swore he was relieved to have her once again safely at his side. She didn't know if it was because he was the most inept man she'd ever seen in a kitchen or whether he was slightly afraid of what Rebecca might try next.

"We're ready for your apples," Rebecca said.

"I'm on it," Melody replied. She walked over, picked up the bowl of sliced apples, and handed it to Rebecca. "So, you and Bernard are engaged. When's the wedding date?" she asked.

Rebecca didn't answer. Instead, she looked at George. "Watch closely," she said. "First I'm going to put the raisins and walnuts in. Then I'll add a layer of apples and top it off with the sugar-and-cinnamon mixture."

She reached for the raisin-and-walnut mixture. George grabbed it first and pulled it toward him. "I believe my wife asked you a question." He said it very seriously and even Rebecca was smart enough to realize he wasn't fooling around.

Melody's heart was so full of love for George at that exact moment that it was about to burst out of her chest.

Rebecca turned to Melody, and said, "We haven't set a date."

"Do you plan on living here?" Melody asked.

Rebecca looked surprised, then perhaps a little offended. "My television show *is* taped in San Francisco."

It suddenly dawned on Melody that Rebecca had no real intention of ever marrying Bernard. That, for this woman, it was all about the chase. Specifically, men chasing after her. It made Melody furious and she was just about to press the issue, because after all, her husband would make the woman answer, when they heard the front door open and then the sound of Grandmother's and Bernard's voices. Then it was quiet.

Rebecca pulled her car keys out of her pants pocket. "Anyway, just put the layers together the way I described, bake it for forty minutes, and serve it warm."

She was gone before they could reply, like she couldn't get away fast enough. Melody was sure that her suspicion was correct, and her heart ached for Bernard.

Melody looked at George and he shook his head. "I don't know what her game is," he said.

"Me either. All I know is that we're going to need to be here for Bernard when it all falls apart."

"We will be," he said.

She liked the sound of that. "By the way, thanks for sticking up for me. I mean, I've got at least twenty pounds on her. I probably could have taken her, but it was nice not to have to."

"I'd have held your coat for you." He pulled her into his arms and rubbed his nose against her nose. "You had some flour on your nose."

She kissed him. It was a soft kiss, offering up promises of what was yet to come. "You're sort of sexy in butter-flies," she said.

He put his hand under her shirt and gently cupped her breast. She felt the heat of his skin through the thin mate-rial of her bra. "You're mighty appealing yourself when you don't have any clothes on at all," he said.

She kissed him again. Then she backed away and his hand fell to his side. "Let's get this tart in the oven and get this mess cleaned up," she said. "I think we'll still have time for a *nap*, if you know what I mean, before dinner."

He started carrying dirty bowls to the sink. He washed and dried dishes while she finished putting the tart together. Within ten minutes they were done. They left the kitchen and were headed upstairs when Melody saw Bernard sitting in the family room. He wasn't reading or watching televi-sion. He was just sitting, staring off into space.

Even though all she really wanted to do was go upstairs, she sat down next to him. "How did it go this afternoon?"

"Fine. Your grandmother is right. This may be our best vintage ever."

If so, she'd have expected a little more excitement. "Re-becca had to leave," she said, hoping she wouldn't have to provide too many details.

He didn't look all that surprised. "A headache?" he asked.

"She didn't say."

He nodded and looked rather resigned. "That's usually what it is when she's tired of pretending that she's inter-ested in me."

Yikes. Melody had no idea what to say to that. "I'm sorry, Bernard."

"It's all right," he said, patting her hand. "I'm an old fool but I'm not blind. It was never going to work."

"You gave her a beautiful . . . and expensive ring," Melody said.

"You know what they say? A fool and his money are soon parted. It doesn't matter. By the way, who was it on the telephone for your grandmother, Melody?"

Young Will Beagle was on the tip of her tongue. But then it dawned on her that it was an odd question to ask. The time to ask that question would have been right after the telephone call. The person to ask would have been her grandmother.

Which meant maybe he had, and Grandmother hadn't told him anything.

"I don't know. You'll have to ask Grandmother. Where is she, by the way?"

"Upstairs. Once she got that call, she seemed to be in a big hurry to get finished up. We weren't even done."

Things were not making sense. From what George had said, her grandmother was really looking forward to the blending trials. What would have caused her to cut them short?

She looked at George. "I think I'm going to go find Grandmother."

"That won't be necessary. I'm right here."

Melody, George, and Bernard all turned to the right. Grandmother had changed into what looked to be a new black suit. She had panty hose on and good shoes.

"Are you going somewhere?" Melody asked.

"No. We're having company later."

"Pearl, is everything all right?" George asked.

"It's fine," she said. Her voice was steady. "I need you two to go and find Louis and Tilly and Genevieve, too. I want everyone to meet Bernard and me in the family room in a half hour."

Melody studied her grandmother. She looked calm and the request wasn't outrageous, but still, something didn't seem right. "Grandmother, are you sure everything is okay?"

The older woman nodded. "Please, just do this for me?"

"Of course," Melody said. She looked at George and then nodded toward the stairs. He followed her up. Once they were in their room, she turned to him. "Just what the heck do you think is going on?"

He shook his head. "You told Bernard that you didn't know who called your grandmother. Do you?"

"Yes. It was her attorney."

George rubbed his jaw. "I think we better do what she asked. I'll go get your aunt and uncle and then stop in Genevieve's room on my way back."

Melody shook her head. "I'll call Louis's cell phone. He always has it on him." She pulled her own cell phone out of her purse and dialed.

"Louis, it's Melody. Grandmother asked me to call you. She wants you and Tilly to come to the family room in a half hour."

She listened.

"I have no idea," she said. "Just come, all right?" She hung up the telephone. "Look, I think I'd feel better if I went and found Genevieve. Maybe she knows something that we don't."

On her way past, he put his arm around her and she snuggled into his warmth. "Don't get upset," he said. "Everything is going to be fine."

She wished she could believe him but she had a bad feeling about this. "I just don't think this is going to turn out good. Look, if I don't come back here first, then meet me downstairs."

*   *   *

GEORGE took a fast shower and tried to figure out what might have happened. Grandmother had been polite but her tone hadn't held its usual warmth. Had her attorney given her news that upset her?

After he got dressed, he realized that he still had fifteen minutes. He saw his camera on the dresser. Thinking it might make Melody happy to have the photograph of Pearl, he decided to develop it. He took his camera into the bathroom. He put the stoppers in both sinks and poured a very thin layer of developing fluid in the one and then the same amount of finishing fluid in the other.

He shut off the light and the bath was completely dark. He opened the door just a slight crack, allowing enough light in to allow him to see what he was doing but not enough to ruin his photograph.

He pulled the glass plate out of the camera and slipped it into the developing fluid. He let it rest there for just a moment before he transferred it to the other sink. After a minute, he picked up the glass plate and held it up.

It was a good shot. Melody would like it. He pulled the carefully rolled photograph paper out of his camera case. He uncurled the five-by-seven sheet and laid it flat on the bathroom counter. Then he pressed the plate against it and transferred the image to the paper.

He opened the door to the bathroom and turned on the light. He examined the photograph again. That's when he noticed the marks in the right-hand corner, about an inch from the bottom. And then he remembered that Melody had noticed a very similar mark when she'd looked at the picture of John and Sarah. At the time she'd questioned him, he thought perhaps someone had marked on the photograph.

He opened the box of ten glass plates he'd ordered from the Eastman Camera Company and looked through them. Sure enough, each had the same mark in the corner and it somehow was getting transferred to the paper. It was some kind of defect.

He put the plates back in the box and quickly cleaned out the sinks and put his camera away. He'd wanted to surprise Melody with the photograph but now that he'd seen the marks on it, he knew he couldn't do that. She was too smart. She'd pick up on the similarities and then the questions would start.

All he had to do was keep his secret for a little while longer. Then her child would be born and she'd be better prepared to handle the news. He hated lying to her, but he just couldn't take a chance with her health or Jingle's. Especially not after he'd seen that new baby inside of her. It was too real to do anything to jeopardize it.

He opened the drawer where he kept his clothes and he put the picture underneath his extra things. When he got downstairs, Melody and Genevieve were already sitting close together on the couch. Bernard stood, across the room, looking out the window. George took the chair across from the two women. He'd no more than sat down when Tilly and Louis joined them.

Tilly looked more tired than usual and Louis was smoking a cigarette. They took the chairs next to the couch. When Pearl came in the room, Louis hurriedly stubbed his cigarette out.

"What's going on, Mother?" Tilly asked.

Pearl shook her head. "We'll wait until our guest arrives."

George heard the crack of lightning and not three seconds later, a rumble of thunder. He hoped the guest had a raincoat.

The doorbell rang and Pearl left to answer it. George smiled at Melody but she wasn't having it. She sat quite still, twisting one section of her hair around her finger.

He wanted to take her to bed and make her forget all this

craziness. He wanted to sprinkle cinnamon and sugar on her breasts and lick it off. Hell, he wanted to eat warm apple tarts off her bare stomach.

Pearl returned with a man whom George guessed was close to his own age. He was dressed in a gray suit and he carried a leather case bulging with papers. The man nodded at the group, his manner very serious. So serious that George stopped thinking about having a special dessert and started thinking that Melody might be right—this wasn't going to be good.

"This is Will Beagle. I asked him to come tonight because I think it's important that we all hear the same information." She nodded at the man.

He sat down in the chair next to George and pulled an envelope out of his case. "We are here tonight to discuss the terms of Pearl Elizabeth Song's will."

Melody's mouth opened then shut. She looked at her great-aunt but Genevieve was staring at Louis and Tilly. They both looked pale.

Will Beagle put on his glasses. "Now, this meeting tonight does in no way purport to thwart the court's responsibility to read and administer Ms. Song's will. It is simply an informal session so that all parties may understand the terms and conditions set forth by Ms. Song."

He opened the envelope. "To my sister, Genevieve Louise Song, I give a million dollars." The man looked up.

Tilly made an odd noise. Genevieve, on the other hand, said nothing. Pearl reached out her hand to her sister and said, "You have been my companion, my confidant, and my best friend. I have always known that if I stumbled, that you would be there to catch me and push me forward. The fifteen years that we were separated were fifteen years filled with missing you. And while I applauded your wandering spirit, I yearned for you to return. We have shared what few sisters have shared and I am grateful for every day that we've had together."

George would not have dreamed it possible but Genevieve Song had tears in her eyes. He understood. He was having some trouble keeping dry-eyed himself.

Will Beagle cleared his throat. "Shall we proceed?" he asked.

Pearl nodded.

The man picked up his papers again. "To my grand-daughter, Melody Louise Song-Johnson, I leave—"

"Wait," Pearl said. She leaned forward in her chair and looked at Melody. "I have something to say first."

TWENTY

"I loved you when you were born like any grandmother loves her grandchild. You were a beautiful baby and very happy. Your parents were so proud of you, so delighted with you. When the three of you would come for a visit, we would have the best time. And like a fool, I thought it would always be like that."

Melody got out of her chair and sat on the floor next to her grandmother's chair. The woman stroked Melody's hair and George knew somehow that there'd been many nights through the years that they'd done this very thing.

"But it was not to be. When your parents died, everything changed. And after that, I would hear you crying in your room and I didn't know, I really didn't know, if I could do it. Could I heal your heart when my own was broken?"

Melody was crying. Big tears rolled down her smooth cheeks and it hurt him to see her suffer. He wanted to reach for her, to hold her, but now was not the time.

"You made it easy for me," Pearl said. "You brought joy

and laughter and the energy of youth back into this house and I desperately needed it. You saved me, Melody. You gave me a reason to get out of bed every day, a reason to eat, a reason to live. I owe you, Melody. I know you think you owe me but it's the other way around, I've always known it. I want you to know it now. I love you very much."

She laid her head on her grandmother's knee. "I love you, too," she said.

"I know you do. And you will never know how that has sustained me."

The room was absolutely silent. Finally, Pearl nodded at her lawyer to continue.

"To my granddaughter, Melody Louise Song-Johnson, I leave a 50 percent interest in Songbook Serenade ranch and a 50 percent interest in Sweet Song of Summer wines."

Melody's head jerked up. "But—"

"I want you to have it, Melody. I want you and George to stay here and to raise your child here. Nothing could make me happier." She turned to her attorney. "Will, please continue."

Everyone in the room was looking at Tilly and Louis. That is, everyone, except Pearl. She was looking at Bernard.

Will cleared his throat. "And to my trusted friend, Bernard, who has been with me through both good and bad times, I leave the remaining 50 percent of Songbook Serenade and the remaining 50 percent of Sweet Song of Summer wines."

No one in the room moved. Then Louis jumped out of his chair. "That's outrageous. Insane. Jesus Christ, you crazy old woman," he said to Pearl. He took a step toward Pearl and Melody but George was faster.

He hit him: a quick punch to the stomach, which sent Louis sprawling back onto his chair.

Tilly didn't even glance at her husband. She sat quietly, staring at her hands.

"You can't get away with this," Louis said. "We'll contest the will."

Will Beagle chuckled. "Good luck," he said.

"He's not even family," Louis screamed.

Pearl shook her head and went to stand next to Bernard. He was white-faced and stood still as a statue. She put her arm on his. "When I realized I was dying, my one regret was that I'd never found out more about my father. I'd been afraid for years, afraid to unearth rocks that were no doubt best left lying in the dirt."

She smiled at her attorney. "Young Will here was of great assistance. So tenacious. And before long he'd discovered what I'd always known in my heart. My father had another family, another life."

George heard Genevieve's intake of breath and saw Melody reach for her aunt's hand. Tilly had finally looked up. Louis had moved forward to the edge of his chair, his eyes darting furiously between Pearl and the young attorney.

Pearl squeezed Bernard's arm. "Reginald Song was mine and Genevieve's father but he was your father, too. Not by blood but by all else that was important. He raised you, he loved you, and you were with him when he died."

Bernard closed his eyes and he seemed to shrink into the carpet, like all the breath had been taken from him.

"I'm right, aren't I?" Pearl asked. "And you've known it since the beginning, since you came to work here."

Bernard opened his eyes and looked first at Genevieve, then at Pearl. "I was six when my mother met Reginald Song. She loved him more than life itself and I think he loved her, too. Even so, I don't think he would have stayed. He would have gone back to you and your mother. But my mother was not a well woman. She said that if he left, she'd kill me first, then herself. I think he believed her. I know I did."

The room felt hot and stiff and George desperately wanted to take Melody away from all of it. But he knew the time had come for all of them to know the truth.

"So he stayed," Bernard said. "I called him Father and she called him husband while the two of you had no one to call Father and your mother had no husband to share a life with. Before he died, he told me about you and I swore that I'd somehow make amends." He turned to Pearl. "Your dream, all of this, became my dream. Your joy"—he nodded his head at Melody—"became my joy. I gave some but I received so much more in return. There's no need for payment now."

Pearl shook her head. "You are my brother, in every sense of the word, and I am honored to share this with you."

"Bullshit," Louis said.

George, who had stayed standing up in case Louis tried to do something else stupid, walked over and grabbed Louis by the shirt collar. He yanked him up. "You're done. Get out."

Louis tried to push him away. "It's not your house yet," he yelled.

Pearl stood. "No, but he's right. There's no place for you here any longer. I'm hoping my daughter has the good sense to divorce you, but if she doesn't, once again that's her choice. But I'm not going to let you ruin everything that I've worked a lifetime for. So, you either go to the door nicely or I'm going to ask George to help you find it."

George felt mildly disappointed when Louis picked up his pack of cigarettes and walked out the door. Tilly stood up, moving slow like an old woman. Pearl motioned for her to sit down. "We're not quite finished here, Tilly," she said, her voice gentle.

"It sounds to me like we are," Tilly said. She didn't sound angry or bitter, just very sad.

"Please continue, Will," Pearl said.

"To my daughter, Tilly, I leave the sum of three hundred thousand dollars," he read.

Pearl stared at her daughter. "Here's what I suggest you do with that money. First, pay off your gambling debts and your credit cards."

Tilly's normally pale face reddened fast. "But how . . ."

"I know you tried, but really, you can't think you were successful in answering every phone call and intercepting every piece of mail that came for you?" Pearl asked. Her voice was kind, almost consoling. George thought it sounded like she might have been angry at one time but was now just sad for her daughter.

"I'm sorry, Mother," Tilly said. Her lower lip trembled and her eyes filled with tears.

"I know you are. I am, too. But you made choices along the way that were bad choices. And there are always consequences. You should have enough left after you get your affairs in order to hold you over for a couple months. Find a job, Tilly. Use some of the talent and brains that God gave you. In time, I hope that you'll forgive me and understand why I made this decision. It has been the hardest decision of my life." Pearl smiled at her daughter. "You don't need to leave tonight. Why don't you go back to your room and start making plans. Tilly, I really think that the best part of your life is ahead of you."

Tilly kissed her mother on the cheek. "I love you," she said.

"And I love you," Pearl replied.

Pearl waited until she'd left the room, and then said, "You should all know that I have reserved some additional money for Tilly. It will remain in Will's capable control until such time that it can be determined as to whether Tilly has taken my advice to heart. If she does, then she will receive an additional two hundred thousand dollars. If not, then Will has been instructed to donate it to one of the worthy causes that I have favored through the years."

Neither Melody nor Genevieve seemed surprised at that news. No doubt they'd realized how difficult it had been for Pearl to make her decision. While George had no way of knowing, he thought maybe Tilly would find her way out of the darkness.

Pearl looked at her lawyer. "Thank you, Will. I appreciate all that you've done for me. And I appreciate you driving out here on such a wicked night."

Almost as if on cue, there was a bolt of lightning, clearly visible through the big windows and it seemed to split the sky. Will gathered up his papers quickly. "I think I'll be going before it gets any worse," he said.

"Me, too," Bernard said.

Pearl shook her head at Bernard. "Please stay." She turned to her attorney. "I'll see you to the door."

He held up his hand. "No need, I can find my way out. Good night."

Once he was gone, Pearl glanced around the room, looking rather expectantly at each of them. George wondered what could possibly be next. His gut tightened when her gaze settled on him.

"George," Pearl said, "I like you. I might even love you. And I can see that you have made my granddaughter happy. But I can't leave this earth without knowing that you've told her the truth, the whole truth."

He felt the room start to spin. "What?"

Melody looked from her grandmother to him, then back to her grandmother. She was clearly confused, concerned.

No sudden shocks or other stressful situations.

He looked at Genevieve. She didn't look confused but neither did she look happy. She stared at her sister. "Pearl, some things are better left alone," she said.

Pearl shook her head. "I used to think so, too," she said. "But if I have learned anything over the years, it's that the truth, as ugly and scarred as it may be, must be dealt with. If Bernard had told us the truth years ago, we would have had a brother to share our lives with. If years ago I'd have been more truthful with Tilly, had forced her to see the truth about herself, about Louis, then tonight could have been a very different night. I won't keep making mistakes like that."

He couldn't think. What did she know? What was she expecting him to say? "Pearl," he said, keeping his voice low. "Now is not the time or the place."

She smiled. "Interesting choice of words, George. That's what I'm interested in hearing. Is exactly how you've come to be at this particular time and place."

Melody got to her feet. "I don't understand what's going on," she said. No one answered.

He knew he should be a man, he knew he should tell her. But he was scared. She'd been lied to once by a man that she'd thought she'd loved and it had hurt her. Would she understand why he'd lied as well? "Melody, it's a difficult thing to explain."

"Somebody tell me . . ."

She stopped, her face paled. She was looking past him, toward the door. Before George could move, she said, "Louis?"

George turned and he saw the man. He was drenched, his clothes sticking to him, and water ran off his bald head. He waved a rifle around, his motions as wild as his eyes.

"Put down your gun, Louis," George said.

"Shut up," the man screamed. He waved the gun and stepped into the room. "It wasn't supposed to be this way.

It should have never happened like this." He paced back and forth, swinging his rifle. "This should have been mine. All of it should have been mine."

He whirled toward Genevieve. "You got your share," he screamed. "All those years ago, you got yours. And more now. It's not fair."

Pearl reached out her hand. "Louis, you need to leave. Now."

"Don't tell me what to do. You've been telling me what to do for years. I should have been the one giving the orders."

Bernard stepped forward. "Louis, it's over," he said. Bernard looked somewhat apologetically at Pearl. "I didn't want to say anything until I had all the proof." He turned back to Louis. "I know that you've been having an affair with Mickey Maloni's wife. I know about the men who are trying to blackmail you."

The late-night visit to the tasting room suddenly made more sense. George looked at Melody and could see by the look on her face, that she was also putting the pieces together.

"Shut up," Louis screamed.

Bernard shook his head. "Mickey Maloni is one of the most powerful men in Reno. And he doesn't play nice."

"You're not going to be telling anyone," Louis said, pointing his gun at Bernard.

George shifted and got ready to move.

"I don't need to tell anyone. The men who are trying to shake you down are not the only people who have a copy of the photos, Louis. I've got a set, too. They're locked in a drawer in my office. I've given instructions to my own attorney that upon my death, the drawer should be opened."

Louis made the kind of sound a cornered animal makes.

Genevieve stood up. "You're a desperate man, aren't you,

Louis?" she taunted. A man like you is probably desperate enough to pay someone to run my sister and my great-niece off the road?"

"Damn you," he said, his eyes darting back to Pearl. "I couldn't wait any longer. You needed to die now. But then again, that's before I realized you were going to screw me over."

Now it was Melody making sounds, like she was gasping for air. Louis swung his gun toward her.

George charged him. And there was a terrible sound, a mixture of screams and storm and the crack of a rifle. And terrible pain as a bullet tore into him.

Melody. Melody. He struggled to hold on, had to. But the pain and the darkness and the evil grabbed at him and it took him. And as he slipped away, he heard another gunshot and he knew he'd failed again to protect the woman he loved.

HE woke up to a soft whiteness and he wondered if it was heaven. It took him a minute to take it all in. He was in a room, in a bed. The walls were white, the curtains on the windows were white, even the sheets he lay on were white.

But yet the room was almost dark, lit only by a small light on the far wall. He could hear a terrible wailing that seemed to come from outside the window.

He moved and pain streaked from his shoulder to his arm.

"I'd move a little slower than that if I were you."

Jesus. He turned and saw Genevieve standing next to his bed.

What the hell? "Where am I?" he asked.

She looked amused. "Calm down. You're in the hospital. The power is out. They're working off emergency generators. And by the way, you're going to be sore for a couple weeks but your shoulder is going to be fine. The bullet nicked an artery—that's why you lost consciousness so fast."

"Melody?" he asked. His throat was dry and it hurt to talk.

She patted his hand. "She's fine. You know you saved her life."

That couldn't be right. "I heard another shot."

Genevieve nodded, no longer looking amused. "Louis is dead. Tilly shot him in the back. None of us, including Louis, I'm sure, even knew she'd been carrying a gun in her purse for months. She came back when she heard Louis yelling."

Oh, God. It was all so senseless. But what mattered was that Melody was safe. Her child was safe. "Melody wasn't hurt?" he asked again.

Genevieve shook her head. "No. But she knows."

He jerked his head around, causing his shoulder to move and a whole new pain almost took his breath away. He struggled to sit up. The room started to spin and he felt like he was going to be stomach-sick. But none of that mattered. "What?"

"She knows everything. Who you are and where you came from. Pearl and I told her."

He had a thousand questions but none of them mattered. "I have to see her."

Genevieve put her hand on his arm. "There's no time," she said, her voice serious. "Or you won't be able to go."

"Go where?"

"Back. Back to your time, your place." She pulled back his sheet. He was wearing the same kind of gown they'd put on Melody when she'd been in the hospital. When he pulled at the neckline of the gown, he could see the thick white bandage taped around his shoulder.

"You need to get dressed, now. I know it hurts like hell but you'll make it back. I'll see you through."

"See me through? You told me before that you couldn't help me go back."

She sighed. "I lied. I'm sorry about that. And while you have every reason not to trust me, you're going to have to go on faith. I can do it. I can get you back to your time."

"How?"

"People like you have the ability to negotiate the portal but not at their will. There are only a few like me, who can choose to go and come back."

His head was reeling and he didn't know if it was the pain of being shot, the worry about Melody and her child, or the craziness of what Genevieve was saying. "So you've been to my time?"

"Yes." She handed him a sack. "Put these clothes on."

He waved the sack away. "You brought me here?" he accused.

"I did not," she said. "I didn't even know about you until you'd arrived and then I realized what my sister had done."

"Pearl?"

"Yes. She's never traveled although I suspect she could if she tried. We are, after all, sisters. She limits herself to helping those who need it. She guided you here. When I found out, I went back to your time. That's where I was the night you came to my room. I should have told you right away. I had no right to keep what I knew to myself. I did it for Melody but it was wrong."

He couldn't think. It was too much. And the noise from outside the window was deafening. "I don't understand."

"I know about your wife and how she died. I know about the two men who've already died. More important, I know who and where the third man is."

He grabbed her hand. His head was beating so rapidly that he thought it would jump right out of his chest. "What are you saying?"

"He's a circuit judge. Funny, isn't it?" she asked, looking disgusted. "A man like that getting to cast judgment on others."

"How do you know?"

She shook her head and looked nervously toward the window. "George, you don't have time for this. Just know that I know. And I will take you to him. But we have to go now."

He couldn't leave now. He had to see Melody. Had to explain why he hadn't told her the truth. Had to explain why he was leaving.

She'd been left behind by so many others.

"I can't go now. I need to talk to Melody first."

"George, you don't have that choice. If you wait, if you delay, you'll never be able to go back. It's now or never."

The screeching and screaming from outside was so loud he covered his ears. It was a horrific sound and he knew that he'd only heard a similar noise one time in his life. Right before there had been complete and utter silence. Right before the footprints had appeared outside the changing station. Genevieve wasn't lying.

He grabbed for the clothes that Genevieve had tossed on the bed. It took everything he had to pull on his jeans. He was sweating like a pig after the effort. "Untie this," he said, motioning to the strings around his neck. She did and he let the gown fall on the floor. He slipped one arm through the sleeve of his shirt but let the shirt just hang loose from his body. He wasn't even going to attempt to put his other arm through.

How the hell was he going to manage the journey back? The first time had almost killed him and he'd been whole. "Let's go," he said.

Genevieve nodded and held the door open. The hallway outside his room was dimly lit, too, and absolutely empty. He'd taken five steps when suddenly, it was as if all the noise in the world had suddenly been swallowed up.

"It must be now," Genevieve whispered. She grabbed his arm and with amazing strength, pulled him to the door at the end of the hallway. In his heart, he knew what he was going to see.

And he was right. When she opened it, he was looking down the row of grapevines that practically butted up to the building. Between the vines, the saturated ground was a mass of mud. But leading away, as clear as if they'd been carved in dry stone, were the footprints.

He had to go. Had to fully pay his debt to Hannah. He'd failed to protect her once and she'd paid the ultimate price. He could not fail her again.

Tears ran down his face. He'd loved two women in his life. One had been brutally torn away from him. The other, he was about to leave. She would hate him for that. Probably already hated him for lying to her. "Will you tell her," he begged of Genevieve, "will you tell her that I never meant to deceive her? Will you tell her that I loved her?"

"Yes. Hurry. Go."

Forgive me, Melody. He looked up into the swirling dark gray clouds and for the first time in thirty-four years, he prayed. *Protect her and the child, God. It's the only thing that matters.*

He took his first step. He felt the ground shake and he could smell the sweet scent of the lilacs that grew outside his back door. He took his second step.

WHEN Melody woke up, her grandmother was holding her hand. They were in the living room and a candle burned bright on the piano. It was daylight but the sky was so gray that no natural light came in through the windows. She didn't know how long she'd slept, only knew that when she'd closed her eyes, she prayed that somehow she would survive for the sake of her child.

George was gone. Had to be, by now.

Her grandmother and her aunt had told her everything. Melody had demanded it. They sat in the waiting room of the hospital and she had listened and known that crazy as it sounded, it was all true. She remembered all the little things that she'd dismissed. The odd use of language, the fascination with the radio, the inability to drive a car or to operate a microwave.

And when the women had finished, she had sat for a while longer, hoping and praying that he hadn't lost too much blood, that he would be saved, knowing in her heart that if he was, he was still lost to her. He was a man of honor and could do no less than honor the memory of his wife by bringing her killer to justice.

If she'd needed more proof, it had been waiting for her when she'd finally come home from the hospital. She'd gone straight upstairs, intending to remove George's things, knowing that she couldn't bear to open a drawer and see the things they'd bought at Target or the silly straw hat that he wore when he rode Brontë. It had taken less than a minute for her to find the photograph of her grandmother, the one George had taken with his camera. On it were the same thin scratches in the corner that were on the photograph that hung on her wall. The photograph that her aunt Genevieve had told her was Sarah and John Beckett—the photograph George had taken before he'd left his own time.

She'd put the photograph back in the drawer, unable to look at it, unable to throw it away. She'd left her room, come downstairs, and curled up on the couch. Some time later, her grandmother had come in and sat with her. They hadn't talked, had just sat quietly, each lost in her own painful thoughts, and finally, she had slept.

She heard a noise on the porch and she turned on her side, away from the door. She closed her eyes, pretending to be asleep. She didn't want company.

"Melody."

She flipped over, flat onto her back.

He smiled at her.

"What the hell are you doing here?" she yelled. "You're not supposed to be here." His shirt was hanging open, unbuttoned, one arm in a sleeve, the other cradled to his side. "Oh, my God," she said.

"Calm down," he pleaded. He pulled the loose shirt tighter around his body, hiding his shoulder from her view. He glanced at her grandmother. "Good morning, Pearl."

Her grandmother was crying. "Good morning, George. I must say I'm very glad to see you." She stood up and walked toward the hallway. "I imagine you'd appreciate some privacy."

Melody struggled to sit up on the couch. "Where is Aunt Genevieve? You've got to get out of here."

He shook his head, "It's too late."

She put her hand over her mouth, terribly afraid she was going to be sick. "Oh, no. The storm passed before you were ready to go. That's it, isn't it? Oh, George, I'm so sorry."

He took another three steps toward her and sank down on his knees in front of the couch. "I started to go. I could have made it." He rubbed a hand across his face. He looked so tired. "I was wrong, Melody. I should have told you the truth. I'm so sorry."

"George. Do you understand what this means? Aunt Genevieve said you only had one chance to go back."

"Please, just listen. Hannah was right. She told me that

vengeance will not heal the pain. But you know what does?" He reached for her hand. "Love. Love heals. I love you, Melody. And I want to stay with you and help you raise your daughter. I want to be here, now."

She thought her heart would burst with joy. "I thought I'd lost you," she said. "And I knew that for the sake of my child, I was going to have to get up every day and eat and work and pretend I was living. But I didn't know how I was going to be able to do it." She pulled their linked hands up to her lips and kissed the back of his hand. "I couldn't ask you to stay here with me. I couldn't ask."

He smiled at her. "You didn't have to." He placed his hand on her belly. "Everything still fine?"

She nodded. "Actually, I had a little time to think while somebody was in surgery. I know you're not crazy about the name Jingle. What do you think about Sarah Miguella Tyler?"

"Sarah Miguella Tyler." He repeated it, almost reverently.

"I want to name her for the three people I have loved."

He couldn't hold back the tears. They rolled down his cheeks and he made no effort to hide them. She opened her arms and he gathered her close.

"I love you, George Tyler."

He pulled his head back and looked her in the eye. "I love you more than I ever thought possible. Will you marry me, Mrs. Johnson?"

EPILOGUE

AS they rocked on the porch swing on a warm, early October night, George kept one arm around his wife. In the other, he cradled his one-month-old daughter. She was up to nine pounds and he swore he'd seen a smile yesterday.

He looked up when he heard the front door open. Genevieve stood there. She plucked a pink feather from behind her ear and brushed the soft part against Sarah's baby face. "I missed you, pumpkin," she said, before nodding at Bernard, who sat in his chair, across the porch, like he so often did in the evenings. "It's the middle of the crush, Bernard," she said, her tone teasing. "Shouldn't you be out fretting over the grapes?"

Bernard shook his head. "Give me a break, Genevieve. This is the first chance we've had to sit in two weeks." He inclined his head toward George. "Besides," he added, sounding satisfied, "my partner already took care of that."

Melody sat up and smiled at her aunt, who'd been gone for several days. "Safe travels?" she asked.

Genevieve nodded. "The Becketts send their love. Their boy just turned one and Sarah's pregnant again. She's proud as can be of her family and I swear he's one of the happiest men I've ever seen."

Through Genevieve, they'd been able to reconnect with Sarah and John. "No happier than me," George said.

"I told them about Pearl," Genevieve said.

They'd buried Pearl a little over two months ago. The days leading up to her death had been painful and sad but there'd been moments of quiet joy. They'd all been there. Even Tilly. The woman had been sober, thoughtful, and mother and daughter had shared much. George and Melody had been by Pearl's side when she'd passed from this life to the next and they had taken comfort when she'd told them that she was content to go now that she knew everything was in good hands.

"It's over," Genevieve said suddenly.

"What's over?" George asked. Keeping up with Genevieve was always a challenge.

"He's dead. The man who killed Hannah."

George felt his heart lurch and he handed Sarah to Melody. "How?"

"Pack of wild dogs attacked him. Crazy how things like that happen."

"George?" Melody asked, her voice filled with concern.

"You don't need to feel bad," Genevieve said. "You didn't ask that it be done. I just thought you should know."

It was finally over. Justice had been served.

Melody leaned toward him. He stretched out his arm and pulled her and Sarah close. "She knows, George," she whispered. "Somehow, Hannah knows."

He smiled. The fall breeze carried the scent of freshly brewed tea.

STAY WITH ME

Beverly Long

Something strange has happened to Sarah Jane
Tremont. One moment, she was walking along
a beach outside Los Angeles. The next, she was
wondering through Wyoming Territory, 1888,
taken in by a rugged cowboy whose wounded
heart she believes she is destined to heal.

"A Perfect 10."

—*Romance Reviews Today*

0-425-20062-0